I0451695

The Future Queen

by

BK Crawford

Edited by Mandy Cummins

Published in the United States of America
Mind Key Publishing ©2013
All Rights Reserved

Mind Key   Publishing

ISBN: 978-0-9912936-1-2

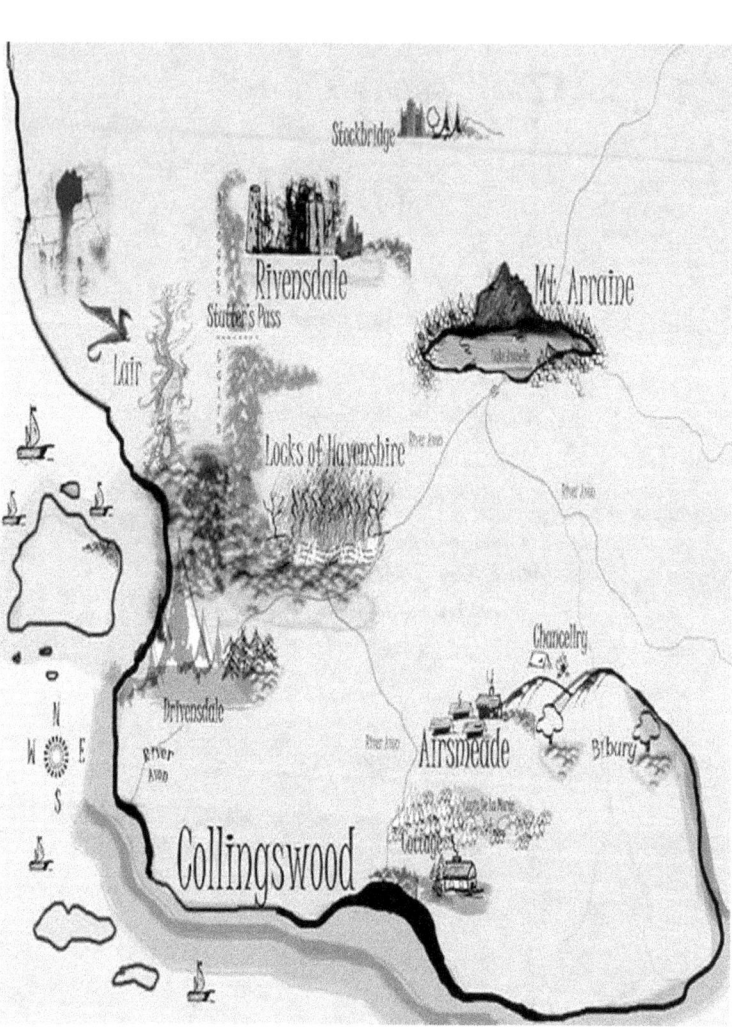

I dedicate this book to Angie, my devoted soul mate who allowed me the love, freedom, and time to explore the depths of my imagination.
Also, to my trusted editor, Miss Mandy Cummins, without her devotion and skill, this work would not be possible.
And to my sons, Nick and Chris, around whose light and love my world revolves.

"They say patience is a virtue, the way of divine wisdom, the path to a balanced soul. What they must really mean to say is it's a complete waste of time." ~Farrin Lockwood, the Future Queen of Collingswood.

ξ℀ξ

The night air felt cold for late October and bit at Farrin's face where her hood failed to cover her tingling cheeks. Not a star in the sky and no moon to speak of. She took care to follow a pine path, other trees drop mounds of leaves that send harsh alarms into the night when trampled, pine needles make no such complaint.

The skies reflected the colorless face of a demon, black and eerily still and if she didn't know the way to Airsmeade by heart and soul she would easily become disoriented and quite lost. But, she did know the way and ten minutes had already passed without breath or hair of another living soul inside the wooded thicket. Feet moving soundlessly over the padded ground, she allowed herself a smug grin. Soon, she would be sipping Sarina's newest brew and listening to how she had discovered the recipe. People say Sarina descends from Mother Earth. She is a famed and incurable herbalist, a fact that pleases her immensely.

Nearly halfway there and no sign of trouble.

Orchestrated in a low hush, the song of the night consisted of an occasional flutter of leaves as lazy winds whistled through the trees accompanied by the low moans of a bullfrog bathing in a nearby puddle. Farrin breathed deeply, immersing herself in the soothing aroma of earthen pine as she moved with confidence through the sleepy forest.

The creature sprang from above, pinning Farrin on her back before she could grunt a proper protest. Its matted fur smelled of smoke and dead fish, its eyes bulging with a ravenous rage, bearing down on her chest like a boulder sprung from a catapult, drool lolling from its bared fangs, ready to rip the prize from her chest. Mithragog's hellhound. A young pup, thankfully, and not nearly as weighty as its adult counterparts or the battle would already be lost. Digging her fingers into its flesh, she held the slobbering muzzle at arm's length while the dog snapped its jaws and tensed its muscles, leaning in with all its weight, trying to break her grasp, its breath an atrocious mix of barnyard excrement and scorched vomit. How lovely.

She could use a spell to reduce the animal to a whimpering toad but the use of even the slightest bit of magic would create a trail Mithragog could trace. He wouldn't hesitate to send an entire army of ghoulish creatures in search of his spoil: the heart of the first female born in the line of Gwenevere. Which, if he could cast the spell correctly, would guarantee an eternal reign of terror meted out by the black-hearted dimwit who fancied himself a descendant of the great Merlin. Nothing could be further from the truth. Truth, however, had never caused Mithragog the slightest concern.

Without magic, Farrin's options were severely limited. The dog proved immovable and her muscles were already weakening under the strain. She must be quick. Her pocket held the solution (only fools travel the forest without protection) but she would have to let go with one hand to reach into her pocket, giving the advantage to the dog. Sensing her hesitation, the hound backed off slightly, effectively breaking her grip. Thrusting its muzzle, it took a quick stab at her face. She twisted her head to the side and dropped her chin to protect her jugular. An indescribable pain seared through the side of her head as the hound ripped into her lower ear lobe, tearing away a chunk of hair. Despite the surging pain, she stiff-armed the mutt, knowing it wouldn't last long. What she needed was a brief distraction.

Fake as Mithragog's proposed lineage, she sneezed. When the dog flinched, she reached into her pocket and withdrew a clove of garlic, planting it deeply inside the mongrel's right nostril. Slumbering peasants as far away as Drivensdale must have heard the yelp and howl. While the hound writhed in pain and attempted to snort the garlic from its nose, Farrin ran with all the speed her legs could muster. If she could gain the advantage of distance, the hound could not follow—dogs are nothing without their sense of smell.

Obviously, Mithragog could find no better way to while away his hours and intended to continue this merciless hunt.

Now what? Twenty minutes to the cottage, twenty minutes to Airsmeade. Should she return to the safety of the cottage? Putting a hand to her ear, she brought it away, fingers wet with sticky fluid. Press on, or turn back?

ξɔжξ

Once a year, the kingdom of Collingswood vibrates with anxious energy and oozes eagerness. The annual fall festival. Three days of music, dancing, games, and ale. It's the one time when a person, regardless of her stature, can get sloppy drunk and trip over her own feet without ridicule. You do not miss the fall festival to cultivate cobwebs.

And yet, for a brief moment, Farrin felt a twinge of guilt for leaving McFleegle behind at the enchanted cabin. It wasn't his fault the king's council had sequestered her...locked her up like a common criminal, banished and shunned her, sent her away to rot until her skin turned moldy and gray. Granted, that's stretching the truth like a batch of taffy but it felt that way, despite knowing that her father, the king, had sent her away for her own protection.

McFleegle had been her only companion for nearly a fortnight and the line between sanity and madness had begun to blur. That wasn't McFleegle's fault either. However, although he thought himself quite special (with six toes to each paw), except for the occasional gift of slaughtered rodent that he pranced through the door, he was just a typical cat, that is to say, a fur-covered narcissist with little concern for anyone but himself as was clearly demonstrated in his dastardly way of showing appreciation for Farrin's affection. Arching his back and twisting his tail, he rolls over and swats, full claws, snapping until his teeth find flesh. And that is why Farrin's guilt for leaving him behind quickly dissipates.

Still, deciding to abandon the security of the cabin was not an easy decision. Farrin knew the dangers. She had already come within an inch of her life at Mithragog's hand when he returned to Collingswood several months ago. But, he had mistaken Farrin for a common woman, unaware of her talent and skill. That error alone had saved her life. Now that he knew about her witchy wiles, he would be on guard to fend against her magic. Thus the hours Farrin had spent trying to tame her temptation.

"What do you think, Flea," she had asked, "is it worth a trip through the forest to join the festival, or am I a fool to consider it?"

The cat had jumped onto her lap, engaged her with a foul stare (his way of saying he didn't much appreciate the nickname she had given him) and took on an immediate air: *Whatever you say, you'll do what you want regardless of my opinion.* And, of course, he was right.

In the end, she had decided that if she took care not to use magic, if she kept her wits about her and remained especially stealthy, she could join the festivities and return before daybreak. She had twisted her copper hair into a long braid, slipped into her darkest leathers and made one last attempt to reason her way out of this irresponsible, idiotic decision, but it was no use. Over the course of her nineteen years common sense had never won a battle over desire.

Now, with blood leaking over the nape of her neck, she called her sanity into question.

Sane or not, she was still midway between the cabin and the festivities in Airsmeade. The festival ends tonight. She had come this far already and had bested Mithragog's hellhound. She could let all of that be for naught, or press on and claim a few tankards of ale as a reward for her struggle.

ξЖξ

Mithragog stepped away from the viewing pool and slammed his staff onto the slate rock that comprised the floor of the cave. In the reflection of the still water, he had seen one of his best hellhounds take a proper thrashing from a young *girl*. Where, pray tell, does a wizard of exceptional quality go to find sufficient help? Hiking up the hem of his robes, he turned away in disgust, ascending the stairs that led from the grotto two at a time, mumbling incoherent curses along the way.

Of course, he could send another hellhound after the girl, but he trusted only one of them to do the job properly. Unfortunately, it was Wednesday evening, and his best hound, Adonadon, had his bath and massage on Wednesday evenings. Come whiskers or high tails, nothing would drag the hound away from his lavish spa. Mithragog had already attempted to bribe the hound with every conceivable gift and treasure, it was simply a useless endeavor.

The imps plainly weren't smart enough. Oh, they were a vicious adversary, once they actually located their prey, a rare occurrence without a proper guide. That left Kachar, the formidable demon. Mithragog would send him after the girl and he would bring her back, too, shredded perhaps, but Kachar had enough wit to leave the important organs intact. If only the demon hadn't come to him recently expressing a sudden concern for his...what had he called it? Oh, yes, *Karma*.

It was no secret Mithragog's minions thought him weak—too young and inexperienced to harness and execute the powers of the great Merlin. So what if he'd skipped a few years of instruction? His mentor, Spinel the Wise, had clearly held back the better part of his magical arsenal, not trusting an apprentice with intricate and useful bits of wisdom. The ancient mage had obviously lost his steel, reverting to the practice of only mild forms of magic. Tea brewing of all things! What apprentice could possibly have patience for such a thing? So, yes, Mithragog had taken his leave of Spinel, but not before he had collected every whisper concerning the cursed heir and had learned that the heart of the heir will grant its possessor access to powers that could easily surpass the feats of the great Merlin.

Arriving at the throne room, Mithragog pointed the tip of his staff at the door and released a spell far too powerful to shut the door gently. He winced as the stone slab crumbled to a pile of dust. Unable to recall a repair spell, he determined to order a mason to fit a new door in the morning.

Sitting stiffly upon his throne, he listened to his own labored breathing, his breath expelled in flaming bursts.

He almost had her! Clearly, she was within an inch of her life. What dastardly jinx had she pulled from her pocket?

No matter, it's finished now.

Lowering his chin, he brooded, moaning with sour despair. He couldn't allow her to get away. It could be months again before he had another chance to take her. What could he do?

Rising, he crossed the room to look auspiciously at an oversized text resting on a pedestal to the right of the throne, a highly prized codex he had lifted from Spinel. The gutless wizard owed Mithragog at least as much for the years wasted in his worthless company. The Book of Deeds. Dirty deeds. Surely, there was a spell he could conjure to put that witch in his grasp once and for all. He fumbled through the pages, scanning the text, waiting (none too patiently) for inspiration to strike.

There, on page five-hundred and eighty-two, was a bit of a spell that just might work. He rubbed his hands over his scantly bearded chin and considered the possibilities. A cloud of dust erupted from the book as he slammed it shut and rushed through castle corridors, knowing he had only a few minutes to spare.

The spell room housed an awaiting cauldron and shelves filled to the brim with ingredients, some ordinary herbs and roots, others not so ordinary, not so easily acquired. He flicked his wrist toward the base of the cauldron where a sturdy fire sprang up. In a whirl, he twisted and turned, throwing bits and pieces into the steaming brew. If he managed to do this right, he would have his treasure within the hour. Then the powers of the ages would finally be his and the insubordinate minions lazing around his castle would no longer deny him, for they (and every other creature breathing under the sun) would become subject to his desire. The corners of his lips rose with a twitch.

ξɔʞξ

Farrin stopped running and searched for any hint of pursuit. Nothing there. The hound hadn't followed. Smiling with satisfaction, she listened to the cooing of a pair of owls, informing one another of their state of affairs, perhaps relaying where one might find a juicy mole, or perhaps asking about the identity of the witch creeping so brazenly through their territory. The angry chitter of a squirrel seemed to beg the owls for silence and a lone howl from a wolf or coyote was barely discernible, sounding off in the far distance.

Gingerly, she touched her ear. Her fingers came away wet and sticky, the lesion still oozing. Sarina would dress the wound and use a mysterious compound to heal it in half the time normally required.

Farrin adjusted her hood, which, in a frustrating but predictable cycle, continuously slipped off her head, the fabric repeatedly snagged by low pine branches. This part of the forest grew particularly dense, she was bound to suffer a scrape or two as she twisted and twirled to fit her slender frame between the huddling trees.

Lapis De La Morte rested on the far side of the grove, a large unattended cemetery used mostly to house the last brigand of Frenchman who had come seeking England's glory only to find the king's knights cunningly prepared for their arrival. Les Monsieurs, consequently, have been spawning maggots for nearly fifty years.

Clouds scattered off and exposed the moon, its light permeating through the trees, resting softly where it fell.

Squeezing through the last of the overgrown pines, Farrin squinted in an attempt to identify an odd figure perched atop one of the larger headstones. Drawing nearer, clinging to the lush cover of pine arms, she saw a man sitting nonchalant, one leg waving inches above the ground, the other knee drawn to his chin, his foot resting on the crest of the stone, a dark hood drawn over his face as he busily carved into a small stick with a knife much too large for the intricate job. Moving to the right, she searched for another angle, hoping to get a better look at the oaf without alerting him to her presence.

"If I meant you harm," he said, his tone subdued and relaxed, "you would already be explaining yourself to St. Peter."

"Ozzie?" She ventured, certain she recognized his dulcet tone.

"And who else would the council dare disturb at such an ungodly hour to come fetch your mutinous backside from the throngs of this horrid thicket?"

Emerging from cover, Farrin burst through the clearing and knocked him off his stoop in an awkward attempt to embrace him.

"Heavens to Merlin, you make it seem as though we haven't enjoyed one another's company for an entire lifetime. It's been but a few weeks."

She pecked him on the cheek with a hurried kiss. "It felt like forever."

Righting himself, he dusted his breeches off and threw back his hood. Handsome as always, he towered over her and gazed into her eyes, the slightest hint of a smile spreading over his lips. "Still, it would do you well to learn the proper way to treat a knight."

"Excuse me, *Sir Oswald*, for I am a complete buffoon in your honorable presence." Performing an exaggerated curtsy, she laughed, slipping her hand ever so slowly into her pocket.

"Don't," he scowled, grasping her wrists.

"Please." She implored, batting her eyelashes, as if that would have any effect at all. "I only want a few minutes at the festival and then, I swear to Merlin, I'll go back and play the prim damsel. I swear it."

"The hound nearly took you to pieces. Do you think Mithragog will leave you to wander the rest of the way unencumbered? What sort of knight would I be to leave you here to die, hmm?"

Aha! Ozzie had seen the hound attack and had done nothing to intervene, which meant he had complete confidence in Farrin's ability to deal with the mutt, or he was a coward. But no, there wasn't a trace of fear in this man's blood, far from it, which could only mean he knew Farrin could handle the slobbering hound. She smiled and felt a blush burn into her cheeks. But, how had he managed to get to the cemetery before she arrived? Oh, he was a cunning and resourceful rogue and, once again, she was grateful to have him on her side.

"Mithragog," she said, "can kiss my..."

The ground beneath them began to quake as if affected by the sound of Mithragog's name. Ozzie glared at Farrin and she knew he suspected she had conjured a spell to secure her freedom. She shook her head and he seemed to know without her having to say, whatever was upon them was not her scheme.

Thirty long-dead Frenchman began to burst from the ground. Shattered stone crunched and broken sod erupted, forming a large circle. Within the space of a fraction of a second, lurching skull and bone had surrounded Farrin and Ozzie.

ξжξ

Sarina threw the bolt on the door and inspected the disarray left behind by her jovial guests. The crowd had been quite merry this evening and she was glad, though not overjoyed with the muddle. As usual, pools of ale stained the rough wooden tables. Empty tankards scattered the bar, chicken and turkey bones stripped of all edible flesh were piled high on pewter service trays, lemon and lime rinds littered the floor and one exhausted minstrel lay passed out beneath the candlelit chandelier slowly swaying over his head.

The minstrel had an exceptional talent that kept the patrons singing well into the night, his dashing looks adding an extra bonus to the festival's pleasantries. In fact, he had spent nearly every moment of his intermissions fending off tipsy maidens. Smiling, Sarina decided to allow him to sleep while she bit into her task. It would take at least an hour to put things back in order, perhaps two.

It seemed safe to say the marigold tincture she added to the brew had produced a cheerful effect. Her pub, *The Belching Bra*, had always drawn a large crowd, especially during the festival and, though she would like to think its prosperity due to the herbs she added to the ale, she must give credit to the locals who utterly enjoyed one another's company. Many elements played into the successful running of her establishment, but none quite so important as the unbreakable bond she had formed with the villagers.

She carried empty tankards into the kitchen and thought about the wonderful time she had had this evening. The laughter, the music, the ale, the food—all of it quite perfect. One thing would have made it better, though. If only Farrin had been here. And yet, Farrin's absence constituted a blessing, it meant she was keeping herself safe and that mattered most.

Still. A curse on Mithragog and his minions! The council continued to search for a way to disarm the weasel but had yet to arrive at a suitable solution. Blessed be the day of that discovery though, for on that day, Mithragog would surely wish he were never born.

Sarina drew a bucket of warm water and hefted it back to the bar, soaping down the tables with a flourish. The minstrel expelled a pig-snout snore and Sarina allowed herself a peek. Knees tucked into his muscle-laden chest, he was unabashedly sucking his thumb. Bless him. Poor man! Every wench within a hundred mile radius had severely mauled him during the course of the night. T'was his own fault though, running around the countryside looking like an angel accidentally escaped from the heavens. Long locks of golden hair, muscles nearly ripping the clothes off his back, a square jaw, bright blue eyes and a voice surely meant to melt the soul. Oh yes, the bloke had as much as asked for it. Then, too, Sarina had been grateful to the maidens for keeping the minstrel at arm's length, as it was immediately evident Sarina had sparked his interest. Sarina, however, had come to Airsmeade specifically to escape the chains of marriage. She would not be tempted into the dungeons of male domination and ownership, even if it meant becoming a spinster. The minstrel wasn't the first smitten man to pass through Airsmeade and Sarina had no desire to crush the heart of yet another love-starved puppy. Fortunately, his exhaustion had spared her the thankless task.

The wielding of the broom and mop always took the longest to complete. People don't seem to care much about dropping whatever they have in their hands and leaving litter where it falls. Cleaning the floor was the one chore that always put Sarina in the mood for a long night's sleep. She yawned and arched her back, stretching stiff muscles. Thanks be for the fresh straw she had recently used to stuff her mattress, she would be grateful for it tonight.

A sudden crash at the door nearly sent her out of her skin and before she could consider what might cause such a disturbance, another blast hammered and nearly split the bolt in two. Abandoning the broom, she ran for the kitchen. The third assault broke the hinges loose and the large wooden frame crashed to the floor with a clatter. The cold night air rushed into the pub, followed by six large men dressed in black leather, swords extended, their ominous blades glistening in the candlelight.

Sarina cast her spell too late and, admittedly, it was weak. She barely had time to think the proper words, much less speak them. She'd always had more skill with plants than with magic. Now, she found herself bound and gagged, thrown over the ass of a monstrous black steed, the air forced from her lungs each time the horse planted a hoof.

Bouncing on the back of a high-stepping stallion, the handsome minstrel lifted his weary head, searching Sarina's eyes for an explanation.

ᚻᚷᚻ

Farrin and Ozzie crouched, knees bent, standing back-to-back, arms extended toward their assailants. The dead Frenchmen wielded makeshift swords that seemed fashioned from rib bones and, in fact, probably were. Not bothering to count, Farrin was sure each specter would have come up at least one rib short. The tips of bone looked sharp enough to send an unfortunate victim through the gates of hell. She did not plan to make that trip this evening and Ozzie didn't seem a willing traveler either.

"How many are there?" He asked, his voice calm as they slowly turned a circle, eyeing their gaunt foes.

"Thirty or so," she answered, her tone not nearly as calm as his.

"One blade against thirty," he mumbled.

"I don't suppose your men are nearby?" She hoped he'd chuckle and say, 'of course they are,' and yet the knot turning in her stomach told her it wasn't so. His long-drawn sigh answered sufficiently.

"Do they look a bit clumsy to you?" He ventured.

She carefully studied their movements as they slowly stepped forward, closing in. Ozzie was right. They were animated, but not at all graceful. One of them could only inch its way forward as it had a spear wedged between the lower leg bones, preventing it from walking full stride. Another chattered, its upper and lower teeth battering in rapid succession as if the frigid air could bother a mortified zombie. Most of them were interred wearing elaborate hats that slipped over their faces now, past the point where a thick brow might have supported the brim, if they had any brows, which of course, they didn't. Nor could they see, their eyes having decomposed long ago.

"Mithragog is controlling them all," she said, half statement, half question.

"So it would seem."

The tallest of the lot with the widest shoulder girth, lunged forward, stabbing its makeshift weapon toward Ozzie's chest. He maneuvered around the jab, sidestepping.

"They mean business," he grunted, his brow furled in concentration, his focus darting as he surveyed the tightening circle.

"Is it safe to say Mithragog knows exactly where we are?" She asked.

"It is."

The Frenchman closest to Farrin took a wild swing that might have relieved her of her head if she hadn't ducked quickly enough.

"Nice move," Ozzie chuckled.

"Thanks for blocking the blow, Sir Oswald. Whatever would a girl do without her knight in shining armor?"

Now the line of dead men began to swing their weapons in wild bursts, Farrin and Ozzie dancing their way around the thrusts.

"Have we had enough of this?" She panted.

"Quite," he said, jumping over a low blow meant to dispense with his feet.

"Cover your ears and close your eyes," she instructed, "unless you fancy the idea of spending the rest of your life blind, deaf and dumb."

"All right," he answered, "but I may have already mastered the last item on your list."

Farrin made sure Ozzie complied with her instructions and slipped her hand into her pocket, withdrawing a palm-full of silver powder, which she threw toward the nearest ghoul. The silver sparkled as it rained down. She spoke her words concisely, with precision and authority, "Servo diligo. Praemium maximum!"

Once again the ground began to quake as, one by one, the dead Frenchmen exploded in ear-splitting eruptions of blinding white light, leaving nothing but rubbles of dust and bone where they had stood.

Ozzie swiped bone fragments from his hair and surveyed the damage, "Remind me never to piss you off."

ξӜξ

Farrin watched Ozzie tousle his flaxen hair, small bits of expired Frenchmen tumbling between his fingers. She was shaking in her boots. It was one thing to possess a spell like that, using it was another thing altogether. Never before had she conjured such a massive explosion.

Dreadful spell.

Overkill.

Most awesome.

The moon had ceased its game of peek-a-boo during their little soirée and now shone brightly upon the weathered tombstones.

Farrin would be all right, once the trembling stopped.

"I just killed thirty men," she muttered.

Ozzie laughed. "They were already dead."

It took a moment to process the information, but when it sank in, she sighed with relief. Killing wasn't high on her list of ambitions, although she wouldn't mind a go at Mithragog.

Ozzie stopped patting himself and threw an arm around her shoulder. "Let's get you home, shall we?"

She nodded and began to walk away.

"Not that way," he chastised.

"Home," she said, her tone firm, "is *this* way." She increased the speed of her gait, determined.

Unmoved, Ozzie calmly called after her, "Back to the cottage where the council has multiplied the power of protection. It's the safest place in the valley. After what we've just been through, how can you consider putting our lives in further peril? Not just your life, Farrin, mine as well."

Stopping, but not turning, she replied, "You would have that vile rat win the night? I want ten minutes at the festival. That's all I ask."

"It's late. The pub is probably closed."

"I don't want a drink," she countered.

"Sarina will be in bed, everyone else asleep as well."

"Ozzie?"

He sighed, knowing what she was about to say. "What?"

"You're pissing me off."

ξЖξ

Mithragog was livid. Twice in the same hour he had stood on the precipice of untold power, twice he'd plunged into the depths of humiliation. His cheek twitched.

What a spell! He had underestimated the prey and that changed everything. In fact, he no longer wanted the witch dead. Oh, no. No, no, no. Why waste such an impressive talent? Killing the girl no longer seemed prudent. Call it ironic, call it whatever you will, he simply never had the stomach for killing, that's what minions are for. But now! Now he could go after the girl himself. What is that old saying? Oh, yes. 'When you want something done right, do it yourself.'

The witch would teach him everything she knew about the arts. Once that was accomplished, he would have her heart ripped from her chest and use the rest of her innards for stew.

ξ⊁ξ

The witch of Dearbourne sipped the last of her damiana tea and pointed an arthritic finger at her looking glass, a cackled crack of laughter passing through her lips.

As it sometimes happens, air mixed with liquid and exploded inside her esophagus, causing her to choke. Her skin turned an unbecoming shade of blue as she struggled to regain her composure, the coughing fit flaring and increasing in velocity. She slapped her knee with a ferocious swat of frustration. Oh, she *hated* when this sort of thing happened. On top of feeling as though she might choke to death, she also felt the familiar gush of urine escaping as she fought for air. There is nothing—*nothing* worse under the sun and moon than the undignified horror known as aging. If that seems too much of an overstatement, ask any woman who has just entered her one-hundred and eighty-fifth year, as had Helga Dearbourne.

The coughing fit mercifully subsided and her skin gradually returned to its normal grayish hue. She backhanded the wooden cup that had held her tea, sailing the culprit cleanly across the room where it smacked against the mud-patched wall, teetered to the floor, spinning dramatically, landing upside-down on the bare sod.

The tea hadn't been the only culprit, had it? No. Her laughter was at fault as well. And when was the last time she could remember enjoying a genuine fit of laugher, twenty-five, fifty years ago? Try as she might, she couldn't remember what had incited her mirth back then, but she knew what had tickled her funny bone this evening: Mithragog and his potty-training parlor tricks. More careful this time, as it seemed a dangerous activity for a woman her age, she allowed another cackle to escape her withered lips. Cemeteries and zombies! Whatever was the man thinking? Against Farrin the Fair and Sir Oswald no less, both of whom possessed more magic, wit, strength and grace than Mithragog could ever hope to acquire.

Helga softly touched the smooth circular surface of her looking glass and smiled, baring her blackened teeth. The deeply creviced skin on her face wrinkled up around her nose and she discharged an unexpected snort. Mithragog didn't stand a chance of ever catching Farrin the Fair; Helga, if need be, would see to that personally. The clumsy oaf should have known that the most vulnerable prey is a prey unaware of the hunt. The entire country knew Mithragog wanted the girl's heart—the king's council was certainly aware and that constituted a huge mistake. Surely, they had imparted every protection available on the girl's behalf. A bumbling idiot, that's what Mithragog is...a fool's fool.

Helga stood to fetch a tattered rag and returned to her wooden stool, sopping up the puddle she had leaked there. Sitting back down, she slowly traced her fingertips over the potted skin of her face, a face once fabled as unrivaled in beauty and grace.

With the heart of the first female born in Gwenevere's line, Helga could restore her youth and rejuvenate her power. Then, glory to all a faithful witch deserved, unbidden urine would never again escape her thighs.

Hanging from a long nail over the scant wooden door, an aged black hat with a pointed tip collected dust. Helga eyed it thoughtfully then rose and drew nearer to it. Standing there, rigid, she considered many things, consequences first and foremost. After several minutes of quiet contemplation, she snatched the hat from the hook, gave it a good shake and thrust it over the crown of her head.

Croaking in a dark corner, a large toad the size of an overgrown armchair began to expand and contract, repeatedly growing twice its size and reverting to normal.

Blinking hysterically, its tongue lopped out of its mouth, green toad-dribble oozing into a slimy puddle at its feet.

"Enough with the anxiety attack, Edema! Get your warts in order, toad, we're stepping out."

ξ꙾ξ

Mithragog summoned his one loyal servant. Within moments, the boy, Archknuckle, stood before the throne, his tattered rags more haggard than the last time Mithragog had beckoned him to court. The lad looked and smelled as though he hadn't had a proper bath since his mother chewed loose the birth cord. Bowing on one knee, the boy peered through his long, matted, straw-colored bangs, not quite comfortable making direct eye contact, as it should be.

"Sire," the boy mumbled.

Mithragog reveled in the sound of the word, but did his best to mask the smile creeping over thin lips.

"Archie," Mithragog bellowed, "I require my Seer. I am embarking upon a dangerous journey and would like his council before I leave. Fetch him for me."

The sudden drooping of the boys shoulders and despairing grunt did not escape Mithragog's notice.

"I cannot, Sire. If I may remind your highness, you yourself dispatched of the Seer in a most unusual way." The boy lowered his head and deepened his bow.

Mithragog curled his face into a scowl. How could he have forgotten? His Seer, Nostradumbas, when asked to give an account of the future, had begun to spout incomprehensible nonsense, going on about a contrivance he called e-mail, claiming men would one day have the capability to communicate with one another from around the world in an instant, without saddlebags, without horses, even without the men required to carry such correspondence. He spoke of the World Wide Web but refused to say where the giant spiders would come from. This had frustrated and infuriated Mithragog. When the Seer went even further, insisting that man would one day fly, not by magic, not with wings, but by a fearsome contraption he had called an aero plane, Mithragog was sadly forced to admit that not only could his Seer no longer 'see,' but he had simply lost his last shred of sanity. And so, Mithragog had turned the wretched clod into an outhouse, which he believed still stood at the base of the mountain.

Since these events had occurred many weeks ago, perhaps the Seer had come to his senses.

"Does the outhouse still stand?" He asked the boy.

Archknuckle replied with a nod, "It does, Sire."

Mithragog reached for his staff. "Let's have a look, shall we?"

The trek down the mountain was pleasant enough, if not a bit chilly. The boy dutifully followed in Mithragog's steps, saying nothing, but mumbling now and then when he lost his footing.

They soon stood beside the weathered outhouse, small sun and moon shapes carved into the thin wooden door.

"Open the door," Mithragog commanded, stepping back lest he become overwhelmed by the noxious fumes surely present inside.

The boy tugged the neckline of his tunic over his nose and reached to pull the creaking door open.

"You've got mail," the outhouse declared.

Mithragog jerked back with a jolt of surprise and the boy gasped, releasing the door as if bitten.

ξↃҜξ

Maintaining a quick pace, Farrin listened to the reassuring sound of Ozzie's boots slapping the ground behind her. He hadn't said much in the last five minutes but there was little need, she knew he was angry. Still, Sir Oswald was not without power, far from it. If he wanted Farrin back at the cottage, he could certainly put her there with very little trouble. The fact that he hadn't forced her to go back was a testament to his undying friendship and, for that, she would always be grateful.

They were a few moments from Airsmeade. Most of the forest chitter-chatter had calmed down, the animals settled in for the night, only the occasional cricket nest causing a ruckus. Farrin kept her senses on alert for any unusual sights or sounds in case Mithragog decided to concoct another welcoming party. Ozzie hadn't let his guard down

either, but walked with his broad sword in one hand, long
knife in the other, both blades bathed in moonlight. Only
when they stepped out of the forest and into the clearing
did he finally relax enough to sheath the long knife. Farrin
heard him exhale a sigh of relief and realized that she, too,
had been holding her breath.

The festival had obviously ended. Few lights in the
village were still aflame. Torches outside the blacksmith
shop flickered low and would soon extinguish altogether.
Waning candles burned on the windowsills inside a few
huts, an occasional shadow passing by, bearing testament
to the night owls who busied themselves with their late-
night tasks.

Farrin's heartbeat quickened. A few more steps and she
would stand inside *The Belching Bra* for the first time in
weeks. It had been far too long. If by chance Sarina had
gone to bed, Farrin would rouse her. Sarina would be glad
of it.

"Stop!" Ozzie's face was set like stone, one hand
grasping Farrin's cloak, the other wrapped tightly around
the hilt of his sword.

At first, Farrin thought it some sort of vengeful joke, but
when she looked past his shoulder to see the gaping maw
where the pub door had once hung, she allowed the squeal
broiling inside her throat to escalate into a full-fledged
scream.

༻✠༺

Smashed off its hinges, the pub door lay on the floor in a battered mangle. A bucket of water perched on one of the tables held soapsuds. Farrin submerged her fingers into the water. Still warm. Whatever had happened here couldn't have happened more than a few minutes ago. Yet, she and Ozzie had heard nothing when they approached the village. How was that possible?

She touched the crystallized blood coagulating behind her ear. Had she lost hearing when the hound attacked, or during the explosion in the cemetery?

Ozzie made a full sweep of the pub. Sarina was gone.

༻✠༺

An enormous lake resides twenty miles northeast of Airsmeade, surrounded by woodlands and fed by the river Avon.

Fables passed down from long ago speak of faeries and elves, dwarves and trolls, all living on the shores of the mighty Lake Avonelle. Some say a vicious battle took place here among the smoky mists and curling fogs, at dawn's break many years ago and that the spirits of fallen warriors still haunt Avonelle's gloomy banks. Myla pulled her tunic tight around her shoulders, staving off the crisp air, not knowing whether to hope the tales true or false.

She had come in search of a legend. Despite a long acquaintance with the mythical Elaine Viviane, Myla still thought of her in awe. Now, she must find the notorious Lady of the Lake once again and beseech her to take action on behalf of Gwenevere's heir, a young woman in dire need.

Myla made her way around the lake, skirting through trees, fighting against the underbrush, attempting to move stealthily, not always succeeding. Fallen branches snapped beneath the soles of her boots, leaves rustled, frightened animals screeched and took flight. Each time she set off one of these natural alarms, she would stand rigid until it felt safe to proceed. She was no huntress, no warrior either, and embarrassingly clumsy.

Some would not want Myla to succeed in finding the Lady. There are those who would stoop to the lowest means to keep the Lady from using her power to protect the heir and too many knew of Myla's connection to the Lady. Someone was watching Myla now, she could feel the unease crawling at the base of her neck, prickling like a nest of needles.

She yanked at her hood, drawing it further over her face, her pale skin too easy to spy in the moonlight. She must find the Lady Viviane quickly. There she would be safe from this phantom putting her on edge with its prying eyes. Only a fool would take issue with the Lady of the Lake.

The path Myla followed smelled of rich herbs—patches of mint and fennel, yards of chamomile and yellow fern, the sweet scents captured by the night air quite intoxicating and she found herself yearning for a hot cup of tea. Truly, it was an exceptionally cold evening. She watched with annoyance as wisps of white fog formed each time she exhaled. Winter's blankets would soon fall upon the lofty mountain, the valley affected not long after. Then it would be almost impossible to approach the river without leaving a trail.

Would she find the Lady inside her cave, or with the lake? Myla hoped for the cave and a bright fire, if luck had seen fit to accompany her.

The last time she made the journey she had come under less dire circumstances. Lady Viviane was a dear friend to Queen Gwenevere and had always treated Myla in a sisterly fashion as well because Myla had joyfully born the title of head handmaiden to the good Queen.

Since Gwenvere's death, many, many years ago, Myla would occasionally come to visit with the Lady, not to gossip or to give news of recent occurrences, the Lady had no need of messengers as she possessed her own means of procuring information, but simply to offer cordial company, which, sadly, the Lady seemed to lack.

Stepping through a scant clearing, Myla approached the water and watched moonlight shimmer on the surface of the lake, fragments of light sparkling like shards of white fire.

Stooping to one knee, she wiggled her fingers in the icy water and stepped back, expecting the lake to erupt with the Lady's dramatic entrance. The water did not stir. A hint of a smile worked over Myla's face. She would find the Lady inside her cave.

Myla headed toward the western shore. Dew ridden leaves on the short branches of an oak brushed against her face, increasing the chill of the sharp night air.

Veering away from the lake, she trudged inland, toward the base of the great mountain, Arraine. Here she would find the Lady's cave carefully camouflaged by clinging vines and weeds. No one would ever guess an entrance existed. Even with a sharp eye for detail, Myla unwittingly walked by the mouth of the cave several times.

She needed to find it, quickly.

Fixing her gaze upon the ground, she began to search for the telltale signs of ginseng root. Few knew of the Lady's penchant for elixirs prepared with the roots, as such, they were the one clue provided, as the Lady insisted on growing them close to home.

At last, Myla located the root beds.

"Myla," the Lady's voice echoed from within the stone enclosure, "Please, come in."

Myla pulled a throng of vines off to the side and leaned in, squeezing through the narrow entrance. The moment she stepped inside the cave she knew something was amiss.

ξᬽξ

How many times in life does the average person wish for a chance to reverse the hands of time?

Farrin felt as though she didn't have a second to waste on useless introspection but couldn't help thinking, a few minutes less in the forest and she might have reached Airsmeade in time to save Sarina. She exhaled with frustration. Her hands curled into tight fists even as she willed herself to relax. There was a bull, a mighty raging bull, coursing through her veins: nostrils flaring, head lowered, eyes fixed upon its mark, pounding at her chest in a desperate attempt to escape its confines. If *The Belching Bra* didn't belong to Sarina, Farrin might have shattered everything breakable within her reach. The pub did belong to Sarina, though, and it had already sustained enough damage—*just look at that door!*

Ozzie lumbered back inside the tavern, eyes lowered to avoid contact. "There are hoof prints for at least six horses. I found this hanging on one of the hitching posts." He handed Farrin a small piece of black leather fabric then gingerly stepped out of reach.

"For the love of England, I'm not going to *explode*," she blasted, a little hurt and annoyed at the insinuation. He shrugged and tried to subdue a grin, turning away so she couldn't see his face.

Farrin's tone made it clear she had carved her decision in stone, "I'm going after her."

Ozzie turned to face her. "You have no idea where they've taken her," he blurted, his face blooming with vexation.

"I don't?" She asked.

Shoulders slumping, he breathed a quick inhale-exhale. "You do?" He leaned closer to inspect her eyes.

"Of course." She slipped the black leather fabric into her pocket and lifted her chin, pointing it toward the door. "Her father has sent for her...*again*...the obstinate donkey."

ﻉﻜﻉ

Ozzie kicked a lemon rind in frustration and pasted it on the far wall where it slowly slid down, leaving pulpy slime in its wake. Yanking a bar stool away from the bar, he plopped onto it, the way a dying man might reluctantly slump into a coffin. Clearly, his patience walked a high wire.

Raking both hands through his lion-like mane, he sighed. "Tell me, if it's not too much trouble, why Sarina's father might abduct his own daughter?"

Farrin took the stool next to his, her fingers tapping nervously on the bar's wooden surface. "Sarina's father is the Bishop of Stockbridge." Her tone was matter-of-fact, as if this statement was all the explanation required.

"So?" He prodded.

"So, he thinks Sarina is a witch. We know how the church feels about witches, don't we? Midnight meals burnt at the stake, served with a gallon of holy water."

He turned to her, his face wrought with confusion, "But, she *is* a witch. Would her father really condemn his own child to death?"

"No, I doubt he would condemn her, unless she forced his hand. But, she's not just a witch, Ozzie. She's a *beautiful* witch. I'm sure that fact hasn't escaped your notice."

Farrin's gaze hadn't left the door, her fingers furiously tapping, her legs bouncing as if churning butter. She had to go after Sarina. Now. Every moment spent here delayed the rescue. On the other hand, Ozzie had a right to know what he was getting into should he decide to tag along, a right to make an informed decision.

"While her father is a man of the cloth," Farrin explained, "he, apparently, has not come across those scriptures written in his Holy book concerning the iniquities of greed."

"Greed?"

"Yes. Sarina left home three years ago when she realized her father meant to marry her off to the highest bidder, the Duke of Devonshire."

"You're kidding?"

She sighed heavily. "Now is no time for jest."

"How can you be so certain this is the Bishop's work and not some frightful spell cast by a ghoulish witch or warlock? Maybe this is Mithragog's doing."

"Look," she said, retrieving the black fabric Ozzie had given her. "The leather is branded with the family crest."

Ozzie slipped off the stool and stood to stretch, his elbows reaching for his back, his chest puffing out like a rooster at dawn.

"It's time to get you back to the cottage." Eyelids set at half-mast, his exhaustion was evident, "As long as her father doesn't intend her harm, she's safe."

Farrin stared, aghast, jaw slack. He was serious. She kicked off the stool and headed for the door. There, she turned back, cheeks burning with fury, "I said I'm going after her. I know you can stop me, I've seen what you can do when you put your mind to it, even if you insist on denying your wizardry. But I swear to Merlin, there will be a duel if you try to stop me and you *will* have to kill me."

ᛷᚹᛷ

Myla had never seen the Lady weep before, had never seen her in low spirits for that matter, but she was crying now, shoulders heaving with great sobs, tears shining on blanched cheeks, eyes red and swollen, hands wringing the fabric of her tunic as if attempting to squeeze out its deep blue dye. What in creation could reduce the most powerful woman in the world to a sniveling child?

Rushing to her side, Myla knelt on the floor and slipped her hands over the Lady's trembling knuckles. "My Lady, what has upset you?"

The Lady pulled a handkerchief from her cleavage and used it to blow her nose, her sobs growing louder. Long, soulful minutes passed before she composed herself well enough to speak and Myla did not pressure her, but stroked the back of her hand and brushed away strands of golden hair when they covered her face. When the Lady finally spoke, her voice was raw, her words interrupted by the occasional skittered sigh.

"I took tea," she said, "earlier this evening with a woman who appeared as Carrin Swathmore, an old friend for many years. Of course, now I realize the woman wasn't Carrin at all, but a shape shifting hag."

Myla gasped. Shape shifting is a power quite rare, devious, and often lethal. If someone had used this power to beguile the Lady, it would require great skill.

"Needless to say," the Lady continued, struggling to subdue her sobbing, "the tea wasn't merely tea. When I awoke from a drugged slumber I realized what had happened..." A torrent of tears broke over her cheeks.

Myla threw her arms around the Lady and held her, fluids spilling into the fabric of Myla's cloak, her shoulder soon soaked in a puddle.

Slightly composed, the Lady exclaimed, "She took the crystal globe. Pray with me, Myla. Summon the Goddess.

I must retrieve the globe or I will simply perish. I cannot live without it!"

"Globe? Whatever for? Did it have some power, some magic?"

"It holds more than power, Myla, more than magic, it holds the great Merlin."

ξℳξ

Helga Dearbourne stood on the banks of the river Avon, hunched stealthily behind a large sycamore, eyes wide, barely able to believe what had just scampered by in a hell's rush. Dezva, one of the most vile creatures in this world (or any other), had just blazed his way through the thicket. Was he running *to* something, or running *from* something? Hard to know the difference, impossible really. Who knows the ways of demons?

Helga hadn't laid eyes on Dezva for at least a hundred and fifty years and believed the demon had met its final fate along with its mistress. Apparently, she had been mistaken. That posed a problem, a very *big* problem.

Inching her way from behind the sycamore, she glanced left, then right, and did it again just to be sure she and Edema were alone. Edema had taken full advantage of their current location and sat belly deep in the water, soaking her warts. Perfectly still, she had seen the demon as well and enlisted what little defense a toad has, attempting to blend inconspicuously into the environment. Say what you will, but a wise toad understands that there are times when cowardice comes in mighty handy.

Using her staff for leverage, Helga lowered herself to the ground and sat beside the black river. There, she took a moment to collect her thoughts. Hopefully, she wouldn't have too much trouble getting back up when the time came.

"He's gone, toad. You can breathe now."

Helga had yet to take her own advice, her hands still trembling with shock.

Dezva stood three and half feet tall, small as demons go, his size not at all indicative of the tremendous power he wielded. Helga would like to believe she was mistaken, convince herself she hadn't seen the demon at all and, if it weren't for the tail, which she clearly saw, she might have half a chance at pacification.

The tail.

She'd seen the accursed tail.

Dangling from the back of Dezva's head like a wayward ponytail, the ill placed caudal was a mild reminder from the lord of Hades that no demon found un-loyal to said lord could walk away unscathed. Dezva, however, remained loyal only to his mistress, Morgana le Fay.

Morgana was a problem, a very *big* problem.

Apparently, she lurked nearby, for wherever you find Dezva, Morgana is not far away. Helga grew nauseous with the thought, more queasy than the time she had accidentally dropped a pair of spoiled donkey balls into her soup. And, since Morgana had chosen this time to resurface after a century and a half spent in silence, little question remained as to what she wanted: the heart of the heir. Ironic, considering Morgana had placed the curse on the heir in the first place. Now, she had come to reap what she had so spitefully sown.

Surely, Queen Gwenevere was spinning in her grave.

Swatting at a swarm of gnats attempting to feast upon her face, Helga offered them a few choice words and took a tight grip on her staff, pulling herself to her feet with a grunt and moan.

A battle loomed. Helga could go home and wait it out, or take sides. As much as she had hoped to procure the heart of the heir for herself, that no longer seemed probable, not with Morgana le Fay in the mix.

"Come, toad," Helga barked, walking away from the riverbank toward the great mountain Arraine, "We seek the Lady of the Lake."

ξжξ

Panting from the maddening pace required to match Farrin's brisk and angry strides, Ozzie pleaded his case. "I did not intend to leave her to her father's cruel fate. I simply thought it prudent to wait until morning when I can gather troops to go after her properly."

Men. You ask them to do something for you and they act put off and offended, but if you set out to accomplish something on your own, they are even more so. How do you win?

"I agree with you, Sir Oswald," she answered, raising her legs over a very large and irksome fallen tree.

"You do?"

"Yes, it's a wise decision."

Farrin noticed the ground beneath her boots had begun to give way and tufts of high grass were popping up in large sections, muddied splotches of swamp riddling the terrain, so she circled around to avoid one of nature's most vile traps.

"Go home, Sir Knight, sleep well. In the morning, you and your men can deliver Sarina the last two miles to safety, as I will have already brought her back twenty. Fear not, I will gladly give you the glory."

The ground became more and more muddied as Farrin moved along. There are two ways to Rivensdale, the long, safe road and the shorter, not so safe way. Time was of the essence. Unfortunately, the shorter route meant passing through the Locks of Havenshire, chockfull of haphazard dangers and foul creatures, not to mention a dead zone where magic doesn't work. That fact, Farrin realized, would be to her serious advantage if Mithragog still had his sights set on her. The power of his minions would not manifest here. He alone could approach. Two against one.

Speaking of two... Farrin stopped clomping through the brush and listened for the sound of Ozzie's footsteps, but failed to hear them. Turning back, she scoured the immediate terrain but found no sign of him. Had he actually returned to Airsmeade? Had her words insulted and shamed him into a quiet retreat? Sir Oswald, the gallant knight? Improbable. She worked her way back through the brush, calling his name, listening carefully for a reply. Seriously, she didn't need this delay, no time for hide-and-seek.

And then she saw it, the tip of Ozzie's sword jutting from the ground, barely moving, moonlight oozing lazily off the blade. The sprint toward the sword seemed an exaggerated promenade as time regressed to a pace slower than a porcupine mating session. She frantically scampered about and fought for ground, finding it impossible to cover the last five yards where a pool of quicksand lay between her outstretched arm and the sword blade. She stood too close now, her feet sliding in the mud, no rocks or roots to anchor them. The quicksand would have her for dessert if she moved any closer—it was already devouring the entrée.

ξӜξ

Myla was unclear as to who had ensnared Merlin inside the crystal globe. She didn't ask immediately, but when the opportunity presented itself in the form of an elongated silence, she made the inquiry.

"Of course, it was me," the Lady confessed, spent and clearly agitated.

All these years! Myla would never have suspected, nor would anyone else. Most assumed Merlin had left the realm for more interesting parts, or had expired and withered away. Who would have guessed he'd been outwitted? The very idea seemed preposterous, impossible for such a powerful wizard. How had the Lady managed it?

"He was my mentor," the Lady mumbled, her tone a collapsed whisper, "and he was smitten. I too, felt an irresistible force at work but refused to succumb as completely as he. I used his passion against him and made him promise to teach me everything he knew, vowing to give him his heart's desire if he did so. Gladly he made this pact and happily taught me, year after year, all the while his yearning burned ever more brightly. When he had transferred all of his wisdom to me, that, too, I used against him. You see, with the passing of the years I grew fonder of him, but realized a man such a he could never be truly content with me as I had already betrayed him, and so..."

"You trapped him?"

The Lady's cheeks burned bright. She lowered her chin to her chest, tears streaming off her face, her guilt and grief emanating, the air bound with tension.

Speechless, Myla moved to stand before the fire blazing in the hearth. She was familiar with the cunning and conniving ways of the mind's subterfuge. From the first glance, we sum one another up, forming opinions, forging glorious images in our minds, images not necessarily representative of truth, images we hold high and firm until they shatter. Fantasy always outflanks reality. We kick, claw and scream to protect our delusions. And now, Myla's image of the glorious Lady Viviane lay in ruins.

A lump caught in Myla's throat. Thoughts refused to gather. Emotions, like so many chameleons, took shape and reformed. Anger, bitterness, incredulity, shock, dismay, and yes, envy. How much must a woman love a man to want him near for all eternity? Myla had never met such a man and had since given up on whimsical hopes. But this tryst, this companionship, this sordid arrangement between Merlin and Viviane, was it romance, or a criminal affair? Where, exactly, do you draw the line?

During the lunar eclipse when no magic, no spell, is strong enough to hold its power, Merlin would have been free to take task with the Lady. Surely he had the ability to break her grip then, if he so desired. Why hadn't he? What transpired between them over the course of those moon-shadowed hours?

Myla turned back and knelt at the Lady's feet. Searching Viviane's eyes, she implored, "My Lady, the eclipse. Did he not beseech you to set him free?"

The Lady's tears flowed heavily then, her eyes swollen with sorrow.

"Of course," she said, her speech burdened by trembling lips. "He promised to stay at my side, made this oath and others, pleaded with me to see reason. I have seen reason, and I have seen many a man wander once a woman quenches his thirst. Although Merlin used every opportunity to express his gratitude for being near to me, I could not bring myself to find faith in him."

"You were never tempted to set him free?"

Staring into her lap, the Lady spoke sternly, "I knew only that, in time, he would leave me in pursuit of other quests and adventures. Selfish, I know. But, he must have sensed this as well, or he would have forced the issue. Not once did he attempt to undo what I had done. But now he is in grave peril. I have no way of knowing if the hag means to destroy him, or if she simply wishes to control his power. Either way, it does not fare well for the world to have such power in the wrong hands."

"My Lady, I can think of only one witch capable of what you suggest."

Viviane nodded and, in unison, she and Myla spoke the name together and with much foreboding, "Morgana le Fay."

ξжξ

With nothing but swamp grass and the silver drape of night for a canopy, a lurking presence slunk low to the ground, creeping forward inch-by-inch, careful to keep the glint of moonlight reflecting in his eyes undercover. He had been following the future queen since she left her charmed cabin two hours ago. Mind you, it is not easy to amble through Airsmeade without casting a shadow, but he had managed to avert detection.

He licked his fingertips and marveled at the taste of the salty, smooth flesh, then drew up a knee, dug the toe of his boot into the mud and pushed forward another half-foot or so without causing the slightest sound.

From what he could see, his decision to follow Her Heady Highness had been a divine inspiration and a stroke of good fortune. Twenty yards ahead, he could see the tip of Sir Oswald's sword, jutting out of the murky ground like a flailing church spire. The girl, wild-eyed and blithering about in full panic, did not have the slightest clue for remedy.

He began to braid long tendrils of grass, moving his fingers with blinding speed. It would take a minute or two to combine them into a rope sturdy enough to pull Sir Oswald from the muck. He worked without regard to maintaining his stealth, Farrin's constant cries would prevent her from hearing much else. Besides, once the rope was finished, he would have to come out of hiding in order to make the rescue. Perhaps it was time for a proper introduction.

Best hurry, the sword had sunk another six inches already.

ξжξ

Submerged in black waters without a hint of light, no shadow, or movement whatsoever, the pressure in Ozzie's lungs compounded a hundredfold with each passing moment. A fuddling place to be, a horrid place to die. How had he come to be here? He couldn't remember approaching this hell-pit. The last thing he heard was Farrin's sarcastic promise to give him glory, and then, *whoosh*.

The water seemed like liquid ice at first, he'd become numb since. Just a minor bother, he'd fallen into a puddle, he would simply pull himself out. But the hole hadn't let go and the sand beneath his feet refused to support his weight. The more he fought for freedom, the more the pit drew him in. He had determined it best to remain calm and still—not an easy task when your lungs are about to burst and the only sound you can hear is the rapid thrumming of your own heart as it prepares to beat its last.

Was Farrin aware that he had fallen, or was she still stomping off to Rivensdale, spouting her unending reprimands? God, if ever there was a time to hear a man's prayer, let her be near.

Good Lord, had his testicles just fallen off? Felt like it. Hard to say.

The sword began to slip.

Fading.

BK CRAWFORD

Lungs burning.
Darker.
Darker still.

ξᴊᴋξ

Nostradumbas, bone thin and possessing more wrinkles than a month of tall tales narrated by a mindless bard, was long and lanky with milky eyes that appeared consistently troubled by cloud cover. He kept his beard so long, he tripped over it whenever fate seemed in need of a good laugh. He anxiously stroked the white hairs of his beard now and carefully considered the immediate situation. He was grateful to have shed the outhouse form and to occupy flesh and bone once again, yet not overly thrilled with the misfortune of returning to Mithragog's service.

Despite Mithragog's self-proclaimed divinity, he was not particularly fond of truth. Nostradumbas must choose his words wisely when answering the king's requests (if 'king' constituted the proper word to describe the bumbling wizard, or if the term 'wizard' fit the oaf any better).

"I seek the heart of the first female born in the line of Gwenevere," Mithragog was saying, leaning forward with a certain air of authority, perched upon his counterfeit throne. "She has left the protection of the council and travels toward Airsmeade. I must know the fastest route to her current location. Also, you must reveal if this quest will bring me glory."

"Certainly," Nostradumbas humbly replied, "give me but a moment's contemplation."

Mithragog nodded. Nostradumbas turned away and walked to a far corner where a pair of long drapes provided a sufficient shadow. There he would seek to see.

Oh, who was he kidding, he didn't need to 'seek' to see, it was a simple matter of directing his mind to whatever question had been posed and—*presto!*—the information instantaneously swarmed through his mind as clearly as if it were a scene playing out before his eyes, no seeking involved. He would use this time in the shadows to calculate how he might handle the delicate delivery of the information he already possessed.

Mithragog had indicated the heir was near to Airsmeade: not so. He had also inquired as to whether his endeavor would bring him glory: quite the opposite. And so, the question was, what manner of truth would Mithragog accept without ire?

A tactful lie seemed the obvious solution. Frankly, the conveyance of truth had not been kind to Nostradumbas as of late. For the love of Arthur, the backwoods fool had turned his greatest asset into an outhouse! How barbaric, how stupendously childish. It would not happen again.

Nostradumbas returned to face Mithragog.

The tyrant lifted his face with grave anticipation, "Have you seen?"

"I have, my lord. You will find what you seek on the sacred acre. There, you will meet glory."

Mithragog's triumphant snickering was more than Nostradumbas could bear. Adonadon, the hellhound, might share his hot pool with a man in need of a bath and Nostradumbas would welcome the opportunity to shed the spider webs and outhouse excrement caked on his skin.

ξ🜍ξ

From the cover of the tall grass, he carefully watched the hardened glower ripen in Farrin's sapphire eyes. He had seen this look before, only a blink of time remained before she made a grave mistake. Should she do what he thought she had in mind, it could very well be the end of her. Sir Oswald would fare no better.

Sure enough, and to his great horror, Farrin made the plunge, one hand clinging to a feeble clump of grass, the other exploring the waters for Sir Oswald, her form slowly sinking into the muck.

Who has ever seen the mother gazelle challenge a lion for the life of her fawn? No one? There's a perfectly good reason for that...it's absurd, a losing battle, two lives lost instead of one. Who knows why humans do not possess this healthy measure of common sense, clearly they do not.

His fingers twisted the grass with heightened anxiety. He had nearly finished the rope, but it wasn't strong enough to pull two from the mire. The best he could hope was that fate would give him the opportunity to throw the rope twice.

Time to *how-do-you-do*. He sprang from the grass and threw the rope. Who grabbed on first didn't matter, what mattered was pulling one of them to safety fast enough to attempt a rescue on the other. Sir Oswald couldn't possibly have but a moment of life left in him. It would be advantageous, then, if he were the first to return to solid ground.

A prominent shadow eclipsed the moon and the fluttering of a mighty wing broke his concentration in a way no other sound could. He had heard this undulation only once before, on an evening when an entire village succumbed to ghastly horrors. A sense of dread and nauseous foreboding shuddered through him.

Just as Sir Oswald had taken a firm grip on the rope, the raptor swooped out of the sky and picked Sir Oswald and Farrin out of the muck with its mighty talons, much in the way a morning robin takes the early worm. Pluck and fly. They were already gone.

That was no morning robin. That wasn't a bird at all. That was nothing else but a dragon.

Scampering up a tree, he searched the skies but found no trace. Muscles tensed to the point of tearing, he cursed the night, screaming until his lungs begged reprieve.

Dragons are nasty creatures. They say a firedrake once took a dump on the village of Bibury and it took nearly three months to clear away the mess and stench. Of course, he had no way of knowing if the tale held any merit, but he had no reason to doubt it. These overgrown lizards throw their weight around easily, they're forty times the size of a man and able to barbeque an entire city with one sneeze. No one knows much about the vile temperamental creatures, though stories of conquering heroes abound, blah, blah, bullshit, and blah. As far as he could tell, a dragon dies of old age and not much else. However, and more specific to the situation at hand, it is common knowledge that a dragon never eats dead meat. In fact, dragons often play with their food, seeking amusement for hours, days, weeks, depending on how amusing the prey is and, of course, how long it's been since the firedrake's last meal.

He may yet find an opportunity to intercede on behalf of the future queen and her companion.

The nearest lair was located southwest of Rivensdale.

Hopping down from the tree, he licked the tips of his fingers, no longer salty, no longer smooth, and raced through the night on all fours, hoping the dragon hailed from the lair near Rivensdale.

ξ⭑ξ

Hands tied securely behind her back, Sarina couldn't cast a full-powered spell, which left her with only those she could perform telepathically. She didn't have a spell to make the horses lame, or one to give the men bad bowels, or one to lift her off horseback, nothing to help her escape. Just a hailing spell, which wasn't technically a spell at all, but a focused energy directed toward a designated recipient. Farrin had never failed to return one of Sarina's hailing spells, so Sarina sent them one after another.

The hailing spells went unanswered. Only one thing could explain that: Farrin was somewhere inside a dead zone. But why? She should be safe at the cottage, the closest dead zone was located miles from there. Had someone gotten news to her about the break-in at the pub? If so, she would be trailing Sarina now, probably crossing the Locks of Havenshire, fully exposed to Mithragog and his minions once she stepped out of the dead zone. Unacceptable.

The horses stopped riverside for a short respite, but they would not remain here long. The moon began to tilt on the horizon, dawn only a few hours away. Sarina would arrive in Rivensdale with the sun.

Hushed by frozen banks, the river seemed to flow slower than normal, the sound of its passing but a whisper compared to the roar of summer's rollicking streams. The night air assaulted like a granite embrace, cold and hard. Her abductors hadn't given Sarina a cloak when they grabbed her and showed no mercy along the way while her teeth chattered and her skin rose in defiance. Normally, she reveled in winters' approach, but only an idiot faces the cold without a cloak. If not for the warmth generated by the horse beneath her, she would have frozen to death already.

ξЖξ

Morgana le Fay fondled the globe. She finally had
Merlin at her mercy. Peering into the glass, she searched
for signs of him, but alas, ancient magic is not always
transparent, nor easily undone.

After all the years of traveling, blood and bribes,
searching without finding, she had come upon her treasure
quite by accident when she recently returned to England
and found herself camped outside the small village of
Chancellry. There, she overhead an old woman telling a
story to her grandchildren, a fascinating tale that spoke
admirably of the Lady of the Lake as Merlin's one true love,
a fable that ended when the Lady imprisoned the great
wizard inside a crystal globe—the very globe Morgana now
held within her hands.

The old woman's account had instantly resonated with
Morgana and she wondered why she hadn't considered it
before. The pieces to the puzzle had always lain bare for all
to see and yet, no one had deciphered it. The truth had
become so deeply embedded in whimsy, no one took it
seriously, no one at least, until Morgana came along.

Slicing the old woman's throat and disemboweling her
grandchildren may not have been entirely necessary, but it
did serve to keep the old bat quiet. Besides, Dezva
preferred the tender flesh of children above all other fare.

Morgana had spent too much time in Merlin's company to believe the Lady of the Lake had managed to trap him inside this globe, but it was not her burden to believe. For as long as Lady Viviane assumed Merlin remained helpless inside the globe, all would go as planned.

Slipping the globe back into the black satchel she used for transport, Morgana clung to it like a child's first doll. Dutifully, Dezva covered her with an extra cloak and fussed over her until she hissed him away. The fire dwindled and she was tired, a little sleep would do her well. At dawn, she would continue her quest to acquire the ultimate revenge.

ξӜξ

Despite his panic, it had taken more than an hour to arrive outside the lair. He could hear the dragon panting. Or, was it snoring? What a fateful stroke of luck that would be, yet probably too much to hope for.

The lair was a gaping hole torn into the side of a prominent granite hill; a natural hole, perhaps, or one the creature painstakingly bore. Either way, it appeared as a hollow eye, daring fools to enter.

He licked his fingertips, smooth and salty, and inched inside the lair, holding close to the darkest shadows, hoping to remain unseen.

Observing a dragon up close like this is, well...it just doesn't happen every day and, if it does, those who accomplish the feat do not live long enough to tell the tale (massive piles of crumbling human bone crunching beneath the soles of his boots bore testament to that fact).

He paused—couldn't help it. It was the thing to do. Any other man would have done the same. He could turn around now and walk away unscathed, live his life and grow old. Perhaps marry, sire a child or two. Take up blacksmithing, or some other reputable occupation. Or, he could remain and stare admirably at one of the most terrible creatures he had ever seen.

White as a newborn lily, the firedrake rested upon four haunches, wings folded in, its tail curled lazily around a pointed rock formation jutting up from the ground, eyelids drooping as if prepared for sleep, yet watching with interest as Farrin and Sir Oswald climbed toward the lair ceiling, hand-over-hand upon a series of vines, some of which clung to rock, some of which hung like garland.

He allowed himself a bit of a smirk. It was good, indeed, to see the pair of them still breathing and fighting for their lives. It would be better still to see them outside the lair with a few more miles passing beneath their boots.

They both clung to the same vine, precarious because the vine wasn't strong enough to hold their weight and now they were dangling high over the dragon's head, the vine ripping inch-by-inch off the stone, slowly dropping on a trajectory that would place them neatly inside the dragon's jowl.

Sir Oswald extended an arm, struggling to grasp the nearest vine, which was out of his reach by at least a foot, and the exertion of his effort caused the vine's tendrils to tear, dropping them twelve feet or more and causing a collective gasp, (even the dragon seemed a bit shocked).

Remaining on the same vine guaranteed a gruesome end and yet there seemed no viable solution. Sir Oswald may be wishing he hadn't left the quicksand.

Regurgitated remnants scattered about the lair spoke volumes on just how difficult this situation was. Personal belongings, clothes, shoes, buckles, knives, swords, and even an occasional coin, mixed in with the ghastly rubble.

Slashing through the remains with the toe of his boot, he located a crossbow and a quiver holding one arrow mostly unaffected by digestive acids.

The choices life brings are not always fair; this truth, difficult as it is to grasp, repeats without mercy.

Dragon skin is predominantly impermeable with one exception, perhaps two. The breastplate of the dragon is vulnerable, or so they say, and a soft spot exists beneath the chin. A man armed with a particularly sharp and lengthy sword coupled with sufficient muscle and parrying skill might stand a chance, but a man armed with a tattered bow and a rusted arrowhead would not. Therefore, battling the dragon was not an option.

The vine would no longer hold the combined weight of Sir Oswald and Farrin the Fair. Leaving them there would mean a certain end for both. However, if one were to let go, there would be time to seek a way to rescue the other, especially once the dragon became consoled and preoccupied with a fresh meal.

God save the queen.

He placed the arrow on the crossbow and lifted the weapon, sighting in on Sir Oswald's chest.

Hesitation. Perfectly natural. Perhaps even the cold-hearted would give this moment pause.

Visions of the young knight's childhood began to play before the mind's eye as he recalled watching Oswald grow from boy to man, observing with keen interest the choices the lad made and discovering the meaning of pride when the majority of those choices brought naught but good into the world. No other living being would ever come so close to heart, touch so deeply, matter so intensely. Among those men within his circle, he considered Oswald more like a son than any other. And yet, Oswald had insisted he swear an oath to protect the future queen. What would Oswald say now if he knew a rusted arrow would momentarily pierce his heart? Would he still insist on the keeping of that oath?

God save the queen.

Crossbows aren't normally this heavy.

What choice is there?

Lifting the crossbow once more, he attempted to sight in on the target, but Sir Oswald had begun to sway fervently, like a child on a swing, desperately reaching for the adjacent vine. Crafty.

What now? Should he shoot, or wait?

Fate seemed all too willing to provide an answer when the tension on the vine, coupled with the fervent movement, caused its roots to rip from the stone at a much higher rate, dropping the dragon's prey closer to its maw. Less than thirty seconds remained before the entire country began to grieve their fallen queen.

He hoisted the crossbow with hardened determination, calculating the trajectory and timing. One shot. It would have to be a good one.

The arrow released with power and precision, heading for its mark with the vigor of a cobra strike, fatally accurate.

He turned away. Couldn't bear to watch.

Farewell noble knight.

ξӜξ

The fastest way to raise a dragon's dander is to threaten its food source. Except in situations of impending starvation, dragons don't eat dead meat, so attempting to kill its prey is akin to snatching sweets from the hand of a toddler.

Someone on the ground had sent an arrow speeding in Farrin's direction. Seeing this, the dragon turned its maw and blew a bolt of fire at the jackass. Hopefully, that would deter the dolt from attempting another shot.

Wasn't there enough to worry about without having to concern herself with armed lunatics? For example, where was Ozzie? Only a moment ago, he was swinging on the vine above her. And now? Vanished like a specter in a minstrel's play.

The vine had dropped so close to the dragon's maw, the creature began to drool in anticipation. There couldn't be more than fifty feet between the soles of Farrin's boots and the awaiting gullet.

Now would be as good a time as any for some magic but she would have to let go with one hand to gain access to her pocket. After more than an hour of climbing and scrambling, she simply didn't have enough strength left to hold on with one arm. Frankly, she wasn't certain how long she could keep her grip using *both* hands.

Throwing her legs forward, she began to swing. At the very least, she could keep the dragon guessing and, at the same time, give herself an opportunity to try to locate Ozzie.

Someone scampered behind a group of boulders on the ground, she could see the shadows darken as the slumped form scurried about, but it couldn't be Ozzie, he wouldn't cower like a cornered rat. That only left the vermin who had taken the potshot.

Her heart quickened. Would he shoot again?

Fear is a funny thing, it can completely paralyze, rendering the sufferer incapable of defense. On the other hand, it can also energize, giving the bearer uncommon strength at a time when it's needed most. For a moment, she wondered what made the difference whether a person became paralyzed or energized, but the question passed through her mind unanswered. It didn't matter. The power of fear gave her the strength to cling to the vine suspending her moments away from the end of her brief life.

Where is Ozzie?

The vine dropped another foot as a number of its tendrils lost their grasp. Had she really come into this world only to become dragon chow? What of the grand designs of fate and destiny, was this the best they could do?

The tendons in her shoulders felt as though they might snap, the intense burning sensation in her arms drawing the last of her energy.

She had to let go.

She couldn't let go.

She and Sarina often played by the riverbank when they were children. Someone had hung a rope from an old oak and tied knots in it so you could swing over the water, letting go when you were ready to take the plunge, except Farrin was rarely ready to plunge. The water always seemed frigid, as if it flowed directly from winter's mouth, shocking and an affront to her senses, even on the hottest days of summer.

She had to let go.

She couldn't let go.

Sarina would want her to hold on. Collingswood needed a queen.

Should she have stayed at the cottage under the council's protection? Most certainly. Should she have gone back after the attack in the cemetery? Absolutely. Should she have insisted Ozzie stay behind? Without question. (She wouldn't be here now if he hadn't fallen in the quicksand). And yet, with all this hindsight, would she really have decided any differently? No. Even now, as she clung to the vine, she knew that going after Sarina was the right thing to do, even if it ultimately cost Farrin her life, it *was* the right thing.

It's probably normal to discover a pool of regret when facing certain death, but among the trivial, mundane concerns, only a single regret stood out as significant. She had left Rivensdale against her father's will, knowing he would soon succumb to the fever that consumed him. Sadly, he had obstinately insisted she select a king to rule by her side. While Farrin had no desire to rule Collingswood on her own, the desire to marry was even less. Her life had just begun. Marriage was, at the very least, a prison sentence and under harsher circumstances, equivalent to a death sentence. And so, she had followed Sarina from the safety of their sheltered lives in Rivensdale and travelled to Airsmeade, where they were content to abide (until Mithragog began his dastardly antics). Farrin had long carried the regret that she might not see her father again, that hollow sadness deepened now. News of his daughter's death would surely worsen the king's fever, quickening his demise and Collingswood would lose the royal line.

A common woman might allow a seemingly impossible situation to get the best of her, but not a woman with Farrin's extensive training and education. Her father, ever tolerant, had acquiesced when she insisted on undergoing a knight's training. She hadn't spent countless hours playing cat and mouse in the forest with Ozzie and his men for nothing. Yes, this dilemma was a befuddling puzzle, but if she maintained focus, she might solve it. Clearly, she needed to reassess the situation.

First off, she would never swing far enough to the side to grab another vine. Therefore, she must find another route. She carefully studied the creature staring up at her. Long snout, beady eyes, gaping maw and, growing from the top of its head to the tip of its tail, a series of protruding spikes resembling thorns, situated in such a way as to appear very much like a ladder. A ladder would certainly come in handy.

Now that she considered it, what creature can bite the back of its own head? What would happen if she started to swing forward, toward the beast, rather than away from it? Would it be possible to propel into a position where she could land on the back of the firedrake's head? In such a scenario, one of three things would mostly likely occur: the dragon's reflexes might prove fast enough to snatch her out of midair, she might impale herself on one of the spikes, or she would succeed.

As dire as the situation appeared, remaining positive seemed the best recourse. Success was a possibility and the prospect provided more hope than she had only a few moments ago. But, just to add a bit of insurance to the equation, perhaps she could mesmerize the beast.

Swinging side to side, she watched the dragon turn its head left to right, left to right, left to right, as it followed her movement. Excited by her success, she used a small rush of energy to swing wider and wider still, the dragon surveying her motion as if entranced by an intricate ballet. After some time, the drake began to anticipate her rhythm. Recognizing this, she made a sudden lunge forward and dove for the back of the beast's neck.

The dragon had no time to react, but Farrin soon realized her trajectory was an undesirable one—she would land directly atop one of the beast's spikes. Impalement, then, would be her end. She wondered if she preferred this fate over becoming dragon crumpet, but had no time to decide. Squeezing her eyes shut, she braced herself.

She lost her breath upon impact and convinced herself the spike had gone straight through, leaving her with, perhaps, a few moments consciousness before she passed into the great beyond. It soon became apparent, however, that the so-called spike was soft as potter's clay and had curled beneath her weight, harmless.

The firedrake was not amused.

Bucking and twisting beneath her, the dragon began a fit of wild frenzy, attempting to twist in such a way as to access the back of its head, which of course, was impossible. However, because no one had informed the beast of this particular impossibility, the thrashing continued.

Digging her fingers into the soft flesh of the dragon's spike, Farrin secured her position, attempting to work out her next course of action. That's when she recalled the stupendous acts of one Francois De Beranac.

Part of a minstrel group, Francois had come to Rivensdale for Farrin's ninth birthday. A tall and gangly man, he seemed remarkably unremarkable, until he took to his act. Using a thin, wooden pole crafted especially for his trade, Francois walked a high wire with a grace and balance Farrin had never witnessed before. The crowd beneath him oohed and aahed with reverence and awe, none more impressed than the young future queen. When Farrin insisted he teach her his high wire magic, he struck a deal with the king and remained in Rivensdale for three years.

Had Francois de Beranac arrived from the annals of the past to lend Farrin a hand? She thought perhaps he had.

The drake had widened its wings in the struggle but the lair was not large enough for a full expansion. The shape of the wing now resembled a disjointed number seven, the bone structure such that Farrin might employ it in a similar manner as Francois' high wire, albeit an angry, jittery wire. If the door of good fortune remained open long enough to make it past the wing, she would be near enough to the lair entrance to accomplish her escape.

To Farrin's shock and the drake's as well, flute music began to play, the first notes barely audible above the dragon's tumultuous din, but ultimately giving the creature pause.

Who would make merry at a time like this? Was it Ozzie, or the skulking archer? Farrin had never known Ozzie to play a flute, but who knows what men do when they're not conquering or throwing back ale?

The music grew louder, the drake calmer. Whoever piped that flute had done Farrin quite the favor. If ever there was a time to walk a high wire, this was it.

Sliding slowly down the drake's spine, she used the spikes like knots on a rope to draw closer to the wing joint. As she descended, she visualized her escape. A careful, gingerly walk atop the drake's bones was not an option. She wouldn't get far on the wing before the dragon snatched her up like an irksome flea. She would have to run. Although she could successfully perform a brisk walk across a high wire, she had never attempted an out-and-out run. In fact, she had never seen anyone attempt it. No matter, she simply did not have time for a graceful saunter and since defeat was not an acceptable outcome, running would work.

Hopefully.

Probably.

Maybe.

Standing on the wing joint, she took a deep breath and reminded herself not to think too much about how a fall would crush every bone in her body and whether or not the drake would have time to realize she had moved to a place of vulnerability. Nor should she consider the fact that she had never worn a pair of awkward boots on the high wire.

With a forceful exhale, she began to run, focusing mainly on the line beneath her feet, summoning all the speed she could gather.

Traversing the first part of the wing seemed rather easy, despite her fast pace. Thankfully, the bone was horizontal to the ground and, for the most part, quite still as the dragon continued to search for the flutist. The second part, however, involved a severe downhill slant. As Farrin approached this juncture, she realized the angle was far too severe to continue running and yet it would not do to stop. Still too high off the ground to jump, she pointed her left foot forward and turned the right foot sideways, bent her knees and raised her arms to the side, hoping to maintain a smooth slide. One abnormality in the bone and she would topple off. But there were no anomalies and she was only twenty feet off the ground when the drake realized it was about to lose its late-night snack.

The dragon sharply retracted its wing, dumping Farrin only a few feet from the lair entrance. With a quick tuck and roll, she narrowly avoided an oncoming stream of dragons' breath—so narrowly, in fact, the sole of her left boot was on fire. Dragging her foot on the way out, she made her exit.

Outside the lair, the moon began its lonesome hibernation and birds rustled from within the forests' embrace, anticipating dawns' first light. The air, remarkably colder outside the lair, gave Farrin a shiver. She turned to the northeast, ten more miles to Rivensdale. Her first instinct was to gain as much distance from the lair as possible, but she didn't know where Ozzie was and she wouldn't leave without him. That meant dealing with the drake. This time, she had her silver powder ready.

A dragon screaming in frustration sounds somewhat akin to a high-pitched woman giving birth, or a small child suffering a scraped knee for the first time, amplified a thousand times, add a pinch of warrior thrum. The sound vibrated off Farrin's bones, setting her nerves on edge.

Inching around the corner, clinging to the deepest shadows, Farrin re-entered the lair.

Finding refuge behind a large boulder, she cleared the ground with the soles of her boots, smoothing it out. Finished, she sprinkled a handful of silver on the ground, forming the shape of a circle. Careful not to alert the dragon, she whispered, "Vultus Lasso." The powder began to shimmer as it took shape, a wide lasso forming at rope's end. Transformation complete, she picked up the rope and began to swing it over her head. Again, she employed a whisper, commanding, "Impendo," and the lasso expanded. Quickly, she instructed, "Redimio," and the rope flew over the dragon, encompassing it, landing neatly in a large circle beneath the raging creature. With the trap securely in place, Farrin bellowed, "Partum lacuna!" and the ground beneath the beast vanished, the vast chasm gulping down the dragon.

Running to the edge of the opening, Farrin thrust her powder into the gaping hole, and proclaimed, "Vultus Silicis!" A thick layer of granite formed over the beast's head, sealing its fate. The drake would either die there or bore its way out. Either way, it would not pose a menace for many years to come.

Farrin brushed the palms of her hands over the seat of her pants and turned to wonder, where was her wayward knight?

"Over here," someone called. She didn't recognize the voice. Sprinting to the far side of the cavern, she found a thin, dark-haired man kneeling beside Ozzie, who was lying supine and unconscious, bleeding profusely from a wound in his left side. She rushed to him and, without addressing the stranger, attempted to survey the injury.

"What happened?" She demanded, her voice strained with shock.

"He took an arrow to the mid-section and fell," the stranger reported, his tone emotionally unstable as well.

"You removed the arrow?"

"I did, M'lady."

"Did you pack the wound properly?"

"As well as I could, but it requires pressure until the bleeding stops."

The biggest part of her didn't want to ask, but she needed to know, "Will he live?"

"I cannot say. Admittedly, I am a poor excuse for a physician."

"Broken bones?"

The stranger shrugged.

"You played the flute?"

He nodded.

"Thank you," she said.

Another nod.

While the stranger continued to press upon Ozzie's wound, Farrin kneeled on the ground and brushed flaxen strands of hair off the knight's forehead, hoping for a response. There was none.

"Who are you?" Her tone carried a bit too sharp, especially considering this man had just aided in her escape and she wondered at the mistrust she felt toward him.

"I fear an answer might anger you, M'lady."

"Then anger me." She poked her chin toward Ozzie, "Are you one of his men?"

"Not exactly. I'm his uncle."

Farrin cocked her head. She had known Ozzie and his entire family for sixteen of her nineteen years and yet had never met this man.

"I know everyone in the Kensington family," she said.

"I'm not much for social functions. I stick to the shadows. A bit of a loner."

Farrin made no response, but stared at his blood-drenched hands as he applied pressure to the wound. Oddly, he had an extra thumb on each hand. He had already helped to save her life and was doing his best to rescue Ozzie. Was he really an uncle? What reason could he possibly have to lie? Why were her nerves standing on end with mistrust? The question had barely crossed her mind when the answer struck.

Jumping up, she backed away and took a battle stance. He looked surprised, but didn't abandon his tending.

"Is there anyone else in this cavern?" Farrin blasted.

"No, M'lady."

"Has anyone else been here since we arrived?"

"No, M'lady."

"It was you. You shot the arrow. You tried to kill him."

He nodded and lowered his chin, his gaze fixed on Ozzie's dormant face.

Recoiling, Farrin slowly slipped her hand into her pocket.

"Please don't draw your powder," he begged, "I did only what he asked of me."

Rigid, she refrained. "Excuse me?"

"I took a vow, M'lady, to protect the future queen with my life and, if need be, with *his* life."

She gasped. "I'm to believe you tried to kill him for *my* sake?"

"The vine, M'lady, it wasn't holding your combined weight. I saw no choice but to lessen the burden."

The tension in her neck and shoulder muscles released, leaving her in a slump. This sounded so much like something Ozzie would do.

"How long?" She barked.

The expression on his face grew quizzical. "M'lady?"

"How long have you been protecting me?"

He gaped. When he finally answered, his voice quivered with reluctance, "Since you moved into the cottage."

"And I, trained and skilled, never once saw or heard you? Not once in all that time? Who *are* you?"

He winced and grappled for an answer.

"My name is Bartholomew Kensington, brother to James, whom I am sure you know, is Sir Oswald's father."

Farrin inhaled impatiently. "What aren't you telling me?"

He shifted his weight, careful to keep pressure on Ozzie's wound and raised his gaze to meet hers.

"Due to my... Due to certain special abilities, I am also known as McFleegle, although, some among us have taken to calling me, Flea."

ξЖξ

Helga Dearbourne knew she was in the right place but was having a hell of a time locating the Lady of the Lake's sequestered cavern. Helga had been here before, had even been inside the Lady's carefully camouflaged abode, but that was so long ago even the gods couldn't count that far back. If there's one thing in life you can always count on, it's change. Romans got hold of your native lands? No worries, tomorrow it will be the Saxons and after that, the Normans. Nothing ever stays the same.

The moon grew dim, its somber light swaying on the lake's surface with all the enthusiasm of a sluggish hangover. The night air had grown frosty teeth, biting until Helga's flesh felt like ice.

"Don't just sit there, toad, find the cave. A nice fire would do us well."

Startled, Edema blinked but made no movement to suggest she might search for anything, except perhaps a severely injured dragonfly, the only type she could hope to catch.

Helga tapped at rocks covered in vine and brush, using her staff. At some point, the staff would fail to hit stone. This occurred several times, revealing nothing but minor fissures. When at last she found the entrance to the Lady's dwelling, she rushed inside, hoping to find a fire in the hearth.

No such luck. Worse, the Lady was not at home. Judging by the warmth of the embers spitting in the hearth, the fire had gone out approximately two hours ago. Thankfully, the cave was still significantly warmer than the frigid air outside.

The coming of the sun would warm things up a bit. Dawn's light couldn't be more than an hour away. That settled it, Helga would stay long enough to warm up before she continued her search for the Lady.

Grabbing a handful of dried brush, she tossed the kindling into the hearth and begged for fire.

Perhaps the Lady was with the lake and, if so, she might return before dawn.

Sighing heavily, Helga hoped Fortune was in a kind mood. And yet, she had learned long ago never to cling to hope. Hope is fickle, one minute promising the moon and the stars, the next minute packing up your belongings and marching off with everything you call your own. One of the most devastating types of magic known to man, hope will leave you hollow, angry, and bitter; the wise do well to avoid it.

And so, if Helga dare not hope the Lady would return, she must assume she would not. This being the case, she might as well have a snoop while she thawed.

The Lady kept a fine crystal collection (every color, shape and size) displayed on slabs of granite jutting out from the walls of the cave—natural shelves carved by Mother Earth and a fine job she had done of it, too. Any practicing witch would be green with envy at the spaciousness the shelves created.

Herbs the Lady had dried out during the summer hung from vines, each root carefully tied. Only a seasoned witch with a lifetime of experience could tie an herb so intricately. Nowadays, people rear their young without a care for detail. Helga had seen many a young witch leave her herbs to rot in moist corners—blatant blasphemy.

The Lady kept a neat home. While Helga was a bit of a stickler for the proper way to tie an herb and would never think of being careless with the various specimens and ingredients she kept, she wasn't exactly an exemplary homemaker. In fact, she was quite certain she hadn't touched a broom in well over one hundred years. It looked as though the Lady swept frequently. Call it futility, call it laziness, call it whatever you like, Helga had never seen the point to sweeping dirt floors—you never quite get to the bottom of it, do you?

She had to admit, though, what the Lady had done with this place did look nice, enviable even. A wool loom sat in a far corner, unfinished needlework lay in a basket beside the sitting chair, glazed pots used for cooking and storage lined up neatly on a shelf over the hearth, molds for making wax candles and a short pile of wicks were stacked neatly next to the pots, a large hand-woven rug covered the floor beneath the table and a slab of salted venison hung on a hook to dry.

Although many years had passed since Helga's last visit, something seemed off kilter. Curious, she studied each detail. Everything seemed in its place. But, what was this nagging notion? Closing her eyes, she recalled her last conversation with the Lady, by no measure a pleasant chat. The Lady had severely chastised Helga, warning her to stay on the bright side of magic. Ha! Where's the sport in life if you can't use your given gifts to wither a young maiden or two, or interfere in historical battles for a purse of handsome coin? No fun at all. Helga had ignored the Lady's moral tongue-lashing, completely mesmerized by the crystal globe the Lady kept upon her table...what a fine piece of glass!

That was it. The decorative globe wasn't sitting on the table where Helga had last seen it. Perched on a base made of solid gold, the crystal glowed perfectly in its circular contour. Helga had never seen anything like it. Now that she thought about it, it was a wonder she hadn't come back at some point over the years to try to steal it. Whatever had she been thinking?

Finished with her spying, she situated herself in the Lady's sitting chair and released half a sigh, half a grunt. How arrogant of her to think she could take anything unbidden from the Lady of the Lake. The only reason she sat here now was because it seemed prudent to align with the winning side when a battle loomed. Morgana le Fay would prove an admirable adversary for anyone and in the question of whose power was greater, le Fay or Lady Viviane, the answer is not entirely clear, but most would place their coin on Lady Viviane, as she's older, wiser and more experienced. Still, who could say for sure?

Drawing her cloak tight, Helga allowed her eyelids to droop. A short nap before dawn and she would be on her way. With only a few hours head start, the Lady wouldn't be too far ahead if she wasn't with the lake.

Helga's head lolled, resting on her right shoulder, visions of troll intestines squirming through her head, when a black raven fluttered into the cavern and came to roost on a wooden chair sitting near the table.

"You've come out of hiding," the bird said, without opening its beak.

"I was never in hiding," Helga mumbled, aggravated with the interruption of a perfectly gruesome dream.

"You're not at home," replied the bird.

"You are clever," Helga grunted. "I may never understand why every creature slithering under the sun considers you a bumbling idiot. Surely, it's the cosmic error of all ages."

The bird leaned forward. "Perhaps," it said, "the quality is inherited."

Helga laughed, but not hard enough to cause her to urinate on the Lady's chair. What a shame.

"What do you want, Ogre dung?"

The bird fluttered its wings then settled down. "First off, I want you to know I am near enough to snap your withered neck if I so choose and, secondly, I wondered if you've seen the girl upon your travels this evening."

Helga released an unconcerned "hmph" and leered at the raven. "No, I have not. However, I have seen enough to say with certainty that you would do yourself a favor by crawling back to Spinel for a few more years. You will not have the girl's heart, that much, I assure you."

"Do tell, dear Mother. What have you seen?"

Helga's skin recoiled when Mithragog called her 'Mother,' a fact he was well aware of, and she wasn't fond of his penchant for remote viewing, even if that was the one bit of magic he had skillfully mastered. Some things in life are difficult to undo, but if it were possible to un-bear and un-birth, the dolt speaking through this possessed bird would no longer have his existence.

Helga answered through tight lips, "I saw Morgana le Fay and her imp, Dezva. You don't stand a chance in hell."

The bird squawked a high-pitched grating caw. "That is unsettling," it said.

"Unsettling? *Unsettling*? You *are* an idiot." Reaching into the satchel belted around her waist, Helga withdrew a pinch of powder and flung it at the bird. "Intereo!"

The bird burst into flames, its ashes falling like black snow flittering onto the Lady's immaculate floor.

Oops.

Rule number one when visiting the home of a magically inclined immortal: Never cast a spell in said home as it often trips an alarm, which in turn, activates a series of booby traps. Nasty magic.

The water had already risen above Helga's head. Nice touch. No warning at all. As one might expect from the Lady of the Lake, the lake itself defended her home.

Helga hated water, the cold type most of all. Waving her arms about, she turned in the direction of the door and swam to it. Always the good and faithful toad, Edema waited just outside. Taking hold of a prominent wart,

Helga gave the toad a prod. Soon, they were making their way over the surface of the lake. No reason to hold her urine back now.

ξЖξ

McFleegle. Farrin should have known, what with the two thumbs and all.

Ozzie had presented the cat on the very day the council sequestered her. She recalled thinking how sweet it was of him to ensure she wouldn't spend all those hours alone. Little had she known. How many times had she undressed in front of that cat? Bathed? Sang off pitch? How embarrassing.

"The bleeding has slowed, M'lady."

Farrin yearned for the skill to heal Ozzie, but medicinal magic had never been the focus of her training. The temptation to try anyway pulsed through her, but the fear of doing more harm than good loomed greater. *Sarina is the most gifted healer in Collingswood. The wisest course of action meant transporting Ozzie to Rivensdale and retrieving Sarina to tend to him. The question was how to move him without complicating his wounds. Conjuring a horse seemed a viable solution, but the unavoidable jostling involved would only increase the bleeding.*

McFleegle had tied the wound nicely. Farrin bundled Ozzie using McFleegle's cloak. Ready to depart, she drew her powder and commanded, "Consurgo Insisto Prope."

Ozzie slowly rose five feet off the ground, his head near to Farrin's shoulder. When she moved forward, so did he. He would float there until she commanded otherwise.

Leaving the dragon's lair, they headed northeast, toward Rivensdale.

The journey, though seemingly uneventful, was far from pleasant. The entire way, Farrin thought only of how she had put Ozzie's life at peril. He had warned her himself, back at the tavern, but she hadn't listened. She had risked Ozzie's life three times since leaving the cottage. What if he died? How could she possibly live without him? The guilt, alone, would be the end of her. A knight, if he must succumb, wishes only for glory. Where was the glory in dying to save Sarina from the inconvenience of an arranged marriage?

There was no way around the bitter truth—Farrin had acted irresponsibly, foolishly, childishly. It was one thing to prance around acting like an untouchable immortal, another thing altogether to expect others to play in the fields of her lunacy. She should have done as Ozzie suggested and waited until he had the opportunity to gather his men, waited until morning and gone to Rivensdale prepared. Now, all she could hope for was the chance to save his life.

The sun rose, slathering a bright golden hue over Bodach Cairn, a formidable mountain range safeguarding the west side of Rivensdale. From here, they would continue through Stutter's Pass, arriving in Rivensdale in less than an hour.

Small tufts of icy clouds escaped through Ozzie's nostrils and Farrin checked frequently to make sure they were still forming. He was breathing. She wouldn't ask for more. As long as he continued to breathe, hope remained.

Still, she wished he would awaken, say something, mock her for having been right all along, anything, but he hadn't made the slightest sound the whole way.

With eyes finally set on Rivensdale, Farrin quickened her pace.

Outside the castle walls, she used a counter-spell to lower Ozzie; she and McFleegle would carry him inside. While it wasn't strictly unlawful to perform magic in Rivensdale, many frowned upon the practice (the church most of all). Those without a magical penchant often showed signs of fear or envy, neither emotion conducive to peaceful living.

Seeing that an injured man had entered the castle walls, a local farmer brought his ass and wagon, offering them to McFleegle, asking only that he return them by day's end. Grateful, Farrin and McFleegle carefully placed Ozzie on the wagon bed and took him to the physician's quarters on the east side of the castle. Farrin had seen these physicians render some rather barbaric treatments: bloodletting, leeching and worse, (they had once tried to heal a man's spinal curvature by stretching him with ropes and gear wheels. Suffice to say, that poor fellow is half the man he used to be). The sooner Farrin brought Sarina back to tend to Ozzie, the better.

McFleegle agreed to stay with Ozzie while Farrin made her way to court. She would visit her father and then, if need be, they would make way for Stockbridge, a few miles north, where they would find Sarina.

The king was sitting up in his chambers and looked vibrant, not at all what Farrin had expected.

"You look well, Father."

The king's gaze fell upon her and his brow furled, eyes dimming in the shadows of a sudden anger.

He thrust a rigid finger toward her, "You! What are you doing here? Have you no mind? No wit about you? Have you any idea what special treatment you were given when the council agreed to protect you?"

His face contorted with each word spoken, his skin effusing a deep shade of purple, the veins in his forehead so pronounced, you could see them pulse.

"Have you no grace? No heart? Your mother, God rest her soul, gave her life for you. And what do you do with her sacrifice but squander it?"

He turned his face away and sat in fuming silence.

A wave of hot tears ran over Farrin's cheeks as she fell to her knees, "You're right, Father. I made a grave mistake, one I will regret for all my days."

After a long and grueling silence, he motioned for her, inviting an embrace.

"Forgive me, please," she begged.

"My heart gives me no choice," he said, tightening his embrace.

"Have your physicians found a remedy, Father? You look well."

He released a mocking grunt. "Those bumbling idiots couldn't find their own navels without a map. Your friend," he said, "the Bishop's daughter, sent herbs and tonics in hopes of breaking the fever."

Farrin smiled widely. Sarina never mentioned she was treating the king.

"Are they working?" She asked.

"I have good days and bad. Today's a good day and I'm grateful. I confess, it's wonderful to see you, daughter. Tell me why you've come."

She took his hand and told her tale from the beginning, starting with Sarina's abduction and leaving little to the imagination. The king listened thoughtfully throughout her oration, brow raised with concern.

His grip on her hand tightened, "You left Sir Oswald with the court physicians?"

"No choice, Father. Until Sarina returns, your physicians are his only hope. Will you order the Bishop to release her?"

Letting go of her hand, he stood, his balance unsure. Moving gingerly to a window that faced the court balcony, he lowered his head. "I cannot," he bemoaned. "It's a family matter, no concern of the royal court. Besides, the Bishop of Stockbridge has ties to Rome. It wouldn't be wise to risk inciting another Holy war." He turned to face her, pleading for understanding.

"We could claim the Bishop has succumbed to old age," she suggested, not entirely in jest.

He answered with a gentle smile.

"I can't order her release, but perhaps I can help even the odds." Clapping his hands, he summoned a page.

A young boy skidded into the room and bowed in reverence.

Retrieving a key from a satchel tied around his waist, the king handed the key to the boy and asked him to take it to the treasury room where he would find Sir Worthington.

"Give him the key and ask him to retrieve the Lady's relic. He will know what I ask. Ask him to bring the relic back straight away. Make haste."

Bowing, the boy scurried from the room.

Sir Worthington appeared moments later with a lengthy sack made of plush red velvet, which he placed into the king's hands before taking his leave.

"This was meant as a gift for your coronation, but perhaps today is a better day."

Judging by the reach of his smile, he considered the item quite special.

Hands trembling, he removed the fabric from the relic, revealing the most magnificent broadsword Farrin had ever seen.

"In the hands of the unworthy, this sword has the weight of ten men and simply cannot be wielded. However, in the hands of a light bearer, it is weightless and agile, wielded without effort."

"Father! It can't be... Is it...?"

"Yes. Excalibur."

"But, Excalibur was returned to the Lady of the Lake long ago. How could it possibly be here?"

His smile was genuine and wild with mirth. "A gift from the Lady for the future queen."

"I couldn't possibly..."

"Oh, but you can," he said, handing her the sword.

She hesitated, certain she would drop it, an unbearable weight in her hands. When he insisted, she took the weapon and found it light as a goose feather. As she removed the sword from the scabbard, the blade shone so brilliantly one wouldn't think it made of steel, or any other type of ore for that matter, but constructed of sunlight, or perhaps a thin sheet of reflective crystal. Rubies and sapphires embedded in the hilt sparkled brilliantly and an intricate pattern of Gaelic words etched into the edges of the blade seemed alive with motion, dancing hypnotically. This sword was, put mildly, the most beautifully ornamented piece of weaponry in existence and quite possibly the most lethal.

Satisfied with her inspection, the king summoned Sir Worthington and asked him to strap the weapon to Farrin's back. When finished, the knight drew her cloak over the sword so that none might see it and instructed her to continue to take this precaution in an effort to thwart would-be thieves, adding that although most would not be able to wield the weapon, many would risk their lives for the chance to try.

Once they were alone again, the king spoke solemnly, "Your decision to leave the cottage was not wise. The council breathes with wrath. I'll hold them at bay, but you must begin to think more carefully. The Lady of the Lake has sent messengers with grave news. She claims Morgana le Fay has stolen an orb, which the Lady swears contains the great Merlin. The Lady Viviane has never given me reason to doubt. I fear dark days are upon us."

Reaching for Farrin's hand, he took it in his own. "Consider, daughter, a kingdom without a king is thought vulnerable. If only you would give more thought to marrying Sir Kensington." Farrin began to interject but the king shushed her by placing his finger on her lips. "Oswald is a good man."

"I know, Father. But, he's like a brother to me, I grew up alongside him."

"That is of no consequence, my dear. Royal marriage is merely a political arrangement."

"A political arrangement for others, perhaps, but I've seen the way he looks at me, he would never settle for a mere arrangement. However, none of this will be of any consequence if he dies. I must get to Sarina."

ξℳξ

Helga Dearbourne, soaked to the gills and frozen to the withered bone, was grateful to have escaped the Lady of the Lake's booby-trap with no more than a bruised ego. What bedlam.

The trip across the lake had been long and arduous, Edema's subsequent exhaustion understandable. Helga allowed the toad a nap and approached the edge of the lake to wash away some of the mud and muck pasted on her face and hands. There's nothing like genuine lake slime to increase a woman's overall appeal.

Thankfully, the sun had risen and the air would soon grow warmer.

On bended knees, Helga peered into the water and winced. Only those who have once known great beauty can understand how it feels to watch it waste away, little by little, until nothing remains but a lump of rump-ugly. The skin develops wrinkles deep enough to hide furniture within its crevices, growths pop up like weeds sown by an unending wind, pigment begins to blotch so distinctly one begins to suspect leprosy, and the sagging, the miserable sagging.

Thrusting her hands into the water, she splashed it over her face and rubbed furiously in an attempt to wash away the lake's muddy blemish, spurred on by the frustration and anger incited by the ugliness staring back at her from the water's surface. When she finished, she waited for the water to settle and looked once more. The beauty staring back at her nearly caused Helga's bowels to fail.

Standing with arms crossed nonchalantly, dark hair shining in the sun, smirking ruby-red lips, breasts high, hips slim, and dressed in a cloak made of royal purple, was none other than Morgana le Fay.

"The years have not been kind to you, have they, Helga?" Morgana sneered.

Unwilling to make a sudden move, Helga shrugged.

Morgana's insolent snickering didn't escape notice.

Turning to face her, Helga asked, "How do you manage to look so young? Is it real, or have you hexed everyone?"

Morgana took a step closer, leaning slightly forward. "Oh, it's real. No hexing. I simply devour youth and beauty to make them my own. I remain powerful by consuming power. You, Helga, were once legendary for your power."

"Not anymore," Helga replied sheepishly. "Have you come to claim the heart of the heir?"

Tickled by the assumption, Morgana laughed.

"If I wanted the heart of the heir, I would have taken it long ago. However, I am not certain I can resist killing you simply for sport. You understand, don't you, dear?"

Taking hold of her staff, Helga pulled herself to her feet.

"If it's not the heir you're after, what are you up to?"

Just then, Dezva burst through the brush, stopping at Morgana's side. "Say no more, mistress," he cried, his voice a broken thing, raspy and gurgling, a sound you might expect from someone trying to speak with a throat full of fractured glass and molasses.

Morgana swatted at him, irritated.

"Can't you see?" She gestured toward Helga. "She is already naught but worm droppings. Now go and see if you can find something yummy for breakfast. No more fish, I tire of fish."

Dezva bowed, the glare in his oversized eyes searing until the moment he darted away.

"I do apologize for the interruption, Helga. What were we saying? Ah, yes. You inquired after my purpose. The answer is quite simple. I seek Friar John."

"John of the Templar brotherhood?"

"The very same. Do you know where I might find him?"

"What could you possibly want with that old wart crust? He hasn't been good for anything but a bourbon belch for many a year."

"Let's just say the good Friar has hidden talents. Where might I find him?"

Helga ran her fingertips over the hairs on her chin. "If I reveal him, will you ensure my safety?"

Morgana's face suddenly took on an expression of pained insult. "Surely, you don't believe I would harm you?"

"I'll take your vow, Morgana. Even then, do not assume I would trust a single word issuing past your lips."

"You have my vow, Helga. I'll not harm you."

Helga stared, studying Morgana's face, particularly the twitch at the corner of her mouth, which indicated she was not being entirely truthful.

What choice was there? It wasn't as if Helga could outrun Morgana. Her powder was still wet from the trip across the lake and face it, even if it were dry, she wouldn't stand a chance against a sorceress with Morgana's talents. Still, it couldn't hurt to back away from the water and try to get a little closer to Edema.

Helga spoke slowly as she walked away from the water, "Last I heard, Friar John lives in a cabin atop Bodach Cairn with a bloke going by the name of Nothinghem, on the south side of Rivensdale, just north of Stutter's Pass."

Morgana nodded. "When did you hear this, Helga? Was it recently?"

Helga walked quickly, pacing her words with lengthy pauses between. "No. Not recently. Let me think. It hasn't been more than three years. Since I haven't heard another word, the man is either dead or still there. You know how it is...small world and all. Word gets on."

With another nod, Morgana slipped her hand into her pocket. Smooth. Helga widened her stride. Given the chance, Morgana would draw her powder and attempt to obliterate.

Fortunately, Edema was only a few feet away now and had awakened at the sound of Helga's voice. A simple hand gesture did the trick.

Edema let loose with a bellyful of toad vomit aimed directly at Morgana's midsection. Pushed violently by the spew, the sorceress flew into the lake, making quite a splash upon entry.

Helga mounted the toad and delivered a sharp kick, making a narrow escape.

Now she'd gone and done it. Not that she'd been given a choice in the matter, but what fool makes an enemy of Morgana le Fay?

ξЖξ

Myla ran her hands over the splintered branches of a sapling at an awkward stage in its growth, no longer a runt weed, not yet a tree. Jagged and sharp, the shattered fractures revealed the heart of the plant, still wet with a life that would soon dry up and wither away.

A line of reeds and tall grasses growing along the edge of Lake Avonelle emitted an acrid stench as they smoldered, small sparks of flame dying and reigniting, the once thriving vegetation soon to join large patches of dry brush already reduced to mounds of black soot.

Footprints and small pools of mud indicated that someone had recently come out of the water, furious by the looks of it. A curious green slime oozed off pine branches, puddles of it coagulating on the ground where it expelled an overwhelming fetor.

Aside from the intermittent snap and pop of dying embers, silence breathed its quiet hush, making it seem as if every bird, cricket and squirrel had evacuated en mass, which they probably had.

Myla felt tense, surrounded by the remnants of the magic exacted here, not at all an enjoyable sensation, but one that raised the short hairs on her skin and incited an uncommon shiver. Dark magic always leaves a trail of dread behind, a discernible weight, a cloud of foreboding that even the insensitive can perceive.

The Lady Viviane had gone into the lake in search of something she would not likely find after surmising Morgana had hexed the foliage burning here. Myla agreed with the possibility. Only someone truly evil would take their frustrations out this way, casting it upon innocent plants and animals. And so, convinced Morgana may have lost the globe in the lake, the Lady had gone to look for it.

Certain the globe was not in the lake, Myla made no protest when the Lady went after it. If someone had forced Morgana into the water, she had obviously survived the attack, thus the blistering foliage. The sorceress would not go to outrageous lengths to procure the globe only to leave it behind due to an unexpected dunking, but Myla understood the Lady's need to search and had said nothing to delay her.

When the Lady resurfaced, not a drop of water clung to her, her clothing and skin were dry, her hair rippling in the breeze, a miraculous sight for anyone fortunate enough to witness it. She strode toward Myla with empty hands—her eyes, emptier still.

Following a recent trail through the forest, they headed west toward Rivensdale, away from the Lady's beloved lake. In all the time Myla had known the Lady, (and the years were many) she had never known her to leave the lake; her willingness to do so now spoke directly to the gravity of the situation.

Focused mainly on dodging nature's diabolical obstacles, (while trees provide much needed shade and medicinal gifts, they also have no qualms about slapping a passerby in the face when the opportunity arises) Myla occasionally glanced in the Lady's direction, seeing the same thing each time—a woman who wore her worry like a crimson scarf. Viviane hadn't said a word since leaving the lake and Myla grew weary of the silence.

"When I came to see you, I sought your assistance in protecting the future queen. I fear for her."

Pushing a tree branch out of her way, the Lady quietly replied, "As well you should. For as long as there are those who believe Farrin is the true heir, her life will remain in danger."

Myla rushed through the thicket to catch up with the Lady. "You speak as though you don't believe she is the true heir."

"Of course I don't."

Myla gasped. "What reason have you to say she is not the true heir?"

Beams of morning sun filtered through the trees, a frightened rabbit skittered across the path and birds chirped their secrets for all who could hear and understand. The air, though warmer than the night's frigid chill, still waxed cold and damp inside the forest canopy.

Pausing briefly, the Lady studied Myla's face with a worrisome squint. "Perhaps," she said, "I have already said too much." As though she thought her words adequate, she resumed her trek through the woodland.

The Lady's words were far from sufficient; in fact, they only bolstered curiosity. Why would she suggest Farrin Lockwood wasn't the heir and then drop the subject as if it were a burning coal? Surely, she didn't expect Myla to dismiss the issue without a care, not while the future queen's life remained in peril. This wasn't a make-believe scene in a minstrel's play, this was a matter of life-and-death.

"Viviane, if there's something you know about the heir, please confess as it concerns the future of all Collingswood. How can I possibly help the heir if I don't know who she is?"

Moaning with exertion as she navigated a steep incline, the Lady turned to speak with broken breath, her demeanor sharp and agitated, "Perhaps it is not for you to aid the heir, but to help retrieve the globe, an act which will also determine the future of Collingswood."

Manipulating low tree branches, Myla propelled herself uphill, her feet occasionally slipping on dew-ridden leaves reduced to piles of sliming rot. She couldn't count how many times she had fallen. The Lady, aside from her breathlessness, seemed to glide uphill, her ascent unstrained.

When, at last, Myla had conquered the hill, she stood by the Lady's side, panting for air.

While she recovered her breath, Myla's thoughts returned to the time she spent with Queen Gwenevere. From the moment Gwenevere summoned Myla to become head handmaiden until the day the Queen expelled her last breath, Myla stood firmly by her side. In all that time, Gwenevere had never uttered a word about having a child. Was it possible she had, though, and managed to keep it secret? Possible, yes, but the entire concept seemed ludicrous, absurd. Myla bonded instantly with Gwenevere, as if they had known one another throughout the course of many lifetimes. Gwenevere confided absolutely everything. But, had she really? If not, what reason could she have for keeping such an immense secret? Why would she not confess? Unless—of course!—unless she knew about the curse and simply never spoke of it. Under such grave circumstances, Gwenevere would have reason to safeguard vital information.

It did seem possible, then, that Farrin Lockwood may not be the true heir. Only the Lady of the Lake could say who the heir was. What would it take to loosen her tongue?

Myla watched the Lady stand against the breeze. Viviane stood tall and shapely with long locks of honey-colored hair flowing down her back. Cheekbones set high, lips pursed full, her entrancing blue-gray eyes stared over the hillside where she searched for signs of her beloved. She was the picture of an immortal goddess if ever there was one—youth, beauty, majesty, grace and power, gloriously garbed in flowing white robes, a timeless gift to humanity.

Because no one knows the Lady's true age, legends abound. They say she is as old as time itself, born with the earth. The first immortal.

Immortals are a fickle bunch. Many credit their station on the basis of personal merit, believing they deserve the honor of becoming a god or goddess. For Myla, that entire misconception was a fuming load of donkey dung. She hadn't done anything to deserve immortality and yet she would soon see her one hundred and eighty-fifth year. What determines who receives the gift of immortality? Who could possibly say? It is certainly not by personal merit. No one proves that point better than the witch of Dearbourne who has used her gift for nothing but mischief for all her years and Morgana le Fay whose evil knows no bounds.

Myla had never witnessed self-aggrandizing in the Lady's demeanor, quite the opposite, as she often expressed a desire to become more human. Now she would follow her heart to the ends of the earth if it meant returning her abducted lover to her side. It was up to Myla to see that the Lady did not allow her heart's quest to jeopardize the heir.

"Lady Viviane, please tell me about the heir."

At the sound of Myla's voice, the Lady began to walk with wide, determined strides as she traversed a small patch of meadow leading into another shaded forest. Myla matched her stride for stride.

"I know who the heir is," the Lady declared, "That is enough."

Not even close, Myla thought. "Please forgive my tireless inquiry, M'lady, but powerful people are on the heels of the heir and in possession of the globe. It seems to me, the more wisdom and knowledge we have on our side, the better our chances. Leaving me in ignorance can only cause harm." Reaching for the Lady's arm, she grasped tightly, "Is your trust not mine?"

The Lady Viviane stopped to survey Myla's face, staring in uncomfortable silence. The Lady's misplaced trust had brought them to this crossroad, it would not be a minor feat for her to overcome the pain and embarrassment of Morgana's shape-shifting transgression.

Minutes passed in reverent silence. Myla waited patiently.

The Lady finally nodded her acquiescence.

"Come, walk beside me," she said.

Entering the forest, they ducked branches, the Lady speaking frankly, refusing to take her eyes off the tracks left by those who had forged this path less than an hour ago.

"Put simply, Farrin Lockwood is not the first female born in the line of Gwenevere. One hundred and eighty-five years ago, a nunnery in Almesbury released two female children to an orphanage in Bibury. Although no one ever spoke a word of it, one of the two infants was Gwenevere's daughter. That child is the true heir."

Stunned, Myla nearly tripped over her own feet. *She* was one hundred and eighty-five years old. *She* had grown up in an orphanage in Bibury. Could it be...?

Gwenevere had summoned Myla on Myla's sixteenth birthday, insisting she become head handmaiden. She had always wondered why the Queen specifically asked for her, but had never found the courage to inquire. Taken from a world of poverty, where every day might be the day to die of starvation and given over to a life of luxury, she had vowed never to complain.

As the years passed and she watched those she loved wither and die while youth clung to her, she wondered why immortality had come upon a simple handmaiden, as it seemed it had, but once again, she would not complain. Now, the Lady of the Lake may have answered many of these questions and more.

If what the Lady had said was true, Farrin Lockwood's life was in danger to spare the true heir, an heir who had no idea who she was until this very moment.

ξℵξ

Proposing that the six 'little' people glaring at Farrin and McFleegle were trolls would convey neither fact nor truth and yet, somehow, it seemed an accurate portrayal.

Farrin and Flea had travelled twenty minutes north of Rivensdale and were approaching the outskirts of Stockbridge when, emerging from a sparse wood to meet the road, they found themselves surrounded by what Farrin had initially assessed as a group of filthy children.

Upon closer inspection, she could see her assumption had been a poor one. Though short in stature, each of the snarling bandits sported a full beard, blackened and missing teeth, fully developed muscles and empty eyes dim in a fashion children seldom display. One of the horrid fellows had an ear where you would expect to find an eye. Their arms were much longer than their legs and hair grew in places normally reserved for warts and moles, which abounded. Frightful disfigurements and abnormalities aplenty, it required no stretch of the imagination to presume these men miniature trolls by nature.

Despite their size disadvantage, they had Farrin and Flea outnumbered six to two and seemed quite pleased to have corralled their prey so easily.

The tallest of the lot (and that wasn't saying much for the entire concept of height) leaned forward, the tip of his knife jabbing toward Farrin's side as if to say, *do or die*.

Highway robbery—an ancient art sure to live on infamously in the human repertoire of treachery and deceit.

Farrin's recent lessons weighed on her mind. The choices we make on a daily basis will do or undo each of us. Turn right and live, take a left and die, or perhaps, go left and live, turn right and die. Who knows? The point is to make your choices carefully and thoughtfully.

These bandits had made a poor decision but remained unaware. For thieves, it may have seemed a perfectly wonderful day to procure riches by force, but for Farrin it was an ill-timed attempt. Precarious were the moments between now and Sarina's return to Rivensdale. There simply was no time to waste.

"What do you want?" McFleegle ventured, his hand tucked beneath his cloak, probably grasping his knife.

Three of the beastly creatures laughed as though Flea had asked the most moronic question ever uttered, while the other three glared, not amused.

"Silver!" the lead man declared, his growl a deep bass you wouldn't expect from a man of his inadequate stature.

McFleegle shrugged nonchalantly, "We have no silver, no gold."

"That's a shame," the gnarly blighter snarled. "If what you say is true, we have no choice but to cut our supper from your greasy backsides." Punctuating his point, he made a wide swipe aimed at Flea's midsection, forcing Flea to jump back and draw his blade from beneath his cloak.

Now the two stood toe-to-toe, short blades glistening in the sun, circling, twisting, turning, each man parrying for position.

Farrin raised her hands in protest, "Stop! If it's silver they wish, then silver they shall have."

Hearing this, the bandits began to nod enthusiastically, their blackened smiles wide with anticipation.

As she reached into her pocket, the lead man rushed forward, extending a greedy hand that trembled with excitement.

The powder filled the air with a dazzling sparkle as Farrin spoke her words quickly and precisely, "Vultus Silicis!"

Passersby, from this day forward, are bound to wonder if the goddess Medusa had visited this land and rendered these men immobile in their granite state, eyes wide with expectation, hands extended in greed. Or, perhaps, some stately Duke would whisk the stones away to his gardens where children could wonder at the realism in the facial expressions of six small-souled men who would never again weave their treachery upon the living.

From here forward there would be no more bandits springing from behind trees as the landscape had grown dry, the road a dusty sod bristling with pebbles and rocks, a scant patch of low brush protruding here and there. If so much as a squirrel presented itself on the road, Farrin and Flea would see it well before it had time to drop its nuts and run.

Gravel crunched beneath Farrin's step as she watched the sun climb higher over the horizon, mid-morning already.

"Perhaps there was a more delicate way to deal with those thieves, M'lady." Flea spoke contemplatively, relaxed, obviously attempting to relieve some stress, a little conversation to entertain their travel.

"What would you suggest, sir?"

"Well, you might have identified yourself and offered them employment in your court."

Farrin tipped a whimsical nod, she recognized jest when she heard it. If Flea had been alone when the bandits struck, they would be lying in the road with bloody smiles carved into their throats. Reaching over her shoulder, she touched the hilt of the sword her father had given her, it was so light on her back it felt as though it wasn't there at all. She breathed easier when she felt the hilt beneath her fingertips.

"Perhaps, sir. But, you fail to see the reasoning behind their attack, which was, at its base, immediate hunger. Did they choose to seek a stag or a wild boar to satisfy that need, or did they choose treachery instead? Promise of future employment would not persuade them and if I had revealed my identity they would have reacted only to the hope of a hefty ransom."

Flea donned a sly grin. "Well said, M'lady."

As the sun came to rest upon his cheek, Farrin could see more clearly now that his facial features were not as menacing as first perceived. Tall, dark, thin and unshaven, one might have easily mistaken him for a sinister man, but his deep blue eyes told tales of a plentiful soul, a man of conviction, one to reckon with should anyone challenge his loyalties. By that merit alone, it would seem Flea was, in fact, Ozzie's kin.

Farrin spent the remainder of the journey thinking about her father, a man known throughout the realm as one who could produce from his sweat the iron nails required to build impermeable fortresses, until the fever took him aside. He really did look well but, if his improved health had been the result of Sarina's herbal tonics, his continued recovery would depend on Sarina's safe return to Rivensdale.

Farrin believed the king's malady a manifestation of his grief for her long-dead mother. Her father had never remarried despite a continuous onslaught of willing courtesans. What is the cure, then, for a grieving man's soul? Farrin could certainly think of no remedy strong enough to overcome such a powerful emotion. May the Goddess shower her blessings upon Sarina for not giving up on a cure so hastily.

While it was widely known that the king had loved Lorraine Lockwood more than his own soul, Farrin had never seen her mother's face outside the portrait frames hanging dutifully on the castle walls. She was a beautiful woman, yes, but her eyes were unmoving, her lips spoke no comfort, her arms offered no embrace, and her hair and skin gave off no smell but that of the linseed oil the artists had used to incite her image.

For some, growing up without a mother constitutes an insurmountable disadvantage, not so for Farrin. Although everyone understood that no woman could ever take the queen's place, many attempted the feat regardless, chiefly among them Esmia Kensington and Dalphine Caldwell, Ozzie and Sarina's mothers, respectively. Not only did these women coddle and fuss over Farrin, they also supplied her with two playmates that had since become more important than life itself.

When Dalphine died of cholera several years ago, it seemed more than anyone could bear. It surely would have been the end of Sarina and Farrin if Ozzie hadn't brought them back from the brink of self-destruction by forcing them into the forest on a summer-long camping escapade, an adventure that ultimately revitalized Sarina's interest in healing herbs and fueled Farrin's desire for battle training.

Rest in peace good and joyful Dalphine. As for the scheming Bishop you once called husband, with his greed and lofty station, may he rot in hell.

Lurking in the back of Farrin's mind was this business concerning Morgana le Fay and the return of Merlin, a stolen globe and sudden intervention from the Lady of the Lake. This news had been disturbing on so many levels it threatened to split the seams of reality, but now was not the time to consider the issue. All that mattered was getting Sarina back to Rivensdale.

As they arrived in Stockbridge, Flea suggested skirting around the village to approach the Bishop's home from behind, hoping to preserve an element of surprise. He also proposed a cat might easily scout the premises, hopefully unnoticed. "Whatever the situation is up ahead," he said, "it's wise to garner every advantage."

Duly noted.

ξℋξ

Red-eyed and irritated, Sarina listened to the muffled voices coming from the other side of the door and fought against the shackles binding her ankles and wrists.

The scent of the Duke of Devonshire's cherry leaf pipe was sickeningly recognizable. The pipe, a ridiculously long and antiquated instrument that stretched from his lips to the floor, was a relic he had acquired from some exotic market many years ago. His use of the pipe lent him the air of an eccentric idiot and it aged him fifty years. All this for a man who already appeared old enough to have given ill-advice to Adam and Eve.

While many extol the scent of burning cherry leaf for giving off a pleasant odor, Sarina had long associated the scent with the Duke of Devonshire and, thus, the slightest hint of it caused her stomach to heave. His laugh—*cackle-cough cough-cackle*, which she heard faintly through the door, was just as offensive as the pipe odor. She had suffered the rasp of the Duke's laughter since the age of five when he had first come sniffing about her panties. Forcing her onto his lap, he would bare his yellow-gray smile and say as sweetly as if promising candy, "One day, you will be my wife." Each time he spoke these words of prophetic doom, Sarina would run away screaming as though the moths and maggots nesting in his beard had suddenly risen from the dead. Into her mother's arms she would rush, trembling until Dalphine reassured her she would never allow such a thing. 'Never' isn't such a long time when caught between good intentions and the cholera that claimed Dalphine's life. And so, the Duke's appointed day had arrived, uninhibited.

He would pay handsomely for his bride, having promised the Bishop (a man Sarina refused to call Father) an entire commonwealth to lord over, stables filled with exotic quarter horses, countless livestock for butchering, a small castle and a full regimen of knights, not to mention coffers of gold and silver. And since the Duke was willing to part with riches so vast, he probably did not intend to keep his wife for the sole purpose of fine cookery and petty laundering.

Another wave of nausea, another dry heave.

Servants had already dressed Sarina in a fine white gown plaited with lace and had pinned a veil in her hair. The silk dress should have felt soft against her skin, instead, it itched.

Voices outside the door grew louder, footsteps closer. They were coming and she could do nothing to stop them.

If this ceremony actually took place, if she was destined to become the Duchess of Devonshire today, she would not soon forget that there are certain herbal tonics meant to expel the souls of men born to a malicious nature.

Enough time remained to perform another summoning spell before the wedding party arrived. Closing her eyes and lowering her chin, Sarina focused her energy on Farrin.

This time, the summons did not go unanswered.

ξЖξ

Farrin scrutinized Flea. A look of mortal pain contorted on his face as he slumped forward, hands clinging to his ribs.

"Is it painful? Morphing from man to cat and back again?"

"No more painful than growing a beard, M'lady. I took a boot on my way out of the rectory...seems the cook doesn't tolerate cats in his kitchen."

She shouldn't laugh. It isn't right to indulge mirth when a friend is in pain. Still, she could imagine the fat, red-faced cook with a look of murderous intent blooming on his face, shouting profanities as he discovers a cat in his kitchen, his boot connecting and the feline flying through the air as if jettisoned from a catapult.

It really wouldn't be proper to laugh.

Searching Flea's face, she desperately tried to convey a serious measure of concern. He met her gaze and chuckled. It felt so good to laugh she would have liked it to last longer.

Flea rubbed the pain from his ribs and stood erect, a wince crossing his face. "They've gone to the cathedral," he reported. "I overheard a servant say she'd never heard such filth escape a lady's mouth on her wedding day."

Farrin led the way. Having practically grown up in Stockbridge, she knew every nuance and hidden corner on the grounds. The cathedral stood a stone's throw from the rectory.

"If the Bishop is half the rat I believe he is, we may be able to resolve this issue peacefully. If not, I need to know you're in fighting condition."

"My ego is purple and puffy, but I'm fit to fight, M'lady."

"How do you do it, change into a cat, I mean? Is it a spell, or something else?"

"Something else. All it takes is the slightest desire to change and *presto*."

"Really?"

"Imagine trying to raise a child with such a gift...my poor, dear mother."

Farrin's laughter projected so loud she feared she might have given away her position. Was it nerves? Partially. Add a pinch of giddiness. When had she slept last?

Two heavily armed men draped in black leather stood guard at the cathedral door, but it didn't seem as though they had heard anything.

Taking her by the arm, Flea guided her behind a hay cart where the guards would not see them.

Whispering, Farrin drew him close, "We may yet need that element of surprise you suggested earlier. Can you become the cat and get inside the cathedral without anyone seeing you?"

"As you wish, M'lady," he nodded. His eagerness to engage seemed infectious. His smile revealed a gentle beauty that had gone unnoticed before. No question remained, this man was Kensington kin and it was clear now where the daring Sir Oswald had come by his sense of adventure.

Once Sarina was free, they would return to the castle where she could look after Ozzie and this entire fiasco would finally end. A few hours sleep would come well received.

"Go," Farrin said, nudging Flea with an elbow, "I'll meet you inside."

Inching alongside the building, she withdrew a pinch of powder from her pocket and waited for a sufficient gust of wind to release it. "Somnus iam," she whispered. The sound of two bodies slumping to the mortar immediately followed. "Sweet dreams," she chuckled, stepping over the unconscious guards.

The dreadful notes of a minstrel singing off-key assaulted Farrin's senses. As her pupils adjusted to the low light, she saw the singer standing at the altar, chin hung low, hands shackled behind his back. Merlin help him, he was purposefully butchering the Ballad of Logary.

Sarina, shackled hand and foot, her skin bearing a purple hue, looked angry enough to explode. The old man standing beside her, on the other hand, looked as though someone had served him the entire roast pig compliments of the chef, ale on the house. And the Bishop, a man who would put a price on anything, simply seemed to glow as he basked in the thought of the riches he was about to procure through the sale of his only child.

Farrin intentionally slammed the cathedral door, making a boisterous entry. Heads snapped to attention and eyes nervously scanned the cathedral in search of the uninvited guest. Most thankfully, the minstrel stopped his sour braying.

"Forgive my intrusion," Farrin projected, her voice booming with regal authority as she strode down the aisle, "I require but a moment of your time, then I'll be on my way and you'll be free to resume your frivolities."

Standing face-to-face with the Bishop, Farrin squelched the desire to strike his gaping jaw. He offered an apologetic shrug to the Duke. Poor Duke, forced to wait all these years to acquire his prize and when the moment finally arrives, someone interrupts.

"What do you want?" The Bishop barked.

"Is that any way to address your future queen, sir? I'm sure you must know what I have come for. What you don't know is what I'm willing to pay for it. The answer is double whatever the Duke has promised you."

"Double?" The Bishop suddenly lost his stern appearance and took on a misty gaze which, coupled with a sly grin, made him appear every bit the village idiot.

Quickly catching on as to exactly what (or whom) the bartering concerned, the Duke loudly protested. "By whose authority..."

"By my authority, as future queen of Collingswood," Farrin spat, gaze locked. "Dare you question my authority?"

She watched the Duke's face transform. Shadows passed over his eyes, the muscles in his cheeks softened and a look of resolution replaced his fury, a countenance submissive in its expression. By the time Farrin realized what was going on inside his mind, it was too late. The blade was already in his hand, poised at Sarina's throat. If he couldn't have her, no one would.

A growl worthy of a full-grown panther punctured the moment as a large ball of black fur flew from the rafters, landing on the Duke's face, the cat's claws digging for purchase in the flesh behind his ears, fangs sinking into his cheeks. The Duke lost his grip on Sarina, who screamed as she slumped to the floor, blood spurting from her face where his blade had sliced her. In a fraction of a second, that same blade cut into the cat, which screamed a ferocious and spine-chilling wail as it fell limp at the Duke's feet.

There appear events in every life when thoughtless reaction is the only action available, especially when it comes to self-defense or the defense of a loved one. Farrin's reaction to what she had just seen was mind-bogglingly swift. Unsheathing Excalibur, she cut the Duke in two, the blade slicing through his flesh as if he had already taken the form of a ghost, crown to groin, the two halves falling left and right, landing with a thud. One quick wave of the arm and the tip of Excalibur came to rest securely on the Bishop's Adam's apple. He whimpered and waved his hands in surrender, gawking awkwardly at the Duke's spilled remains.

Farrin's entire body radiated with nervous energy, her hand trembling so that Excalibur's blade drew a trickle of blood from the Bishop's throat even though she hadn't meant to cut him. She spoke in a rage, her voice filled with venom, "I have a moody spot in my stomach for men who believe women mere possessions to be used or traded at whim, especially when said women prove more valuable to society than a rat turd such as yourself. Don't you agree?"

The sound of gushing urine answered for the Bishop as he promptly soiled himself. Eyes wide with horror, he sobbed, "Are you going to kill me?"

How tempting.

"Give me the key to the shackles."

Reaching with an unsteady hand, not willing to lower his chin against Excalibur's blade, the Bishop fumbled to retrieve the key. Key in hand, Farrin lowered the blade and commanded him to leave at once. He eagerly complied.

Sheathing Excalibur, Farrin unbound Sarina, then did the same for the minstrel.

The Duke's blade had cut along Sarina's jawline, ear to chin, and she bled profusely, but it did not seem a mortal wound. The minstrel was completely unharmed. But Flea...

The cat was lax, respiration faint, blood matting the better part of his coat. Farrin held him gently, taking him to Sarina.

"Please, tend the cat."

Cupping her chin with the fabric of her wedding gown, Sarina looked to Farrin with an expression of utter disbelief.

"It's a cat," Sarina moaned.

"He saved your life!"

"I know! But it's still a *cat*. I'm bleeding. I'll need to stitch this or the scar..."

"He's dying, Sarina. Fix him!"

Farrin felt hot liquid trickling over her cheeks and Sarina acknowledged the tears as well, but tried once again to minimize the situation, "Sweetheart, it's a *cat*."

Farrin shook her head negatively and Sarina's eyes flared with sudden understanding.

"Why didn't you say so! Give him to me."

Moments later, Farrin was running through the rectory searching for a straight razor, a packet of herbs and stitching utensils. Sarina said she needed to cut away some fur for a proper examination and claimed the herbs would slow the bleeding.

Why do these terrible things keep happening? Why had Farrin continuously managed to walk away unscathed while her friends fell damaged and dying by her side? Did she have a vexing spirit attached to her that insisted on putting her loved ones in peril, or was she just a festering pustule of bad luck?

Bad luck, that was putting it mildly. She had just killed a man and this time it wasn't a man who had already been dead for fifty years, but one who was breathing one minute and no more the next. Yes, he deserved to die and, yes, he probably only had three days left in him before he keeled over from a heart attack, but none of that made her feel any better. The king had told her long ago that killing someone created a pact, a haunting, as it were. Killing the Duke invoked an onus she would carry for the rest of her life. She would be forced to think of him when, otherwise, she could have easily forgotten him. Flea's death would only add another unbearable burden. And Ozzie...she had to get to Ozzie.

What a tangled noose she had woven by leaving that cottage when she damn well knew she shouldn't have.

Tears blurred her vision, making it almost impossible to see, but she managed to find the supplies Sarina needed.

Stumbling out of the rectory, Farrin rushed back to the cathedral.

ξӝξ

Lady Viviane ached for the comfort of the lake. Many years had passed since she'd ventured this far from Avonelle's shores and, although the distance wasn't unnerving, her yearning for the water would not cease until she returned to it. It has always been thus, the lake as integral to her being as the filling of her lungs or the beating of her heart. She often wondered if her immortality depended on her connection to Avonelle, or if it was the other way around. Did the lake depend on her for its survival?

Returning from a short scavenger hunt, Myla offered Viviane a handful of berries and nuts. Viviane declined, her stomach was weaving knots. Peace would remain aloof until she had safely secured the missing globe.

Hairs rising on her arms, foul scents riding upon the wind, Viviane sensed Helga Dearbourne's presence long before the witch came barging through the forest. Wild-eyed and clearly out of breath, Helga sat astride an immense toad, twigs and leaves dangling from her unruly hair. The toad, stopping twenty feet from where the Lady stood, drooled green slime and produced a croaking grunt, a strange and unnerving cacophony.

Helga toppled off the toad's back and approached with purpose, albeit with her head held low.

"Your Ladyness," the witch blurted with an anxious tone, "I bear dire news. An hour back, near the shores of Avonelle, I was nearly killed by none other than Morgana le Fay. This I swear on any grave, have your pick."

Lady Viviane caught Myla's troubled glance and returned it. They had seen the carnage at the lake.

"If not for my toad," Helga blared angrily, pointing a nervous finger at her familiar, "I would be naught but fish meal."

Ah, it was Helga's toad, then, that had forced Morgana into the lake. Impressive.

Viviane took a deep breath and spoke calmly, "You must thank the Goddess for such a brave familiar, Helga."

Helga nodded emphatically. "Indeed I shall!" Slapping at her mud-caked robes as if they had molested her in some way, Helga stepped forward. "Morgana inquired after Friar John. She said he possesses a certain talent. Any idea what she meant by it?" Pulling the twigs and leaves from her hair, she grimaced and waited for a reply.

"She must believe he has the power to manipulate the globe," the Lady mumbled.

"What globe?" Helga countered.

"It is none of your concern."

Helga's facial expression turned immediately sour. "Well now," she sputtered, "since my life was threatened for information regarding this globe, it certainly does concern me. In fact, I'd say it concerns me from the tip of my hat to the soles of my shoes."

The Lady looked to Myla, whose skin tone had blanched a grayer shade of pale than any living being had the right to possess. Fear coursed through her veins, it was clear to see, and not without merit. The presence of Morgana le Fay was no longer speculation, but an established fact.

Turning back to the witch of Dearbourne, Viviane asked, "Why have you come, Helga?"

"To join forces, of course."

"Is this to say you suddenly possess a conscience?"

Helga laughed, not daintily, but the type of squealing one might expect from a cornered boar.

"It's not a matter of conscience," she snorted, "but a matter of survival."

Viviane raised an eyebrow. "Are you expecting me to prevail in a dual against Morgana le Fay?"

Helga nodded emphatically, "Certainly."

"I am flattered, but your faith may be ill placed. Did you tell Morgana where she can find Friar John?"

"Yes. Bodach Cairn, last I knew."

Peering at the ground, Viviane observed the tracks she and Myla had been following. They headed west. Searching the sky, she turned to get a sense of location.

"We're not far from Stutter's Pass," she said and took Myla by the arm, pulling her off to the side. "I cannot imagine Morgana intends to allow Merlin to live. We must get to her before she locates Friar John."

ξᴊᴋξ

If anyone were to ask, Friar John would say honeybees are the most evil creatures ever created. Waving a smoke-wand under the hives, he grunted and stepped back with trepidation, knowing the smoke should pacify the bees, intoxicate them even, but these hives squirmed to the brim with vicious assassins. He had tended these bees for twenty-five years and had yet to walk away with less than ten raised welts. When he first began working the hives, thousands of the little demons got a piece of his flesh. Friar Francis had once assured John that malefic behavior was not in a honeybee's nature. The bees, he's said, attack only when they feel threatened. Considering the only way to procure honey was to destroy the hives and kill the bees, Friar John readily assumed the bees felt threatened. He had since learned to wear leather gloves, to cover his face with a strip of thin-meshed burlap he could barely see through and to keep at least an arm's length away, one foot planted firmly for escape.

He snorted at the thought. What chance was there really? Even when he was a much younger man he couldn't outrun a swarm. Since then, his mustache and beard had absorbed countless winters, his gut had grown pregnant with overindulgence and his joints flamed with time's ire. He was an old man of sixty now and didn't stand a chance against a swarm. Still, he would keep his foot positioned at the ready, thank you very much.

BK CRAWFORD

His was a love-hate relationship with the savage buzzers. He hated the way they despised his intrusions, but loved the mead fashioned from their honey. No other ale, no other luxury, could compare to the golden liquid and the heaven it offered a man's mind when he fills his gut to the brim. Joy in a cup, that's what it is. Why, you could take a man desperate with the burdens of life, ready to hang himself for all his misery, and three tankards of honey mead returns laughter to his lips. Before you know it, that same bloke is dancing a jig atop the tables and passing gas for wagers.

Friar John moved closer to the hive, expecting to see some activity and yet, detecting none. A little closer. Another step. One more. Still nothing. Not a single bee. This time of the morning, most of them would be off attending to their affairs but there were always stragglers left behind. Where were they? Stepping back, he inspected a clear sky. Sometimes, the bees will leave en masse if a storm is brewing, though it's rare. They left a few years back when a severe drought dried up everything from here to Marksbury (two hundred miles east), not a bee in sight for eight months. The most miserable months of his life. Water, you see, is useless without fermented honey.

Picking up a nearby twig, he tapped on the hive and quickly retreated ten steps. Nothing still. Lifting the burlap from his face, he moved in closer, braver now.

After ten minutes inspection he hadn't found a single bee in any of the hives. On the bright side, he would collect honey today without the price of pain. On the other hand, given what he knew about honeybees, something terrible approached.

ξЖξ

Even when the sun is bright overhead, there are places inside the forest where the canopy is so thick, darkness engulfs all. Helga Dearbourne found such a spot and located a small puddle filled with stagnant water. Squatting next to the pool, she pulled dead leaves from the surface, exposing the face of the water. Sprinkling a touch of silver powder over the puddle, she poked her finger into the dark liquid, twirling three times clockwise, three times counter-clockwise, and spoke to the enchanted element, "Mithragog."

A daring chipmunk scampered toward Helga, looking every bit as though he thought it a good time for a swim. When his approach brought him near enough, she snatched him by the neck and twisted.

Reflected on the water's surface was the picture of Mithragog traversing the roads north of Rivensdale. Surrounded by dust, rock, and rubble, he strode over the bland brown terrain.

His voice carried through the water as if he were standing near, "Mother, to what do I owe the sudden nausea?"

"I have news," she whispered, not knowing exactly where the Lady of the Lake and Myla were. It would not do for them to overhear. "Important news. However, if you insist on being yourself, perhaps I'll hold my tongue."

Mithragog chuckled. "Where are you, Mother?"

"I'm traveling with the Lady Viviane, just south of Rivensdale."

"We grow nearer, Mother. I shall sharpen my blades."

The sound of Mithragog's sniveling laughter irritated Helga to no end, second only to his insistence on calling her 'Mother,' which he knew enraged her.

"You're right," she sneered, "I should keep this news to myself. I have no right to interfere with your life, even if you are on your way to losing it."

Mithragog lifted the back of his hand and rested it on his brow, tilting his head back dramatically, "Oh! I'm so frightened."

More spine-splitting laughter. Wouldn't it be wonderful if she could reach into the water and snap Mithragog's neck as easily as a chipmunk's?

"What news do you have, Mother? Get on with it. I haven't got all day to waste on family re-unions."

Leaning closer to the surface of the water, she responded sternly, "Listen to me, maggot meal. You are seeking the wrong prize."

"Oh, I think not. The heart of the heir will bring untold power to its possessor. Everyone agrees, it is the most coveted prize in the land."

"Perhaps, but that was *before* I overhead the Lady of the Lake confess her secret. Merlin lives."

Helga watched with deepening satisfaction as Mithragog's jaw fell slack and his face blanched white. It took several moments for him to regain his composure. Once recovered, his face grew stern with determination.

"Then I'll have them both, Mother, the heart of the heir *and* Merlin. Can you imagine the power?"

Indeed, she could.

"Leave the girl alone, she is of no use to you once you have Merlin. Dealing with Morgana le Fay to get to Merlin is task enough. Come join forces with me."

"Hold on, Mother, while I inscribe your words of advice on an oak leaf I'll use later to spread my cheeks."

Without breaking the enchantment on the water, Helga pulled herself to her feet and straddled the puddle. Her urine shattered Mithragog's reflection.

"Whatever they say about you, Mother, you are at least refined."

ξжξ

The axe felt heavy in Friar John's hands. He still hadn't cut the cord of wood he started three weeks ago. Although the air churned crisp, he sweated profusely, one more slice and then a rest. Raising the axe, he was about to pull down in full swing when a woman garbed in purple robes emerged from the eastern forest and began to cross the field leading to his door. Cupping his hand over his brow to block the sunlight, he squinted, but did not recognize the legendary Morgana le Fay until she was only a few feet away. No time to run.

Smiling like a long-lost lover, she extended her hands, leaving him no choice but to take them in his own.

"Friar John, how good to see you!" she proclaimed, her sinister smile warm as an icecap. Drawing him near, she threw an arm around his shoulder. "Look how busy you are! Come, you must need relief. I've heard you brew the sweetest mead in all the land. Perhaps you might have some to spare?"

What else could he do? The woman had a man's grip and tugged on him as if to say he had no choice, which he supposed, he didn't.

Inside the cabin, she took a seat, looking as though she owned the table and waited for him to pour a tankard of mead. She sipped and forced a smile that didn't quite lift her ears.

"It's true what they say. This is the best mead I have ever sampled."

Friar John wondered if she'd ever had mead before. He doubted she had come for the ale. Rumor has it she travels with a demon. Where was the dreaded beast? Friar John imagined himself making the sign of the cross and prayed God would spare him the presence of the dreadful minion.

"I'm pleased you enjoy it," he muttered, "this particular batch was made with a rare pound of butter. I don't have the opportunity to add it often." Gulping at the liquid, he summoned the courage to speak his mind, "We assumed you dead, long ago. I wouldn't have recognized you but for an old painting the spiders feed upon in a crypt at the cathedral in Rivensdale."

"I don't get out much," she replied, her eyes thinning at the insult, "but I did have opportunity to visit with your mother in the early hours of the morn."

"Excuse me? You are mistaken. My mother died fifteen years ago, God rest her soul." Crossing himself, he swallowed past the knot that formed in his throat at the thought of his mother's passing.

She patted his hand and nodded, "I speak of your *real* mother."

What was this? A sorceress, up to no good, full of trickery and beguilement, what else should he have expected?

"Listen carefully, Friar. Over the course of many years I have discovered a certain number of credible witnesses who would attest to all I am about to tell you. And you, of all people, have the right to understand what I have learned."

Her words seemed filled with genuine concern while the sordid dance playing out in her eyes betrayed them. She was enjoying this. Whatever she said couldn't amount to more than a stewing pile of bull droppings and whatever she had in mind, he wanted no part of it. He had no desire to hear twisted tales from the lips of a walking corpse that should have had the grace to lay down a hundred years ago. This creature breathed by Satan's command. Just sitting in her presence set his hair on end. Only by the grace of God would he survive this encounter. Rising from his chair, he took a step toward the door.

"I must return to work," he muttered, "the wood won't chop itself."

Morgana grabbed him by the elbow, "It will if I tell it to. Sit down. I wish you no harm."

Thrust back into the chair, he rubbed his elbow where she had surely bruised his flesh. "Harm comes in many fashions," he said, wiping a fresh batch of sweat from his brow.

She twittered a wicked giggle.

Reaching for the earthenware jug at the center of the table, he refilled his tankard but left hers alone, she had barely taken a sip.

"No doubt, you will find the truth stretches all imagination, but your real mother has no idea of you," she claimed, her facial expression softening into a solemn sadness, as if it pained her to make such a report.

"My mother made the best rabbit stew this side of the Holy Roman Empire, she could sew a frock in less time than it would take ten other women to do so. My mother was a God-fearing woman who blessed everyone she ever met and some who never knew her. She was as close to a saint as any woman can hope to come. I knew my mother, she knew me. As to your pretense," he sharply retorted, "it isn't possible to carry a child for nine months and be unaware of it. The idea is absurd."

She addressed him as her eyes scanned the interior of the cabin, "Oh, it is more than possible and that is precisely the case. Your father saw to it. Your real father, that is to say."

"You have me confused with someone else."

She returned his gaze. "Not at all, in fact, I'm surprised no one ever noticed the resemblance," her words seemed filled with awe as she ran the tips of her fingers over the lines of his face in the way a young girl might cherish a doll.

He flinched at her touch.

"If you've taken a fall and hit your head," he suggested, "I know of a woman in a nearby village who has extraordinary healing prowess. You can be there by nightfall."

Throwing her arm over the back of her chair, she laughed. When she'd had her fill of mirth, she leaned forward and spoke as if conveying a coveted secret, "What would you think if I told you your real mother is Viviane, the Lady of the Lake, and your father, none other than the great Merlin?"

A spray of mead spurt from his lips and she wiped away the droplets that landed on her face, clearly annoyed. He rubbed the dribble from his chin and glared at her. She was serious. She had obviously lost the last of her sensibility.

When he attempted to avoid her fixed glare, she kicked him in the shin, as if chastising a disobedient dog. Clearly, he had no choice but to listen to her venom.

"Overflowing with unfathomed virtue, the Lady Viviane entrapped Merlin inside an enchanted globe, believing him bound to her whim, except on those nights when the moon is in eclipse. Curiously, though, there are many who say they have seen a man they swear is Merlin, walking free and going about his business unencumbered. While others disregard these reports as fancy, I find them rather revealing."

"I don't believe a single word of your ranting. Just tell me what you want."

"I'm getting to that. You see, there is one thing on this earth that consistently drives Merlin over the edge of insanity—the Lady Viviane. And so, when she schemed to imprison him, he allowed her to believe she had done so when, in fact, he was free to come and go as he pleased. And he pleased. After enjoying a tryst with Viviane, he would hex her memory so that she had no recollection. When she found her belly swollen with their transgressions, Merlin erased all memory of that as well and stole away with his son to have him raised by trusted guardians. You are that child, son of the greatest sorcerer ever known."

Her diabolical words crept over his skin, filling him with dread. She was stark raving mad.

"Cruel and selfish, wouldn't you say, to treat mother and child in such a way, sequestering them from one another for all of their days? Ah, but that is the way of the venerable Merlin, keeping his son to himself all these years."

Her gaze seemed to implore him for agreement.

"Keeping his son to himself? I assure you, I have never met the man. I, along with everyone else, believe him dead. Merlin passed away long ago."

Morgana reached across the table to pat his hand, a patronizing gesture.

"That's what you said about me only a few moments ago and yet, here I am! I can see why everyone believes Merlin gone and I understand the confusion. After all, it took me forever to put the pieces together."

Her expression was smug, like the farmer who sends his sons to harvest carrots knowing full well he planted turnips. Friar John swallowed hard, not quite knowing what to do.

Waving her hands about the room, she spoke coolly, "I hear tell you live here with another fellow, what was his name...it escapes my memory..."

"Barnabus Nothinghem. He is rarely here, a trapper, you see."

She gave a curious nod, "That he is."

Damnation, he hated puzzles, more than that, he disliked smug bullies. Worse, fear had turned the mead in his stomach sour and the bitter acid crawled into his throat.

"What are you on about?" He bellowed, raising his voice more than intended.

"Follow along, Friar! I'm saying Barnabus is none other than Merlin in disguise and keeping in perfect character."

He felt his face flush. No man likes playing the fool.

"This has been an entertaining visit. Do come more often," he forced a smile and gestured toward the door.

She wasn't budging.

His lips trembled with frustration, "What! What do you want?"

"Come now, don't be so naïve. When Lady Viviane is with the Lake, she has more protection than I could ever dream of. But the moment she leaves, she becomes vulnerable. Your father will wish to protect his beloved and their child from the likes of me, which means once she arrives here, Merlin will not be far behind."

Ah. Now he had her. Her logic had failed, as is always the case with liars. Wait long enough and lies will unravel like a knitted scarf.

Planting his knuckles on the surface of the table he leaned into her gaze and made his challenge, "Why would the Lady of the Lake come here if she doesn't know her son exists?"

Morgana's lips turned up in a sly grin, "She is already on her way."

ξЖξ

Flea's wound was a gaping shoulder-to-shoulder slash and although Sarina had done a fine job of stitching, she couldn't say with certainty if he would ever regain proper upper body function. If he survived, he would carry one hell of a scar. Farrin watched as Sarina tied a sling to her chest and carefully placed the limp feline inside.

Flea whimpered a faint meow, the pitiful tone ushering forth an age-old memory: A morning robin trapped inside a brick cooking pit with a thin-mesh metal grate set over the top, four young children using sticks to poke and prod the frantic creature, forcing it to run circles inside the pit in search of an escape route that didn't exist. Their perverted game had gone on for quite some time. Farrin arrived only in time to see the last flicker of light in the bird's eyes, to hear its final squeal of protest.

Fate, have mercy on Flea.

She and Sarina rushed south toward Rivensdale where Sarina could properly tend to Ozzie and Flea.

Early afternoon shadows cast long as Farrin and Sarina maintained a brisk pace on the dusty road that lead back to the king's court. The minstrel had hitched a ride on a northern-bound coach, vowing never to return to Collingswood.

As she walked by Sarina's side, Farrin recounted the events of her journey from the time she left the cottage until her arrival at the cathedral. Sarina held her tongue throughout the oration and Farrin appreciated the gesture. Knowing Sarina, she was aching to slap some sense into Farrin, albeit late, yet well deserved.

A westerly wind kicked up clouds of dirt, blowing debris high over their statures, forcing them to walk with their hoods drawn over their faces. Winds such as these were rare in late October as the annual gales normally subside by the end of August.

Yelling over the growling storm, Sarina asked, "Why didn't you kill the demon who calls himself my father?"

"Because I love you. It is not my place to take him from your life."

"If another opportunity should arise," she bellowed, "don't hesitate on my account."

The wind gained sudden force, making forward progress all but impossible. Small pebbles began to pummel Farrin's flesh, stinging like wasps at war.

"This isn't natural!" Sarina screamed, her voice riding faint beneath the wind's roar.

Farrin felt a pair of strong arms engulf her waist moments before losing her senses.

ᚷᚤᚷ

Thrown like a sack of grain to the floor, Farrin awoke to a pair of probing eyes studying her face with intense scrutiny. Mithragog. She squirmed against the ropes that bound her hands behind her back. Mithragog squealed with garish delight. Who knew the bumbling idiot was capable of conjuring such a wicked windstorm? And why, Farrin wondered, was she still alive? Did her captor mean to delight in a bit of torture before he attempted to rip her heart from her chest?

The air she breathed was overly moist with a prominent mildew odor, a thick, musty, stagnant air capable of extinguishing a weak set of lungs. The room, formed of granite, was not a room at all, but a cavern. Haunting echoes of trickling water carried through the cavern— torturous sounds, she supposed, if exposure continued at any length. An idle cauldron stood at the center of Farrin's view and shelves filled with supplies lined the weeping walls. A large book sat propped on a makeshift table, an ancient text by the looks of it, doubtfully filled with sacred scripture.

Mithragog bent over and tilted his head to gain eye contact, "Show me the spell you used in the cemetery."

Farrin twisted her wrists against the ropes. Ah, here was the reason her heart remained inside her chest. He wants to learn some real magic before he spoils his prey. What is evil without a little greed thrown into the mix?

"Surely a sorcerer of your caliber has no need of instruction," she sneered.

Mithragog's palm seemed filled with fire as it crossed her cheek.

"You strike a woman bound and incapable of defending herself. Let's add bravery to the list of your redeeming qualities."

He delivered a kick to the ribs that left Farrin gulping for air.

"Show me the spell."

"I can't. My hands are bound, loose them and I'll do as you ask."

His chuckle echoed off the cavern walls.

The ropes burned into her wrists as she continued to writhe against them.

"You need silver powder to perform that spell," she asserted.

"No, I do not," he argued, "I use a staff for a conductor, just as Merlin once did. Silver powder is for floundering amateurs."

"And yet, you require my instruction," she countered.

The tip of his staff rammed into the pit of her abdomen and, once again, she struggled to regain her breath.

Recovering, she spoke through clenched teeth, "Where are we? You can't perform an explosive spell if gas pockets are present in the air, unless you don't mind blowing yourself to kingdom come."

"This is my castle and you needn't worry about gas. Give me the spell."

His castle. Only a man of Mithragog's mentality would call a series of caverns carved into the side of a mountain a castle. But, at least she knew where she was—on the northwestern edge of Bodach Cairn, not far from where he had abducted her.

"See the gargoyle etched on the far wall," she instructed, "focus on it and step back. Once you have the target in focus, point your staff and repeat these words...*Amplus erumpo*. I suggest you write them down and commit them to memory beforehand."

Surprisingly, he did as she suggested, recording the spell on the pages of the ancient book and committing the incantation to memory. Considering himself prepared, he did exactly as she had instructed. The gargoyle exploded with a deafening burst.

One look at Mithragog's face and it became strikingly clear, this was a man consumed with a lust for power, a man no longer in control of his base faculties. If ever there was a picture of insanity, Farrin saw it manifested in his giddy laughter, his victorious dance, his short-lived joy.

"Show me the spell you used on my hellhound," he demanded, his voice saturated with avarice, an insatiable voracity that deepened the lines on his face, spittle escaping his lips as he drooled at the thought of gaining more power.

"Spell?"

BK CRAWFORD

"The one you used on the hellhound."

Farrin's gaze caught sight of Excalibur, splayed on the floor like a worthless trinket. She wondered if Mithragog had tried to lift the sword, wishing she'd witnessed the attempt. Obviously, he hadn't managed more than undoing the straps and pushing the blade to the floor.

"The spell I used on the hound?"

He whacked her with his staff.

She hadn't used a spell on the hound, she'd stuffed a clove of garlic up its nose. Mithragog, however, seemed convinced otherwise. Perhaps she could use his confusion to her advantage.

"That spell can't be performed with a staff, I assure you. For that, you will need silver powder, nothing else will suffice."

"No matter," he grinned, "I'm sure you must have some."

He kidnapped a witch and left her with powder?

"In my right pocket. You only need a pinch."

Powder in hand, he waited for instruction.

"Speak the incantation with precision and clarity. *Suspendo Vado Austerus*. Try it without throwing the powder first."

"Austerus Vado Suspendo," he said.

"No. Try again, write it down. Focus."

He did as she suggested and once he had memorized the incantation, she continued to coach.

"Throw the powder high over your head, don't concern yourself with where it falls, it is of no importance. What matters is speaking with precision."

Flicking his wrist, Mithragog threw the powder over his head and spoke the incantation meticulously, only to realize the spell had vaulted him to the ceiling and stricken his body immobile.

Scrambling to her feet, Farrin backed up to Excalibur and used the sheath to cut away the binding rope. Unsheathing the great sword, she poked its tip against Mithragog's throat.

"I'll not kill you now, but if you persist against me, I make no such promise for our next encounter. Perhaps it's best to leave magic to the big girls."

He glared at her with unfathomable loathing, never had she seen such hatred emanate from another human being. Turning away, she recovered his staff and shattered it, throwing its splinters into the cauldron, along with his overgrown spell book and a pinch of silver powder. "Incendia," she commanded, and a bright fire burst to life, hungrily consuming Mithragog's prized possessions.

ξЖξ

About a mile from the base of Bodach Cairn, Farrin heard the clopping of horse hooves combined with the familiar brattle of armor. Sarina must have made it safely to Rivensdale and sent the knights on a rescue mission.

Seeing Farrin, the knight slowed his horse to a gait and reared up beside her. Looking down at her, he gave his neck a sharp twist, his bones crackling with gruesome snaps. She smiled. Sir Charles, the only man she had ever known who could turn his head around in a full rotation without breaking his neck. He was a man with a serious sense of humor. For sport, he would often pop a bright red tomato in his mouth and lie belly down on the ground, head facing upward, red fluid oozing over his chin, just to hear the children scream. Every joint in his body was limber in a way nature never intended, which made him hell to beat in a sword fight. And so, even though he wasn't much older than Farrin, Ozzie had made him captain of his battalion.

Lifting his visor, he displayed a brilliant smile. "My Lady," he said, nodding formally.

Farrin saw no sign of anyone else in the immediate area. "You came alone?"

"No. The rest of the battalion stopped about a half-mile back to see about dinner...an eight-point buck."

Ah, yes, dinner, always a priority over the safety of the future queen.

Heat radiated off the horse's coat and it snorted in rapid succession, Sir Charles had ridden fast and hard.

Farrin leaned on Excalibur's hilt, exhausted beyond comprehension. The sword caught the knight's attention.

"Is that... Ho! Is that *Excalibur*?" He dismounted his horse, eyes wide with excitement and approached with hands extended.

Nodding, Farrin handed him the sword.

"It's heavy," he grunted, straining to wave the sword in a shadow cross parry.

"The fact you can lift it at all says much for your character. Help me strap it to my shoulder."

He spoke as he fastened buckles and tied straps, "You didn't really think we would leave you to your own resources, did you?"

Once Sir Charles had affixed the sword and settled her cloak back into place, she turned to reply, "Thank you. Once again you have arrived in the nick of time, heaven forbid you should risk a dent in your armor."

"Don't mention it, M'lady. Seriously, please don't," he said, his face flushed with embarrassment. Remounting the horse, he helped her saddle up. Wrapping her arms around his waist, she buried her cheek in the small of his back and tried not to fall asleep as they galloped back to Rivensdale.

ξЖξ

Helga didn't like to admit it, but her body was falling apart piece-by-piece, particularly her right hip which was always sore, but more so after a morning filled with strenuous activity. There were times when, despite her stubborn determination, the joint locked up completely, leaving her unable to walk. She would prefer to avoid such an occurrence while scaling Bodach Cairn with Myla and the Lady Viviane.

And so, Helga carefully selected six pieces of common shale from atop a nearby water well and approached a small hut, breathing in deeply as the scent of fresh gingerbread permeated the air.

The farmer who came to the door was getting on in years and the sweat pearling off his brow bore testament to a morning spent toiling in the fields and tending to his livestock. Helga made her proposal without formality. She would give him six pieces of gold if he would allow her to use his donkey to traverse Bodach Cairn. Eyes wide at the sight of the gold in her palm, the farmer readily agreed and fetched the animal for her straight away. So grateful was he, he threw in a complimentary loaf of gingerbread, which his wife bundled in a swatch of fine fabric.

In an hour or two, the farmer would realize Helga had hexed the stones and his gold pieces would slowly return to gray shale but, by that time, she would be well on her way and he, too old and exhausted to chase after her. Blessings on the foolhardy willing to believe everything they see.

Instructing her toad to remain concealed near the farmer's pond, (no toad could possibly survive such a journey and certainly not one as lazy as Edema) Helga guided the donkey to its knees and mounted it.

The Lady Viviane led the march, fifty paces ahead already. As Helga rejoined the trek, Myla took hold of the lead rope and guided the donkey onto the thin path that wound its way up the mountain.

"I remember you," Helga said to Myla, "from the orphanage, long ago."

Myla nodded, "And I, you. Even as a child you threw yourself in with a bad lot of bullies and thieves."

Helga laughed. Those were the days. "And you, Myla, always cowering in a corner somewhere, afraid to stir things up. Before you declare yourself judge and jury, consider—if the world were full of people like me, there would never come a dull moment. On the other hand, if it were filled with the likes of you, the entire human race would wither from boredom."

The reverberation of Helga's cackle raised the hair on Myla's arms.

Myla tugged on the rope, her knuckles white with anger, her chin tucked low. Helga knew Myla was biting her tongue, choking back words she desperately wanted to say, but never would. Blessings on the meek and meager, without them a bully would have no profession.

Unwrapping the gingerbread from its fabric cocoon, Helga broke off a piece and popped it into her mouth. Heavenly. Say what you will about pitiful country folk, but they are generally highly skilled in the culinary arts.

As time passed, the mountain grew steeper, the path thinner and more treacherous. The donkey slipped several times on loose rubble. Helga peered over the edge of the precipice. It was a long way down and would only get worse with each step forward.

Morgana and her demon, Dezva, had left clear tracks behind as they ascended the mountain, a couple of hours ago by the looks of it. One stretch of rock bore fresh stripes clearly made by the demon's nails as he dug them into the granite, leaving black soot imbedded in deep indents. Only a demon can leave such marks. These traces arrested Myla's attention and she beckoned the Lady Viviane to rejoin the group for a bit of chatter.

"Why," Myla shouted emphatically, "would they not take greater care to disguise their path? Why leave a blatant trail unless they expect us to follow? We are walking into a trap."

Hands on hips, the Lady peered to the top of the mountain, its canvas rich with rusty red Beech leaves, golden Larch, hearty Oak, tufts of heather, bracken and bilberry, the autumn foliage bursting with a vibrant appliqué that would become non-existent in another week or two. "So be it," the Lady said frankly and turned as if prepared to resume the trek.

"I presume you have a plan," Myla screeched, fear riddling her expression.

The Lady didn't say a word, didn't have to, the look on her face said it all. She didn't need a plan and, with or without one, hellfire on a crucifix wouldn't turn her away from her quest. There would be no cowering in the corners for the Lady Viviane and, by the look in the Lady's eyes,

Morgana le Fay might wish she were never born before this day drew to a close.

Helga stifled a cackle and tried to hold her urine but when was the last time that worked?

ۻ

After a short visit with the king, Farrin rushed to the infirmary where she found a half dozen handmaidens working feverishly, sorting herbs and grinding roots, quietly focused on the tasks Sarina had set for them.

A thin sliver of light filtered through a small window and came to rest on the forms of the two broken men Sarina anxiously attended. Flea had obviously regained consciousness long enough to convert to human form but had since lapsed into tranquil oblivion.

Sarina acknowledged Farrin's presence with a quick glance and resumed the task of applying a rather gloppy gel to Flea's wound. Farrin approached with trepidation, a dreadful question caught between a lump in her throat and a dry tongue. Swallowing hard, she forced the words, "Will he live?"

Gently dabbing the gel onto the wound, Sarina inhaled slowly, deeply, shaking her head ever so slightly, "Tonight the moon and sun will confer and the dawn will have much to say to fate. Look at him, though. It's no wonder you were so adamant about saving this one. Handsome devil, isn't he?"

Farrin blushed, "I hadn't noticed. Tell me, how did you know where to send the knights?"

Sarina smiled her acknowledgement, "When you disappeared, the winds completely died down. I presumed it black magic and assumed only Mithragog would take you in such a crude way. Did you kill the seeping wart?"

"Not yet, but I suspect he won't find satisfaction in anything less."

A voice, weak and raspy, interrupted from the other side of the room, "Excuse me, your Highness."

Pulling back the curtain, Farrin beamed at Ozzie. It was so good to hear his voice, to see him smiling and alert once again. She traced his face with her fingertips.

"I see you met Mac," he said, his gaze resting on Flea's still form.

"You call him Mac?"

"Do you have a better name?"

She nodded, "Flea."

Ozzie's laugh was guttural and caused him to wince in pain, "Oh, I bet he just loved that."

Flying off her stool, Sarina arrived at Ozzie's side in a blur. "Stop talking!" she scolded. "For heaven's sake, don't make him laugh. The slightest burp and his stitches will rip wide open." Sarina's facial expression was a momentary gargoyle. Ozzie waved her off much like a horse would shoo a fly with its tail.

"Don't give me attitude, mister gallant knight. Remember who mixes the tonics around here. Behave, or

I'll put you down until spring. And you," she said, directing her attention to Farrin, "you need sleep."

"No time for that. Father has received word from the Lady of the Lake. Seems she means to confront Morgana le Fay on the fells of Bodach Cairn. I've been given directions and precise instruction. It's up to me to make sure Morgana does not attain the power she seeks."

"I'm going with you," Ozzie said, attempting to rise.

Sarina palmed him in the chest, pinning him down, "No you don't!"

"You won't hold him like that for more than five minutes," Farrin said with a chuckle. "Step away, I'll make him a deal. If he can use his left arm to hold this tankard over his head for two seconds, he can come along. If not, he will remain here to visualize my triumphant return. Is it a deal, Sir?"

Ozzie nodded and Sarina stepped away. Farrin put the tankard in Ozzie's hand and waited.

It is truly amazing (and often disheartening) to realize how the loss of a single muscle in the human body can affect the completion of a simple task. Ozzie had taken an arrow to the left side and his stitches were fresh. Lifting that arm caused excruciating pain. Though he struggled for five minutes or more, he couldn't raise the tankard at all, much less maneuver it over his head. In the end, the tankard fell to the floor with a clatter.

"That settles that," Sarina said and offered a tonic to Farrin. "This will provide a full night's sleep with only ten minutes' rest. Drink it. I'll wake you."

Farrin had to admit, it felt good to close her eyes and invite sleep. As she drifted off, she thought she might have judged the prospect of marriage too harshly. Clearly, her love for Ozzie was more than she previously realized, coming so close to losing him had stirred up a nest of surprising revelations. But, she was still so young with so much life to live. And yet, they say love is all you need. Ozzie did know her through-and-through and wasn't likely to expect her to change. What's more, he would make a fine king. She would have time to make the decision later, but one thing had become startlingly clear, life would lose all sense and meaning without her chivalrous knight.

May the Goddess reward Sarina's talent, after only a few minutes' rest, Farrin felt as though she had slept for an entire week.

Who could say what events await atop Bodach Cairn, but if youth and invigoration count for anything, the advantage now fell to Farrin the Fair.

ξЖξ

Merlin observed as the future queen approached a farmer's home to ask where she might find the path leading to Friar John's homestead. The farmer, a scraggly looking fellow whose skin appeared as though it had seen enough sun for ten men, did not seem pleased with the inquiry. Face blooming, he screeched in angst, "You and every other mangy witch should like assistance today! Don't bother asking to hire my donkey as it has already been pilfered for six lousy pieces of common shale." At which point, the farmer flung the shale, beaning the young lady upon the brow.

To her testament, she did not exact retribution, but slowly backed away with a splendid display of self-control. She then began to seek the path of her own accord and found her way with only the slightest confusion.

An observer of younger spirit might not think twice about such a display, but one bearing the mark of a master, wise in his years, would find both humor and inspiration in witnessing such an extraordinary event. Why, this observation might even renew Merlin's faith in humankind, however fleeting the veneration may be.

Touched, his curiosity peaked. He would like to meet this valiant young girl, speak with her, guide her perhaps.

Merlin put off his dark robes, which served as camouflage, and set himself upon the path where the young lady could not possibly miss him—ahead of her, but not too far, walking, but not too fast. She would come upon him shortly.

"Ho, there!" She called and Merlin turned to meet the tip of her blade, and a familiar blade at that. Excalibur.

He donned his most charming smile, one specifically designed to mesmerize, and she abandoned her aggression.

"Are you...," she began, her words trailing off in awe.

With a slow, deliberate nod, he bowed, bending crisply at the waist and rising again to meet her gaze.

She opened her mouth to speak, but closed it again, and repeated the ritual thrice more, a blank confusion passing over her pupils. At last, she spoke graciously, "It's a pleasure to meet you."

Bowing once again, Merlin replied, "The pleasure is all mine, M'lady." And, while he perceived her greeting as sincere, he noted that her gaze had left his face and settled over his shoulder as her attention returned to the mission ahead. After all, a man can only be just so famous.

"If you would stand aside, kind sir, I must press on," she asserted, her polite dismissal endearing.

"Of course." Turning aside, he escorted her past with a wave of the hand, "As long as you realize a fool rushes in, while the wise pause to consider."

In haste, she continued on, her strides wide, until they became shorter, slower. Then she stopped altogether and turned to ask, "Consider what?"

Leaning nonchalantly upon his staff, Merlin coiled locks of alabaster beard around his fingers and spoke softly, "If I am not mistaken, we share a common rival. We are both in pursuit of Morgana le Fay who was once my apprentice. If you would like to confer for a moment, I know a lovely place just off the path."

Turning away, he ambled through a small valley carved into the mountainside, which led to a trickling stream.

There he sat, knowing it might take some time for her to follow, but that she would ultimately make the right choice. She didn't keep him waiting long.

Taking a spot on a felled log, she sat next to him, her sigh revealing her impatience, and yet, the fact she had come at all spoke otherwise. Ah, the fabric of youth, torn and re-stitched until it either falls apart or grows to weather the fiercest storm.

"What should I expect from Morgana le Fay?" She asked.

Merlin chuckled. "You can expect unpredictability, my dear."

"You don't know. You beckoned me here to say you don't know?"

"I cannot say with certainty what will happen on the crest of this mountain, but I can tell you what Morgana is capable of. Perhaps having this insight will prepare you, somewhat."

"Somewhat?"

"Somewhat. Shall I proceed, or is peace in ignorance more appealing?"

The stream sounded with a soothing trickle and the sun glistening off the dark stones seemed magical in many ways. Fallen leaves floated over the face of the water, some ultimately tangling on stone while others sailed downstream unencumbered. Merlin visited this place often, content to borrow a little serenity from its soul.

"Do tell," Farrin replied.

Propping his staff between his legs, he took a deep breath and nodded.

"First, you must understand the mindset of a master. A master sees things from a perspective most are incapable of perceiving...this is a strict requirement. If a master focuses only on what others see, the extraordinary escapes while the eyes laze upon the ordinary. A talented student shares in this extraordinary vision and is willing to conceive things not yet understood. Do you fathom the logic?"

Her nod was sharp and determined.

"Good, very good," he said, spinning his staff between his palms, a mindless preoccupation.

"I taught Morgana le Fay many things before realizing she meant to use her power to the detriment of humanity. I consider myself neither good nor evil, but capable of both. Yet, when given a choice, I find my heart leans toward a desire for the betterment of humanity, not for its destruction. Nor do I harbor a desire to subjugate the world at my feet, as Morgana would have it. If I had known her intentions, I would not have shared the slightest bit of knowledge with her."

Again, the young lady nodded and adjusted her seating, indicating an anxiousness to further the conversation.

"As I said, I taught Morgana many things, but chiefly among them, and most likely to cause trouble, are the Principles of Reality. These are an ancient wisdom, put to sleep long ago by rulers who employed the Principals to gain power and control over the masses. Some in power pass knowledge of the Principals on to their heirs but never allow these jewels of information to trickle into the general populace, lest the ruling factions lose control. The Principles of Reality are at the heart of every piece of magic. But, of course, once you understand the Principals, magic no longer seems mystical. As a practitioner of magic, you must already understand this to some degree.

To further this understanding, let us consider the reaction of those who witnessed the birth of the very first fire. Certainly, those in attendance would agree, this element seemed extraordinarily magical in many ways. In fact, many thought fire so mystical, they worshipped it. Of course, we now know fire is not magic at all but simply a natural occurrence. So it is with the Principles of Reality, natural occurrences hitherto unfathomed or misunderstood."

The young lady tossed small pebbles into the stream as if bored by Merlin's illuminations. But when his lips had grown quiet and his gaze met hers, she lost no time in questioning his oration.

"What are they, the Principles of Reality?"

"Put simply, they are the keen understanding that reality does not exist in the way most are conditioned to perceive, but is created on a moment-to-moment basis by each of us according to our vision, faith, and desire."

Her laugh issued forth with a musical quality quite pleasant to the ear, her incredulity, not entirely unexpected.

"Madness," she summated, her tone revealing a twinge of mistrust.

"Is it?" Merlin stood and pointed to the top of a tall oak. "What do you see there, in the branches of that tree?"

"Nothing but bark and leaves," she replied.

"Look again," he instructed, and by the time she had raised her face to peer at the highest branch, he was sitting upon it, swinging his legs, looking down with a wide smile and brandishing a jolly wave. Rapidly twisting to find him no longer sitting beside her, she thrust her gaze back to the tree, but by then he was tapping her gently upon the knee, which caused a bit of a surprised yelp.

"That's your proof?" She scoffed. "You're the great Merlin, known throughout the land for spectacular feats. How does this prove reality doesn't exist as we know it?"

"I did not say it doesn't exist," he corrected her. "I said it is created on a moment-to-moment basis and that you and I create it. To what degree we create depends upon our wisdom, knowledge, and faith. Consider the sword you carry, the fabled Excalibur. It is fashioned from light. There is no other element present in the sword, only light. I'm sure you noticed how it shimmers. Those worthy of it can see through the sword, as it seems translucent. Do you see it that way?"

She answered with a slow nod.

"Excalibur was created by the Lady of the Lake for light-bearers. Anyone unable to see the sword for what it truly is cannot wield it, as it is far too heavy when viewed as a common sword. And so, your ability to carry Excalibur demonstrates your ability to see the world from a perspective most people do not possess. My dear, are you wallowing in the throngs of madness?"

She raised her eyebrows at the assertion. Merlin could almost see the thoughts swirling as she processed the information. She would wonder about the differences between a witch and a common girl, between those who understand medicine and science and those who do not, and she would see how bizarre and frightful an uncommon knowledge might seem to those who do not possess it. Lastly, she would wonder what constitutes madness. Quite comical. No matter how long he lived, one thing still tickled him to the core, the naivety and eagerness of youth—bless them one-and-all.

"How does Morgana le Fay use these principals to her advantage?" Farrin asked.

Merlin clapped his hands. "Now you're on to it!" he beamed, leaning in close to her shoulder, "Clever girl, yes you are. I knew it the moment I saw you." He nudged her shoulder and allowed himself a hearty laugh. She blushed.

"Morgana ultimately lost all doubt concerning the Principals and, after many years practice, used them to summon her demon servant, Dezva. This did not please me as I had higher expectations. I expected she would wish to create something beautiful, something good. Nothing could have been further from her mind. Naturally, when her motives became clear I refused to teach her anything more. This angered her...no, forgive me the massive understatement, she was *livid* and remains so, obsessed with having what I refused to give her. And here we are, come full circle."

Farrin quietly gathered her thoughts, contemplative as the plentiful sunlight highlighted her strawberry hair and revealed patches of freckles on either side of her nose. Merlin allowed her the luxury of silence until her inquisitiveness burst through, "What does this have to do with Friar John, who is he, and why has Morgana chosen Bodach Cairn for this... What is it, a challenge, a duel, an ultimatum?"

"All at once, I suspect," he answered, twirling his staff rapidly between his palms. "Friar John is dear to my heart. Unfortunately, Morgana has chosen to use my affection against me. She has lured the Lady of the Lake, also dear to me, to Friar John's homestead at the crest of the mountain where she eagerly anticipates the ensnaring of the fly."

The future queen stood and gazed over the mountain. Turning back sharply, she asked, "Aren't we wasting time?"

"I suspect you will one day learn that time is subjective. As such, I have taken the liberty to pause it."

Her stern wince implied utter disbelief. "Excuse me?"

What good is life if you can't have a little fun with it? Merlin began asking this question at the tender age of eight. How many hundreds of years had passed since then, exactly? No matter.

Standing, he drew near to the edge of the stream.

"Look," he instructed. "See the small twig with three red leaves ambling over the surface of the brook? Watch it closely. We will see it until it escapes our line of vision. There, you see, it's all gone. Now look upstream, just there, and notice, here it comes again, the very same twig. I've counted thirty passes since our conversation began. How many would you like to count? After all, we have all the time in the world."

Mouth agape, gaze glued to the rambling twig, the young lady seemed genuinely perplexed.

Pointing excitedly at the twig, she ventured, "Can you teach me how to do that?"

"Whatever for?" He asked, a sly grin playing on his lips. "Perhaps I will teach you, one day, if we survive our adventure. I would gladly make arrangements for a future queen."

"You know who I am."

"Of course. Your dark cloak is not much of a disguise and your possession of Excalibur speaks volumes. To be sure, one might expect a princess to twitter about in long gowns and tiaras, concerned with regal things, but you've never been accused of being shallow, have you?"

Self-consciously, she stroked the lapel of her cloak and laughed in the way people do when they truly tickle themselves.

"I don't like being confined to what someone else expects of me," she confessed. "I can't breathe."

Merlin knew the feeling well.

"Is this time spell affecting the entire world?" She wanted to know.

"No, I've limited its effects strictly to the mountain. Why do you ask?"

"Time is a requirement for healing and I have friends in dire need. I wouldn't want to impede their progress."

"Naturally," Merlin said. "Back to the matter at hand?"

She snapped a nod of agreement.

"Morgana will seem ominous, at the very least, and she does have great skill. However, it's what she doesn't have that may be to our advantage. Morgana doesn't put much faith in the abilities of others and often underestimates her opponent. She is expecting the Lady of the Lake and, after the Lady, my timely arrival. What she doesn't expect is you. I suspect we can use this to our advantage. But first, let's see if we can rid you of that blasted silver powder."

Clutching her pocket, Farrin defended her powder.

"You will soon see for yourself how unnecessary and encumbering your powder is, you simply don't need it." Merlin put his staff down and left it an arm's length away. "Kick that stick by your foot, give it a good boot."

Looking down, she located the stick and laid into it. When it hit the ground, it angrily slithered away, the rattle on the newly-formed snake vibrating in wrath.

"If someone tried to convince you it isn't possible to cast magic, you wouldn't believe them because your life experience is contrary to the assertion, but if the same claim is presented to your children or your grandchildren before they've had a chance to experience magic, the outcome might be quite different. Much of mankind's innate capabilities have been lost in exactly this way, whittled away by doubt and inexperience, stolen by those who covet power and control. As such, many sorcerers believe a staff is required for use as a conductor of magic, just as you believe in the use of powder, but this is not true. The true conductors of magic are within the heart and mind...occupants we have come to know as passion and intent. While in possession of these basic elements, our abilities are limitless.

Now you try. Without using powder, direct your focus upon an ordinary object and use your passion to transform the object."

"I don't understand," she confessed, and the pale rose that is embarrassment washed over her face.

"But you do," Merlin patiently replied. "Tell me, what was the last spell you cast?"

"Suspendo Vado Austerus, I used it to suspend and render an assailant immobile," she answered.

"How badly did you want that spell to work?"

"Very much, actually, I believe I would have been killed otherwise."

"There you see, then—passion and intent. When was the last time you attempted to cast a spell without your powder?"

Surprised, she answered with another blush, "Never."

Placing a gentle hand upon her shoulder, he leaned in to whisper, "It is time then, yes?"

She inhaled with determination and nodded, allowing her hands to fall away from her pocket. She then went to the edge of the creek to gather four large stones, bringing them back to the fallen log and arranging them one atop the other. Once satisfied, she flicked her empty fingers at the stones and spoke with conviction, "Incohare dragonfly!" And she stood there, staring expectantly at four stones that had not so much as shivered at her floundering attempt. Merlin suppressed his laughter, concerned with insulting her effort. Instead, he bent near to the stones and pretended to examine them carefully, uttering meaningless grunts.

"I would venture to guess you didn't have much of a desire to see an overgrown dragonfly. Alas. Let's make a few corrections and try again, shall we? First, there's no need to utter an incantation, doing so calls attention to your presence, which can create an extreme disadvantage. All you need is a solid visualization. Secondly, since you're not using powder, there's no need to flick your fingers as if dispelling it. It's never comfortable to abandon a long-used habit, but once you realize how effective you are without these gestures, the habit will fall away rather quickly. Third, consider your immediate need for a dragonfly. If the need is not imperative, the level of emotion will not create enough energy to rise to the occasion. You will fare better when summoning an object of intense desire."

"Your need for a rattlesnake was intense?" She sneered.

"No, but my need to make an effective demonstration seemed rather pressing."

Requesting a moment of solitude, Farrin stared over the rippling waters of the stream, lost in thought, or deep in concentration. Whichever the case, Merlin waited patiently while she gathered her thoughts.

Once satisfied, she broke away from the water's edge and took her place upon the log, her expression taut with determination.

Without uttering a word, she waved her arm over the space before her, closed her eyes, inhaled deeply, and bit her lip, probably forcing back an incantation. Merlin noticed the usual roll of the eyes beneath the eyelids as she focused inward, centering her energy, concentrating on the object she had determined to create.

He felt a grin curling the corners of his lips as he studied Farrin's face. Her hard determination would build until, well...until she most likely fainted from overexertion.

Of the many students he had guided over the years, no one had ever accomplished much of anything on the first try. In fact, the best of his students took weeks to produce so much as a walnut. Some, sadly, never produced more than a ton of sheer frustration. In all likelihood, the girl would fail. The true test of character, however, lies not in success or failure, but in the determination to press on despite the miscarriages life so often endows.

Then again, why be a knot about it and assume the girl would fail? He leaned full weight upon his staff. Who knew better than Merlin the fanciful pleasures taken by Father Happenstance when reminding the haughty that they are not above error, and the amusements of Fate as she drops those things we desperately need into the palms of our hands when we need them most? These are the rare moments in life when the extraordinary transcends the mundane and life takes on a magical quality that often exceeds our comprehension, leaving us to marvel in our simplicities. Thus, the wise refrain from making predetermined judgments. Merlin would observe the girl and simply allow events to unfold.

Following an elongated period of intense concentration that produced nothing more than the red face of exhaustion and a spirit of vexation, Farrin made a humble request, beseeching him for another demonstration.

Arms extended, he placed both palms together, thumbs in the upright position. Keen on the dramatic flair, he opened them quickly, palms skyward, and a white dove briefly appeared in his hands before it lifted off, soaring toward the sun, perhaps in search of an afternoon meal. Six times, he repeated the exercise and six times a new dove appeared, each taking immediate flight.

"Will that suffice?" He asked, noting the studious concentration she held during the demonstration and the yearning apparent in her regard.

"Very impressive, sir, but I wonder what you were thinking when you created those lovely birds."

Merlin's wide smile lifted his ears. This question struck at the heart of the matter and he was encouraged to see the girl recognize the implication so quickly.

In answer, he replied, "I thought of a delicate bird, beautiful and white in its pureness, one that coos ever so melodically, a creature so free no man can cage it without breaking its will to live, one capable of the most graceful flight, fully alive and in perfect health. Every detail you imagine lends credence to the creation."

"But, how did you manage all that thought so quickly?"

"I've had many years to practice, my dear. After some time, the process simply becomes second nature. We must all start somewhere, mustn't we?"

With a curt nod, she returned to her task, her determination significantly intensified.

He left her to her endeavor while he snuggled in the roots of a large tree near the stream where the waters provided a sufficient lullaby for a brief afternoon nap. Twice his own snoring woke him from slumber. Not one to give up easily, he persisted.

It wasn't a ripping snore that ultimately woke him, or his beard tangled in an armpit, as happens far too often, but the smell of a roasting fowl and the sound of a healthy burp.

As consciousness slowly returned, Merlin pivoted toward the fallen log, his eyes filled with wonder at what they saw, his heart leaping with delight. Sitting there, on the fallen log, was Farrin the Fair, tending to a roasted chicken turning upon a spit. In her hand she held a golden slice of cornbread, a triumphant smile beaming upon her lovely face.

"Care to join me?" She asked, urging him with a wave.

Tearing a leg from the roasted hen, he sat next to her and chewed with rapture, savoring the moment of a rare accomplishment and the delectable delicacy of the well-cooked fare. How perfectly wonderful.

"You must have been starving," he noted between bites.

"Quite," she said, handing him a piece of cornbread.

"Bless you, M'lady," he uttered and, because his hands were full, he allowed a lone tear to travel over his cheek and settle on the edge of his beard. After all these years, he had met a student who could apply the Principals after a single lesson. He would never have believed it and yet here he was, eating cornbread.

Mouth bursting with the flavor of the honey-buttered sweetbread, Merlin spoke without bothering to swallow, "Nothing to drink?"

"We are thirsty, aren't we?" She concurred, and two tankards of mead appeared at foot.

"My, my, you do catch on quickly," he chuckled. Tossing chicken bones over his shoulder, he picked up the tankard and drew heavily on the liquid, washing his throat with golden delight. "One would expect a first attempt to taste a bit like donkey urine, not that I can attest to ever sampling such a foul beverage, mind you, but your mead is superior to any brew ever to cross these lips."

She blushed, busying herself with her meal until she had had her fill.

"Is that it, then?" She asked, kicking mounds of dirt over the fire burning beneath the empty spit.

"Oh, I'm afraid not," Merlin answered, his hands resting comfortably on a full stomach. He would deeply appreciate another nap but, alas, they had much to do before ascending the mountain.

He walked downstream a short way, asking her to follow. When they came upon a small pool of still water, he kneeled beside it, motioning for her to do the same.

He pointed at the water's surface. "What do you see there?"

"My reflection," she replied matter-of-factly.

"Do you find anything odd in this reflection?"

Bending over the water for a closer look, she studiously observed the image rippling on the water's surface. "No, nothing at all."

"Look again, my dear, and think carefully about everything you should expect to see. In fact, we may expedite this cruel lesson if you list everything you see."

Turning sharply, she muttered, "Cruel?"

He laughed, "Oh, yes, quite cruel."

"You say the lesson is cruel and, yet, you laugh. Do you take a sordid pleasure in causing others pain?"

"I vow not to bruise anything but your pride," he said gently, pointing once again at the water. "Tell me everything you see."

"I see locks of red hair, blue eyes, a nose, two ears, a forehead and a chin, a dark cloak wrapped around my neck and the hilt of Excalibur jutting over my shoulder."

"Anything else?"

"Yes, shadows from the nearby rocks, faint hints of grass tufts and the colorful foliage from the trees behind us."

"Is that all?"

Her gaze scanned the waters' surface once again and with complete confidence, she replied, "That's all there is."

"Don't you find that odd?" He prodded.

"Not at all."

"Very good, then. Perhaps you can tell me what you don't see."

Merlin had taken great pleasure revealing this particular insight many times in the past and would often leave a student to ponder its perplexities for weeks on end. A man must take joy where he finds it. But, imminent matters pressed at hand and he was quickly becoming very fond of the young lady toiling at his side, searching the water for things unseen, he would not toy with her. Too much.

"But," she protested, "There is much I don't see. I don't see catapults, I don't see horses, I don't see an ostrich, I don't see cactus. There's a whole world of things I *don't* see, we could linger here forever listing them."

"Quite right," Merlin acquiesced, placing his arm around her shoulder, coercing her toward the water. His lips inches from her ear, he coaxed, "Tell me what you don't see."

A gasp revealed her sudden comprehension.

"I don't see *you*," she bellowed, "You're not there!"

He gave her a pat on the back and stood to his feet. "Well done, young lady, well done."

ξЖξ

A riddle presented itself to Morgana le Fay. How had a vicious time coil ensnared her? She and Friar John repeated the same conversation, sipped at bottomless tankards of mead, and when the Friar made a derogatory comment about her mental stability, Morgana laid a heel into his shin. No sooner did her boot bounce off his fleshy leg than the entire scene repeated from the beginning.

Although she could do nothing to break the spell, she recognized the handiwork—only a sorcerer of great mastery could accomplish such a magnificent feat. This was Merlin's doing and that could only mean he was nearby and aware of Morgana's proposed threat.

She would happily suffer the spell, Merlin would have to undo it before he approached the sacred acre. This constituted nothing more than a minor inconvenience while it also provided ample warning of the sorcerer's impending arrival. The old sock was losing his touch.

BK CRAWFORD

§℥§

Helga Dearbourne desperately tried to lean left, duck, swerve, or by any other manner, move out of the way so that the next time the malicious black bird relieved himself, the splatter would not land on her shoulder as it had fifty times already, but her efforts were in vain. With her movements abnormally restricted, the bird splatter hit its mark and spread over her shoulder. Myla released an incessant giggle.

"We keep rounding the same corner," Helga complained, her voice loud and harsh, "Passing by the same trees, catching the same breeze..."

"And receiving the same gifts from our winged friends," Myla chimed in, deriving far too much pleasure from Helga's misfortune.

"Mind your tongue," Helga chastised and turned to Viviane. "Your Ladyship," she said, "What's happening?"

"It's a time spell," the Lady replied, as if it were of little consequence and should have been quite obvious. Perhaps, but Helga had never experienced such a thing before and certainly never imagined it possible.

"And who," Helga griped, "would cast such a hellish enchantment?"

"Only I and one other have the knowledge to do so," the Lady replied curtly, as though concerned about saying too much, or simply uninterested in pursuing the subject. But, the implications of the Lady's answer did not elude Helga.

"If you can cast such a spell, you can also break it."

"Yes, but doing so would most certainly undermine the reasons for it being cast in the first place."

Not sure she really gave a damn for the reason the spell was cast, Helga grunted, "What might that be?"

The Lady spoke as if the conversation had worn out its welcome, "I'm sure I couldn't say."

Splat.

Fifty-two.

ξӜξ

"Seeing," Merlin explained, "is a light reflection process. Without light, there is nothing to reflect and, thus, nothing to see. Becoming invisible, then, is not a pleasant experience at first because it involves creating a cloak of darkness so dense no light can seep through. In order to achieve this, you must remove from your thoughts, from your being, all concept of light and willingly immerse yourself in complete darkness. If you accomplish the cloaking, you will experience an overwhelming nausea and a sense of complete disorientation. It will pass quickly if you avoid panic."

The girl listened intently, fixated on every word, which pleased Merlin so much he felt his pulse quicken. In the past, his students had come begging for instruction and he had chosen among them with great care (especially after making such a grave mistake with Morgana). This time, he offered his wisdom freely, hoping his instruction would benefit both student and master. He couldn't say with certainty if he truly feared Morgana. He would like to believe he had conquered his fears, but doubt is a nagging notion and he simply had no way of knowing what powers Morgana had obtained after leaving his instruction. When in doubt, it's best to devise a sufficient offense.

The future queen had processed Merlin's exposé on cloaking and a profound perplexity crossed over her face.

"If all concept of light is put aside," she bemused, "how is it possible for the invisible entity to see?"

Taking in the question with a jolt, Merlin studied the face of this truly gifted young woman. What a mind, such a rare find. Smiling, he offered his illumination.

"One must learn to separate comprehensive consciousness from the physical senses. There are many among us who see without the capacity to understand what it is they observe."

"You speak of the dim," she interjected.

"Yes. Even though a man may not comprehend what he sees, he sees nonetheless. From this, we can derive the conclusion that comprehensive consciousness is separate from the physical senses, as comprehension is not required for the seer to see, but only for the interpretation of what he sees. And so, even though we may remove all concept of light from our comprehensive consciousness, our senses retain the ability to see."

"But," she said, her expression contorting, "If I have removed all concept of light from my consciousness, then I am no longer aware of light. If I become aware and begin to see, do I not lose the cloak? Further, can I understand what I see?"

Merlin laughed. Sharp and so quick, he hadn't had a student this astute in many, many years.

"My dear," he replied, "You are cloaking your physical body, not your mind. By immersing yourself in darkness, you are willing to become a shadow. What you must understand is that light and dark depend upon one another for their very existence, each a willing canvas the other paints upon. Here, look beneath the water and see the darkest shadows clinging to the banks of the stream while light dances ever so brightly on the surface. Hand-in-hand they go, well aware of one another. Choose to become the darkest shadow and you will achieve the cloaking. As for understanding what you see while cloaked, can you think with your eyes closed and, when you do, can you comprehend those thoughts? Even the most impaired among us can see with his eyes closed. That which we call dreaming is a prime example."

Her face untwisted and softened as she offered a nod of agreement.

"Cloaking, then," she proposed, "is nothing more than a trick of the mind?"

"Yes, but also a trick of the senses. The practitioner has engaged in a trick of the mind in order to create a trick of the senses for all who cannot observe him."

"Does Morgana possess this cloaking skill?"

"Not to my knowledge, but she does use the same principals for shape-shifting which is nothing more than the ability to reflect an image inconsistent with her natural image. For example, if you are in the wood and a fawn approaches, the slightest movement or sound on your part will send the young deer skittering away. However, if you remain still and can thoroughly convince yourself that you, too, are a young deer—you look like a deer, you smell like a deer, and you sound like a deer, then the energy the fawn senses convinces him he is safe in the company of his own species. The ability to accomplish such a feat is truly rare."

"Also a trick of the mind and the senses," she noted.

He patted her softly on the knee, "Precisely."

"I presume you wish for me to learn this skill?"

"I do."

"Why?"

"My dear, the element of surprise is a mighty ally. What's more, because you are honest, you'll admit you want to learn nearly as much as I wish to teach you. So, come. Lean over the water and use your reflection as a measure. I will remain with you until after the scream and then take my leave for another nap while you perfect the technique."

Horrified, Farrin yelped, "What scream?"

Leaning nonchalant against his staff, Merlin spoke with a steady calm, "Don't be alarmed. Everyone screams at first, myself included. Watching your image disappear from existence is a startling thing, but you will survive it."

Emitting a short twitter of laughter, she leaned over the water and mumbled, "I won't scream."

"Yes, you will," Merlin countered.

"No, I won't."

"You will."

"I won't."

"Everyone does."

She turned back to face him directly, "Care to place a wager?"

Merlin chuckled. Not only was she quick in brilliance, but delightfully engaging, too.

"What would you like to wager?" He said with full confidence.

"When I win," she declared, "You will provide me with a month of instruction in your arts."

Merlin cocked his head to the side, grinning. "And when you lose?"

"I won't lose the wager, but for the sake of good sport, I'll wager a position on my court as advisor, for as long as you wish to attend the position."

"Two weeks of instruction in the arts," Merlin countered.

"Two months," Farrin bargained.

"Your negotiating skills leave much to be desired, M'lady."

"Three months." Her tone was firm.

Merlin peered into her eyes. Courage and conviction, an uncommon bravery, and moxie enough for an entire knight regimen. The terms of the wager didn't really matter, *everyone* screams. This was a bet the young lady could not win.

"It's settled then," Merlin countered, "One month of instruction in the arts."

Farrin laughed and turned back toward the water, ready to engage in the exercise.

"You need not stand by. I can handle this on my own. If I were to scream, which I won't, you would hear. Go take your rest while I work this out."

"As you wish, M'lady."

ξ⋇ξ

Farrin stood over Merlin's snoring form with a long blade of grass in hand, the tufts of its dried plume soft and fluffy. Moving slowly closer, careful to stifle any noise her approach might make, she lowered the plume until it touched, ever so slightly, the edge of Merlin's left nostril. Merlin crinkled his nose and snorted, swatting his hand at a pest no longer present. Farrin giggled and pulled back until the sorcerer resumed his dreaming and then lowered the plume again, toying with the right nostril this time.

Tucked in a tree-root embrace, Merlin looked rather ordinary—just an old man, weary with the world, his sharp features softened by slumber, his long white beard flowing over the right side of his chest and spilling onto the leaf-littered ground. Harmless he seemed, fragile even, proof that the sharpest comprehension and the keenest senses are prey to fantastic deception.

Meeting Merlin and attempting to absorb his lessons brought Francois De Beranac, whose gifted influence helped to save Farrin from the white dragon, back to the forefront of her thoughts. It had been a very long time since she stumbled across a man who had mastered his vocation and proved willing to share his gifts. Merlin had awakened Farrin's latent yearning to absorb the knowledge of the world until she burst with it. This training, these lessons, in all their perplexities, excited her to the very core. Imagine taking instruction from the great Merlin. Not merely learning how to turn a frog into a spoon, but to actually create reality and become invisible. What luck. One day, she might learn to pause time. The thought sent shivers rippling over her skin, as did the thought of Morgana le Fay hovering somewhere on the mountaintop, waiting for a showdown with Merlin. Morgana must possess tremendous power after spending years in Merlin's company.

Lowering the grass plume, Farrin tickled Merlin's face until he sat up with a start and emitted an irritated grunt. Looking about, he searched, but could not detect her. Scrambling to all fours, he peered around the tree trunk, his head snapping at various angles, searching in vain, until he caught sight of the grass plume dangling in midair, seemingly of its own accord.

"I heard no scream." Baffled, his words were ripe with disappointment.

"You have lost your wager," Farrin mocked, knowing she wasn't likely to feel squeamish about becoming invisible. She'd spent the better part of her childhood as the reigning champion of hide-and-seek and loved every moment of inconspicuousness afforded to her. "How do I look?"

Merlin stared intensely, studying the space where her image should be but was not, peering especially at the ground where he found no hint of shadow.

"You modified the illusion?" He blurted. "How?"

"I confess I did not completely comprehend the idea of separating comprehensive consciousness from the physical senses. But, when you spoke of light reflection as being the cause for sight, I wondered about light refraction and what might happen if I simply repelled the light I saw in the stream, or deflected the light around me. What you see, or rather, don't see, sir, is the ultimate result of that query."

Clapping his hands, Merlin laughed and began to dance a sprite's jig, his tittering laughter contagious in its heart-lifting mirth. The dance went on and on, his laughter lilting and bouncing off the trees, rising high over their canopies. When, at last, he settled down, he waved his arms aimlessly about, searching for something he could not see.

"Undo it, M'lady," he begged, and Farrin allowed her concentration to break until the hand she held before her eyes became detectable. Merlin rushed in to cup her face in his hands.

"So young," he marveled, "Not so long ago a child and yet you have already outdone your mentor! What made you think to use refraction?"

"Toads and gray owls," she answered, stepping back to take a seat on the fallen log.

Rubbing his chin, Merlin appeared contemplative. "Toads and gray owls," he softly repeated.

"Their appearances cause them to blend into their environment," she explained. "I've heard certain animals can change color at whim to fend off predators. When I stared into the water, I saw a tadpole so dark it was nearly impossible to see against the dreary waterbed and I began to wonder."

"Truly gifted," Merlin beamed. "That should make your next lesson much easier."

Farrin felt her face radiate with delight. Another lesson.

"Now that you can create your own reality and remove your image from it," Merlin bent to retrieve his staff and gave it a twirl, "let's see what we can do about ensuring a silent approach. Would you like to learn to fly?"

ξℵξ

Tales of witches flying about on broomsticks abound, yet, everyone knows these fables are naught but fancy, prescribed for entertainment. However, where you find myth, you will often find a morsel of truth buried deep within, a sliver of fact upon which the myth stands. Without these fragments of truth, we are less prone to suspend our disbelief long enough to allow our imaginations to wander into the frivolity the myths and fairytales provide. Thus, Merlin prepared to reveal a simple morsel of truth for the benefit of the future queen.

Standing before Farrin, a cold wind swaying through his beard, Merlin spoke with a soft persuasion.

"M'lady, when you dream, have you found your feet leaving the ground, fanciful and free, your form moving about unencumbered?"

"Of course," she replied, "everyone has those dreams."

"When you dream these dreams, are you at all afraid of your ability to achieve flight?"

"No, never."

"Very good. Have you ever wondered why?"

"Of course not." Standing, she gave her legs a stretch. "A dream is just a dream."

"I see." Merlin rubbed the short hairs at the corners of his mouth. "Why is it effortless to fly when we dream and yet a seemingly impossible task when we're awake? Can you explain the difference between the dream state and the waking state?"

She gave the path back to the mountain road a hard glare then quickly returned her gaze. "The dream state is an illusion. We dream but then awake and return to reality."

Planting his staff firmly, he gripped it with both hands and spoke over the tip of the brilliant white gemstone affixed to its top.

"The laws of nature, as we understand them, provide a compelling force to keep us grounded. When we drop something, it readily falls to the ground. Should we catapult an object high into the sky, it too will ultimately return to the ground. And yet, this grounding force cannot keep a dreamer from flying. Is it safe to say the subconscious mind has given permission to the dreamer to fly based upon the assumption that dreaming is an illusion?"

"I suppose it's very safe to say," she answered, her gaze probing for a deeper meaning.

"What if I propose the waking state is as much an illusion as the dreaming state and our ability to create reality is merely an ability to shift illusion?"

Her wince suggested a sudden headache. Merlin sympathized and emitted a soft chuckle. This wasn't the first time he'd seen a young mind entangled in the snares of perplexity.

"Consider," he continued, "Alexander the Great. A young man mentored by one of the greatest minds of his time. Aristotle. Fueled within Alexander's being was an intense desire to conquer the world. One young man, one vision, one dream. Through the power of that dream, he created one of the largest empires ever known. What's more, he shifted the illusion of reality for the vast number of people directly influenced by his dream. From this, we can surmise that although a dream may be an illusory subconscious entity, it certainly has the ability to move from the subconscious realm into the conscious realm and when this happens, we alter the illusion of reality as we perceive it. In fact, without the ability to germinate a grand thought, very little in our world would ever change. Do you agree?"

She spoke with a note of uncertainty, "Are you saying I can give myself permission to fly whilst awake because the waking state is as much an illusion as the dreaming state?"

Lowering his chin and lifting his eyebrows, Merlin answered with an impish grin.

"But," she protested, "Alexander the Great didn't conquer the compelling force that causes the weight of a human body to remain tethered to the ground."

"Quite true, M'lady. However, if Alexander had been mentored by a greater mind, he might have." Merlin cackled without restraint, sometimes a man simply amuses himself.

Having had his laugh, he left his staff leaning against the fallen log and took Farrin by the hands.

"Look into my eyes, watch the pupils grow large and small, count how many times they change shape. Count aloud so that I might know."

"One.

Two.

Three. Four.

Five..."

"Very good, very good. Now look down."

Farrin expelled a startled shriek. She was hovering twenty-five feet off the ground. Shocked, she released Merlin's hands and fell with a sharp thump. Scuttling to her feet, she swatted angrily at the leaves and twigs adhering to her cloak. She aimed a glowering stare at Merlin, "Don't *ever* do that again."

A shame, because that was exactly what he had intended to do. The next step, of course, was to guide the young lady up so high that letting go would mean a host of broken bones, or worse. Most students found the experience too frightening to let go and so Merlin did the letting go, leaving the student to realize he could manage quite sufficiently on his own. Much like dropping a swimming student into the middle of a lake where the task becomes a do-or-die situation and, thus, most opt for *do*.

Farrin's unwillingness to accept Merlin's help left him no choice but to leave her to practice on her own. Unfortunately, although she did manage to lift quite easily, she could not maintain her buoyancy. Each time she realized how far up she had gone, she lost focus and fell. To her advantage, she hadn't gone so high yet that a fall would cause any serious damage, but she was beginning to look haggard and probably had a host of bruises to show for all her failed effort.

Face burgeoning with frustration and anger, she railed at Merlin, attempting to pierce his propositions with words that seeped with venom, "What's the point if it's all illusion? If nothing is real, why would anyone continue to fight for justice in the world?"

"Because, M'lady," he answered gently, "this illusion is the only reality we have."

ξӜξ

Until now, the lessons Merlin offered were harmless and posed no real physical threat—not so for attempting to fly.

While Farrin understood the basic concepts of illusion as Merlin had explained them, she could not seem to rid herself of her fear of falling. Hovering a few feet off the ground didn't shake her nerves because tumbling from such a miniscule height hadn't caused any serious physical harm, even if she did sting and ache from falling. All repeated attempts to ascend any higher, though, resulted in an immediate tumble and Farrin had grown frustrated with the effort.

"Tell me," Merlin stepped in, acknowledging her abandon, "what are you thinking when you lift off the ground? And, if you please, what ideas are playing in your mind before you fall?"

"When I lift, I see you, suspended in mid-air as demonstrated. Just before I fall, I recall the vision of a reckless boy tumbling from the castle turret long ago, arms and legs flailing for purchase and the cracking sound his body made when it landed in a splatter."

Merlin gasped. "Is it any wonder?"

Taking her by the shoulders, he spoke as if to mesmerize, "Close your eyes for a moment and imagine the great silver-back goose who leads the flock on its annual migration. Despite a long neck and heavy bottom, she spreads her wings and flaps until she lifts from the ground, rising ever so slowly, over the treetops where her journey begins. She uses the air currents to her advantage and listens to the flutter of wings and the excited honking that follows behind as she bravely leads the way. Her instincts guide her, an innate knowing that flight is not only possible, but necessary."

A pause in Merlin's oration stretched lengthy and Farrin could no longer feel the ground beneath her feet. He had led her, once again, and despite her objections, high over the treetops.

Her eyes squeezed shut. Reflex. She didn't want to see, didn't want to know, but curiosity always gets the last word. Confirming her suspicion, she promptly fell. This time, her head slapped the ground with a sickening thud, her lungs lost their air, and she felt disoriented and dizzy, not to mention completely infuriated. Adding insult to injury, Excalibur had ripped from her shoulder strap upon impact.

"Perhaps we are going about this in the wrong way," she heard Merlin say, his voice fuzzy.

Patting her arms and legs, Farrin searched for broken bones but found them surprisingly intact.

"Indeed," Merlin mumbled, "it may serve a better purpose to teach you how to land before asking you to fly."

Trembling, Farrin pointed angrily. "I told you not to do that again."

His face flushed crimson and he didn't argue, but extended a hand to help her to her feet. Still dizzy, she stumbled to the fallen log.

Merlin reached for Excalibur, suggesting it best to leave the sword off during the commencement of instruction.

That was what this was about? Had Merlin actually gone to outlandish lengths just to get his hands on Excalibur? Perhaps he considered the sword a greater ally than the bumbling talents of a young woman whom, it seemed, would never grasp the entirety of his instruction.

"So, it's the sword you're after," she accused.

Startled, he gaped. It took very little effort to decipher the extreme displeasure bleeding into his tone, "With such a dastardly motive, I would no longer be worthy to wield the sword. No one can gain Excalibur by way of trickery for that very reason."

A queasy regret flushed through Farrin. She had insulted him, made him angry. Who could blame him for being annoyed? She would have taken great offense had she been on the other side of the allegation. She didn't mean to slight him. Her willingness to imagine treachery had less to do with the sword and more with her inability to absorb Merlin's instruction. She had allowed aggravation to slip off her tongue without considering consequence.

"I'm sorry," she said, resolute, "I spoke too quickly and, of course, you're right."

Merlin turned to her, cheeks still broiling, eyes beginning to soften.

"Please," she said, extending the sword, "take it. No doubt you will wield it much more successfully than I."

His cheeks regained an even hue, a gleam returning to his eyes. Raising two fingers, he waved them side-to-side, declining her proposal.

"Thank you for the gracious gesture, M'lady, but that will not be necessary. See here." Reaching over his shoulder, he withdrew a sword of his own—a sword marked with intricate and writhing etchings identical to Excalibur's, its blade nearly transparent.

"Clarent," he explained, "Excalibur's twin." Holding the hilt in one palm and the tip in the other, he brought the sword close enough for Farrin's inspection. When she'd taken it all in, he stepped back and sheathed the sword.

"If powerful weaponry could win the day against Morgana," he remarked, "you and I would already have the battle in hand. Alas, swords, no matter how powerful, will not suffice."

No sooner had he breathed the last of his words than he vanished from Farrin's sight. She sought for him but to no avail.

"Up here!" He was perched on the tree branch he had visited previously. In his hand, he held a large white feather.

"Watch closely, my dear." Leaning forward, he released the feather, which floated weightlessly, turning on the wind like a graceful dancer, slow in its descent. If time were a factor, it would've taken nearly three minutes for the feather to reach the ground.

Farrin picked up the feather and, beaming, projected a knowing smile at Merlin.

"Shall I drop another?"

"Yes. One more," she answered, dutifully studying the flight of the second feather as it meandered in a weightless waltz.

"Another?" Merlin suggested.

"No, I think I understand."

Learning how to fall, with grace and dignity, truly was the key to learning how to fly. Once Farrin had mastered the art of falling, flying was easy. Lift up, twitter about, and descend, nothing to it. Merlin was pleased beyond measure with Farrin's success. "Now," he had said with brightness in his eyes, "we stand a fighting chance." From which Farrin correctly assumed they had concluded their lessons for the time being.

Leaning over the stream, Merlin stretched his hands over the water and snatched up the rust-colored twig, breaking his time suspension spell.

They took leave of the streamside paradise and rejoined the scant road that wound its way up the mountain. To Farrin's shock and surprise, the trees here were bare and a light snow fell, dusting the footpath.

"How long did those lessons take, Merlin? How much time has passed for those unaffected by the spell?"

"Not long at all, ten days, perhaps two weeks."

Farrin gasped. It couldn't be. A few hours perhaps, maybe a day, but not *two weeks*.

Grasping Merlin's sleeve, she forced him to face her.

"Two weeks?" She uttered, incredulous.

"M'lady, you must understand...my best student took five years to accomplish the tasks you've mastered in mere days. Two weeks is refreshing. Besides, who would waste a perfectly good time spell on tasks requiring only a few hours?" Once again, Merlin twittered with amusement, caught in the throngs of a rip-snorting chuckle, his shoulders quaking as he resumed his stride.

ξℵξ

Frigid drafts blustered inside the Rivensdale castle as fall took a bow and departed. Flames dancing on short wicks began their winter sway and antiseptic aromas hung paralyzed in midair as servants scurried about slamming shutters, shielding against the grip of winter whilst pageboys delivered stacks of wood to feed the hearths.

Despite the stinging cold, Sarina felt her face flush with an effulgent heat as she huffed out of the infirmary and ran through the corridors, stopping anyone unfortunate enough to cross her path, assailing them all with the same exasperated question, "Have you seen anyone in this hall?"

Her abrupt interrogations produced nothing but blank stares and wide-eyed bewilderment—no one had seen anything out of the ordinary, which simply was not possible. Or was it? Berating herself for not getting it right the first time, she modified her inquiry, "A cat? Have you seen a cat?"

Harlem Winthrop, a man who has quite possibly frequented these halls since the day the mortar dried and the person to call when fresh linens are required, answered affirmatively. Yes, he had seen a cat scurry though the corridor a few moments ago but had thought nothing of it. Cats roam the halls frequently and are encouraged to do so as they alone control the rodent population, as everyone knows.

Clearly, Mr. Winthrop could see no reason for Sarina's distress and left her standing in the corridor as he went about his business, twirling his finger over his ear when he thought she wasn't watching.

Sarina had no chance of outrunning the wily escapee. It would do her no good to bumble though crowded passageways trying to get to the gate in time to head him off. Instead, she made her way for the turret wall. There, she shouted at the gatekeepers, "Close the gates! Don't allow any cats through!"

The guards lifted their heads in her direction, but cocked them to the side as if they hadn't heard, or didn't understand.

"Do not allow cats to exit the gate!" She repeated, louder this time.

Their jaws went slack. Then, turning toward one another, they laughed boisterously, resuming their duties as if she had issued no command at all.

Men.

Defeated, Sarina headed back toward the infirmary. Hadn't she told Flea he wasn't ready to get out of bed? Hadn't she warned him about the possibility of reopening his wound, about the possibility of infection? Yes, she most certainly had and yet he snuck out the instant she turned her back. What good are the healing arts if the injured ignore honest counsel?

At least Sir Oswald had abided by her warnings and continued to rest comfortably in the care of three handmaidens, one of which, Sarina suspected, fancied him.

When she turned the corner leading back to the infirmary, her stomach twisted at the sight set before her. The three handmaidens she had left to Sir Oswald's care stood outside the door, two with chins tucked low, the third in tears.

Sarina had completely lost her patients.

ξЖξ

"We have company," Merlin whispered. Halting his gait, he scanned the immediate area, inspecting trees, brush, and the white downy sky. Finding nothing out of the ordinary, he stopped walking and closed his eyes, the pupils beneath his eyelids moving rapidly.

"I see a cloaked wizard," he said, opening his eyes, "lying in ambush."

"Mithragog," Farrin assumed. "How do you know this?" She asked, careful to keep her tone low.

"Remote seeing," Merlin answered, "I keep a hawk." Lifting his right arm, he hooked his elbow and waited for the bird to descend and perch, a regal looking brown-speckled specimen with lofty eyes.

"Very loyal creatures," Merlin commented, scratching the bird on the back of the neck. The hawk lowered its head and closed its eyes, immersed in pleasure. Producing a limp rodent from his pocket, Merlin offered it to the speckled fowl and the bird gulped it down. Gently lifting his arm, Merlin coaxed the enchanted raptor to resume flight.

"This Mithragog fellow, any idea why he's stalking us?" Merlin inquired.

Farrin watched the hawk cross the sky until it disappeared behind a series of snow clouds.

"You don't know him?" It was hard to believe Merlin wasn't intricately familiar with all the snakes crawling in the grass.

Merlin shook his head, claiming ignorance. "Has he been in the area long?"

"He was considered harmless until a few months ago. He failed an apprenticeship with a sorcerer in the highlands. Spinel, I believe his name was. Whatever the case, Mithragog recently determined the need to have my heart and has been pursuing it with a vengeance."

"A lover's entanglement?"

Farrin's stomach lurched at the presumption, but she understood the confusion.

"No, he seeks the heart of the heir for its promised power."

"And, he believes you possess it?"

She nodded.

"Is he a gifted wizard?"

"Not entirely," She remarked, amused.

Taking her by the arm, Merlin prodded her to resume their walk. "Well then," he said, "perhaps this wizard will supply us with an opportunity to test your newfound skills."

ξжξ

Wedging himself behind the wide girth of a knotty oak, Mithragog attempted to blend in with the scenery—not an easy task considering the falling snow, he should have thought to wear a white cloak instead of black, and footprints are the most annoying things.

He had her now, discovered her ambling up the mountain all alone but for the company of an old man—it wouldn't take more than a hearty sneeze to dispense with him if he insisted on becoming a problem.

Moments...just moments away from taking the heart of the heir and becoming the greatest wizard of all time. Mithragog's pulse quickened with anticipation as he peered around the tree, waiting breathlessly for shadows to appear, listening for her approach.

A wild hare darted from the brush, startling him and, although tempted, he refrained from casting an explosion spell. He wouldn't want to alert the girl to his presence, now would he?

A flock of robins chattered overhead, another spine-crawling annoyance, as birds seem cheery even when nature pelts them with snow and ice, the best of them devoid of the sense required to be miserable at least some of the time.

When the future queen's shadow finally cast around the bend, it arrived alone. The old man had left her, an act Mithragog supposed had probably saved his life.

Rendering the girl immobile using her own petrifying spell seemed easy, perhaps a little *too* easy, but Mithragog wasn't one to moan at good fortune. He whisked her back to his castle and took care of the first order of business, confiscating her powder.

The girl remained quiet, bound to a stone slab once used by royal bloodlines for human sacrifice, re-initiated for the same purpose today.

The little witch had gotten the better of him last time they met, using his lust for power to her advantage. He would not repeat the error. The heart of the heir was his now. As for the procurement of spells, he would fend for himself once the heart infused him with its power.

Jewel-encrusted dagger in hand, he hovered, leaning close so that she could peer into the last pair of eyes she would ever see. To his great surprise, she smiled—not a cocky grin sometimes produced in an attempt to beguile, but a warm, genuine smile. Surely, she meant to disarm him, or perhaps cause him to second-guess himself. No matter, he did not intend to release her.

Not completely heartless, he recognized the shame in cutting short the life's journey of a girl so young, talented, and beautiful. However, it remained a simple matter of fact: he hadn't cursed the girl in the first place. Therefore, he was not responsible for her fate, even if he was willing to deliver it.

In order to maintain the pristine structure of the heart itself, Mithragog considered it wise to avoid puncturing the chest, thus he placed the dagger in position to slice the girl's throat, its tip poised below her left earlobe. He watched the expression in her eyes grow softer, her smile widening, her face the very picture of contentment. Drawing the dagger away, he spoke incredulously, "Excuse me," he said, allowing sarcasm to dominate his tone, "You are aware you're about to die?"

"I am," she answered, her smile reassuring.

"I assume you're content with the idea?"

"Oh, yes," she breathed, sincere.

Was there no end to her gumption? Despite the admirable theatrics, she was trying to sell an act Mithragog would never purchase.

"I've taken your powder. The straps affixing you to this slab cannot be broken."

"It's just as well," she replied, seemingly unconcerned.

Losing patience with the game, Mithragog steadied the dagger and placed it in position. The girl's smile grew brighter, her eyes fixed on his face as if he was the most adorable creature she had ever seen.

He used the moment to marvel over the fragility of life. Here was a vibrant girl, breathing, blinking, *smiling*. If he released her, she would go on to live a long life, perhaps not always so exuberant, but still vital. And yet, in the moment it would take to rip her throat open, her abundant life would begin to dwindle away, her spirited character reduced to a lifeless lump of leaking flesh. How deliciously delightful.

"I presume you wish me well in my endeavor to become ruler of the world," he sneered.

"Of course," she answered sweetly.

Time's up, wench, he thought, and dragged the dagger across her throat with swiftness of hand and exact force. Only—*what is this!* In his hand, he clutched a long, white goose feather, a harmless object that was, only a moment ago, a lethal dagger. And, where is the girl? *Vanished!* Leaving nothing behind but the sound of a faint giggle.

Mithragog stood transfixed, staring at the empty space where the girl had been, studying the delicate plume he held, dumbfounded. Disappointment, anger and frustration churned through his veins.

Stumbling through corridors, he searched for the girl, his frenzy deepening each time he rounded a corner to find no one there. Still, he left no corner unturned.

When he finally gave up the chase and returned to the throne room, he paced, absorbed in pure awe.

Had he not witnessed this feat of stupendous magic firsthand, he would never have believed it possible. If he could expect this magnitude of power with the heart in his possession, his resolve to procure it only deepened.

BK CRAWFORD

Perhaps, he reluctantly admitted, the time had come to join ranks with his mother, the beldame, who, no doubt, wanted the heart of the heir as badly as he did. Surely, Helga would entertain the idea of sharing, if only as a pretense. The main objective, they would agree, is to secure the prize. They could quarrel over it later.

ξӜξ

Realizing it a vast insufficiency for expressing the enormity of what had just happened, Farrin muttered, "Wow," and repeated it several times.

Ecstatic, Merlin enjoyed another fit of amusement, laughing and dancing so boisterously, Farrin would consider it a miracle if he didn't cough up an organ, or fracture a wildly gyrating hip. Each time it seemed as though he might calm down, his face lit up again and, "Ho!" he would yell, slap his knee, and resume his hilarity.

Farrin's hands trembled.

"He never suspected you were there," she blurted, not caring if Merlin could hear over his jolly antics. "I heard you breathing...I was sure Mithragog could, too. When you sniffled, I thought I would die of fear, but he didn't even notice. He took my invisibility for granted, not thinking for one moment I might still be strapped to his table."

The snow stopped falling, leaving no more than half an inch on the ground, the air considerably colder. Now and then the sun peeked through a crack in the clouds, its bright rays glistening off the edges of the fractured rocks that lined the winding road.

Farrin glanced toward the crest of the mountain.

Pulling the wool over the eyes of an untrained wizard was one thing, hoping for the same result against a seasoned sorceress was another.

"Oh, my dear, what fun, what *fun!*" Merlin wailed, throwing an arm around Farrin's shoulder and giving it a squeeze. "What a gallant performance," he declared. "You will fare well against Morgana."

"Merlin," she quickly interjected, "is it possible to use a time spell during battle?"

Sobered, he turned to her.

"Yes, but it takes time to regenerate the energy required to cast the spell. Time spells burn a great deal of passion. Remember, passion is energy. Just as the body requires food for fuel, the heart and mind need passion and ingenuity to fuel creation. Show me a man without the will to live and I will show you a man who has lost his passion. But, because it's such an enormous endeavor, stopping time consumes nearly all the life energy of the practitioner. As you may recall, I required several naps after casting the spell and not without good reason."

"How long does it take to recover the energy?"

"A year, perhaps two, depending. That's why a wise wizard never wastes a time spell on matters requiring only a few hours effort. What's more, casting the spell during battle can be a tricky matter. If your opponent gains the upper hand during a time loop, you could die a thousand times before the spell is broken."

How awful, Farrin thought. A sense of dread sent a shiver running over her skin. Merlin had used enormous amounts of energy to cast the time spell and had depleted his power. Was it her fate to face Morgana le Fay alone? If so, she would give it her all, but surely there were other options available.

"A great sorcerer must have an army of wizards at his disposal, are there none to aide us?"

Merlin chuckled. "When a master withholds knowledge, even if he does so to safeguard all humanity, he makes more enemies than friends. However, now that I consider it, there are some to rely upon. We could use scouts to report events ahead. A hawk cannot see through walls."

Pursing his lips, Merlin cupped his hands around his mouth and produced a strange sound that was half whistle, half buzz—this he did facing north, then south, east, then west. Finished, he smiled at Farrin, tapping his fingers on the tip of his staff, waiting impatiently. When nothing happened, he smiled again, cheeks flushed with embarrassment and he shrugged his shoulders, resigned to wait.

After several minutes, two male creatures the size of hummingbirds—and with wings fluttering just as fast—appeared and reverently bowed before Merlin. Seeing Farrin, they promptly turned their backs and bent forward.

Flustered, Farrin whispered, "Did they just drop their pants?"

"Don't take offense," Merlin answered, "it is customary among their species."

"I hope they don't expect me to return the courtesy," she exclaimed.

Giggling, Merlin explained, "This is how they greet a female. Dogs sniff one another's behinds...sprites drop their pants."

The sprites resumed a proper posture, smiles wide, eyes sparkling with mischief. The fellow on the right appeared older than his counterpart, sporting a dark beard and a seasoned face. The younger of the two had a fairer complexion with blonde hair spiked on the crown of his head, his gaze more intent.

"M'lady," Merlin beamed, "I am pleased to introduce you to Nyx and Fig Knockbottom of the Knotweed tribe, two of my most prized friends."

"Pleased, I'm sure." Farrin performed a curtsy in an attempt to add a hint of etiquette to the awkward encounter. Her gesture, however, only caused the sprites to repeat their previous offense. Nyx was first to recover a decent posture.

Farrin blushed. When Merlin explained the ritual would occur each time she addressed the sprites, she remained tight-lipped.

Informing the sprites of the situation at hand, Merlin instructed them to scout the area where Morgana lay in wait. With a nod, a wink, and a bow, the unabashed exhibitionists took flight.

Moments after the sprites departed, a squat creature, ugly by every definition and with a tail parked on the back of its head, surged from a dense row of trees and stood, glaring, in the middle of the road. Farrin reached for Excalibur's hilt, but the creature bolted off into the brush.

"What was that?" She screeched.

"Morgana's demon servant, Dezva."

"We're getting close?"

"So it seems." Merlin employed his staff as a walking stick, prodding the ground with its dull tip. "While we finish the last of our journey, allow me to tell you about Bodach Cairn and all its secrets."

ξℵξ

"What is that infernal buzzing?" Morgana wailed, searching frantically for the source of the sound, eyes wild with suspicion.

She had been on edge since the looping stopped and had used the time since to abuse Friar John using words no woman should know, much less utter. He weathered her onslaughts—words are just words, after all, but the tension she created loomed thick as drying mortar and, considering what he had just seen, the situation could become explosive.

Two dear friends Barnabus had introduced to Friar John long ago, Nyx and Fig Knockbottom, had entered the house through the hearth, their wings subsequently blackened with soot and pitch, a substance notoriously difficult to shed. The buzzing that sent Morgana reeling in a tizzy came about when the sprites periodically fluttered their wings in an attempt to rid themselves of the soot.

Most bothersome was Friar John's inclination to stare. It was imperative for their safety that he act as though they weren't there.

The Knockbottom men are efficient and dependable messengers who had twice saved Friar John's life (once from a prowling pack of rabid wolves forced to settle for three hens and a piglet and, again, from a band of murdering thieves who made off with everything they could carry). On both occasions, the sprites had warned Friar John to remove himself from harm's way, he would not betray them by alerting Morgana to their presence.

"I hear no such noise," he protested, reaching for his tankard, finding it woefully empty.

"You deaf old drunkard," she snarled, "I should send you straight to hell." Looking in entirely the wrong direction, she continued to search. "I should," she mumbled, overturning crates and scattering his belongings as she sought the source of her annoyance.

Why she hadn't already done away with him was beyond Friar John's imagination.

The buzzing ceased and a lull of silence drove Morgana back to her chair where she ran her fingertips over the crystal globe. Donning a sly grin, she cackled, "She thinks Merlin is trapped inside!" Morgana's subsequent snorting grated against Friar John's nerves, setting him on edge.

ξϟκϟ

Ozzie normally saddled his own horse, but today he would humbly allow the livery boy to do the job.

Two weeks is not nearly long enough to heal a puncture wound, the searing pain in his side would provide a constant reminder of that, but he had been the benefactor of a truly gifted physician. If not for Sarina, he would lack the capacity to stand, much less ride.

Uncle Bartholomew—correction, McFleegle— correction, Flea—had come even closer to the reaper's sweeping scythe, also owing his miraculous recovery to Sarina's talent. Every man will say the same...it is torturous to lie helpless in the hands of a doting woman, no matter how gifted she may be. And so, Ozzie and Flea had devised a plan of escape. Flea would provide a diversion by drawing Sarina away so that Ozzie could walk out of the castle unencumbered.

For having successfully eluded her, they would render their heartfelt apologies to Sarina when they returned, but for now, the future queen was missing and for far too long without a word to anyone. Search parties sent out on a daily basis ultimately returned shaking their heads. Farrin hadn't left so much as a footprint behind. The rumors making the rounds were dreadful at best—the future queen had run off with a handsome beau, joined the circus, escaped to a faraway land, or lay dead in a ditch somewhere.

Wherever Farrin was, she was alive. Ozzie knew this, because his heart simply said so. It was, however, entirely possible she had met with foul play. She would not go without sending word if it were in her power to do so, a fact that haunted Ozzie with shivers of prickling dread.

Where is she?

Ozzie barked at the livery boy who tended to the horses as if a year to December would do, "Make haste!"

Whatever Farrin's situation, it could only improve if Ozzie and Flea quickly joined her. She had mentioned traveling to Bodach Cairn, but the mountain range was twenty miles long, far too much territory to search inch-by-inch. Who could pinpoint where Farrin was and of whom might they inquire?

Flea leaned a heavy shoulder into the lazy livery boy, knocking him out of the way, and began to tend the saddle straps on his own. "Perhaps, Nephew," he suggested, "it is time to use all of your gifts to our advantage. A little sorcery can go a long way. Our ancestors were high-ranking men in the order of Merlin. You obviously have latent talent. If such gifts had fallen to me, I would not hesitate to use them."

Ozzie felt his face flush, indignant. He had made a pact long ago not to use magic as a way to circumvent the natural order. A man, a real man, can stand on his own merit without using trickery. Believing this, he shunned the order of Merlin and refused to partake in any of its instruction. "I know nothing of magic," he mumbled, wishing for the first time in his life that he had some knowledge he could use to locate Farrin.

"She is the future queen," Flea asserted, "and you are sworn to protect her."

Ozzie's muscles tensed. If any other man had voiced these words, he would have dispatched him to St. Peter with swift regard. Ozzie had no need for Flea, or anyone else, to remind him of his duty. Safeguarding Farrin—oath or no oath—was in his nature, it was his basic instinct to protect her; she was the world and everything in it. He held his tongue, but only because he knew Flea would do anything in his power to ensure Farrin's safety and had spoken without sufficient thought. Taking hold of the saddle horn, he hoisted himself into the saddle, quickly checked his gear, and watched as Flea did the same.

They were seconds from departure when Sarina rushed into the stable, riding gear in hand.

"Well," she huffed, "aren't you two a fresh breath of horse's ass."

Slapping her saddle onto a robust black mare, she spoke firmly, "I suggest we hurry, there's a battle brewing on the sacred acre."

ξЖξ

With the winding mountain road finally behind her, Helga Dearbourne thought only of relieving the numbness that had tormented her hindquarters the entire way. Blast it all to damnation, though, dismounting an infernal donkey is not nearly as easy as one might think, especially if its hide is wet with snow. And so, with nothing else to steady her decline, Helga took a stranglehold on the short hairs of the creature's mane, hoping it would suffice. She managed to throw a leg over, nothing left but a short hop to the ground...shouldn't be too difficult, unless your backside is numb and your bones are older than the wind's first breath.

As she feared she might, Helga fell off her ass.

Myla rushed to her side, slipped her arms under Helga's armpits, and lifted her to her feet.

Sure of her footing, Helga slapped at Myla, insisting she could handle herself.

"You are no more immortal than I am," Helga spewed, her sudden annoyance turbulent, "the same rules must apply to everyone, so how do you, will someone at last explain, manage to retain your youth while I rot like a fermented prune?"

Startled, Myla cupped her hands over her mouth, no doubt thwarting a bout of rude laughter. Pulling her cloak tight around a nauseatingly thin waist, she shrugged, unable, or unwilling to provide an answer.

Perhaps, in Myla's case, Queen Gwenevere had something to do with a special enchantment. Gwenevere was no witch, but she certainly had her resources. How unfortunate an occurrence it had been when she chose Myla for handmaiden, leaving Helga to apprentice with the Witch of Kent who spent most of her time attempting (unsuccessfully) to raise the dead.

Staring intently, Helga deepened her gaze, scowling until Myla realized a response was expected.

"Perhaps," Myla stammered, "an immortal ages due to a condition of the heart and soul, rather than physical malady. Might I suggest you add more joy to your life, more love?"

Helga snorted, "Well then, it looks as though you'll be very busy today indeed."

Confused, Myla retorted, "Excuse me?"

Waving her arms in every direction, Helga blasted, "Look at them all! At least five hundred trees yet to receive a hug."

ξЖξ

When a man lives as long as Merlin, regret looms larger than pride. Many were the events of the past Merlin yearned to change, but he had come to believe that a man is not only the sum of his victories, but of his defeats as well. Failure must always remain a necessary burden, for it is through his shortcomings that a man learns the most important lessons in life. Those things we consider failures are blessings in disguise, as these instances mold and shape us, providing us with character, strength, and wisdom. The soul unwilling to err perishes in a quagmire of stagnation.

The one thing Merlin would never regret, would never change, was fathering a son and forging the subsequent life they had lived together, albeit incognito. Friar John might not have ever realized his love for Barnabus Nothinghem constituted more than just a coincidental bonding. He might not have realized that Barnabus was in fact Merlin, or that a blood kinship ran swift between them, but Friar John had always stood by Barnabus as well as any father could hope from his son and Merlin could not be prouder to know such a fine man.

Merlin's deceit toward the Lady Viviane seemed another matter altogether. As many years after the fact, he had certainly come to realize that hiding a woman's son from her bosom is a dastardly crime that has no redeeming penance, and to do so simply for the sake of maintaining a ruse is only that much worse. But Viviane needed control, needed to believe she had safely tucked Merlin under her wing—he had provided that for her, even if it was a bit of a lie. Could she hope to qualify for sainthood after attempting to ensnare her generous mentor inside a suffocating crystal globe in order to exert power and control over his mischievous spirit, for whatever reasons she may proclaim? And yet—isn't it strange?—it was the cunning and devious side of Viviane that seemed to generate the overwhelming attraction Merlin felt toward her. No other woman would ever compare. On some level, she instinctively knew a curious heart rarely leads a man to laze in the lily fields, but that he yearns for those most keenly when he finds himself immersed in briar. But, she had always underestimated Merlin's devotion.

At any rate, he had some explaining to do and this prospect did not sit lightly. Each step he took toward the mountain summit increased his foreboding. Admitting to his dastardly deceit and trickery might very well cost him the affections of his son and the only woman he would ever love. Yet, Morgana le Fay, heart blackened by her lust for power, would leave him no choice but to confess.

ξϾκϞ

Disappointed beyond measure, Nyx and Fig Knockbottom returned to Merlin with their report. There had been no bloodshed, no gory battle to behold, just a nagging woman testing Friar John's patience.

"She is crazed," Fig declared, "frenzied and short tempered."

"Will she harm him?" Merlin probed.

Nyx shook his head. "If Morgana meant him harm, he would already have his fill of worm cake. As for what is to come, we should hope you think more of our gifts and talents than to consider us mere messengers."

"While I deeply honor your battle skills," Merlin replied, "I cannot ask you to join the fray. It's far too dangerous."

Nyx looked to Fig who bobbed a determined nod. "But," Nyx countered, "I suspect you would not turn your back on two well-qualified archers?"

ξЖξ

Standing in view of a small cottage perched across the fields, the Lady Viviane sensed Merlin's approach and ordered her party to wait on the edge of the wood.

How could Merlin possibly have escaped the enchantment she had placed on the globe? Only he could have cast that time spell, and yet, he could not have done so from the confines of the globe. He was free, ambling his way up the mountain. Had Morgana inadvertently, or purposefully, released the enchantment? It was certainly a possibility.

As to the situation at hand, Morgana's treachery was easily deciphered. She had left a blatant trail for Viviane to follow and planned, as Myla had warned, to draw them into an ambush. She would dangle Viviane as bait to lure Merlin and would manipulate her in an attempt to weaken him. *Let her try*, Viviane thought, the rims of her ears burning hot.

Viviane had no proof, just an instinct, a nagging, but she suspected Morgana had once had more feeling for Merlin than a simple student to mentor kinship. When Merlin shunned her, he may have broken her heart as well. If so, a woman scorned will go to great lengths to exact revenge. At the very least, Morgana coveted Merlin's knowledge and power, which he would never willingly submit. Given the magnitude of the stakes, it was not likely anyone would walk away from this altercation unscathed. If the sorceress so much as harmed one hair on Merlin's head, Viviane would see to it that she spent eternity sucking the pus out of every blister present in hell.

Knowing Merlin was not already in Morgana's grasp was a great relief. And, ironically, there was no better place on earth to commence battle than here on the sacred acre.

ξЖξ

"Mind if I join you," Mithragog pressed, presenting his inquiry as more of a demand than a request. Viviane gave him the once over—a lanky prig in a dark cloak, out playing wizard, come to suckle mommy. There were more pressing issues to consider, so she turned away without replying, but Myla, trained to remain silent at the Queen's side and reluctant to break away from that conditioning, seemed stung by his presence.

"I would thank you to leave," she snarled, her tone oozing with contempt.

Oh, what a development. Viviane had never known Myla to speak unkindly to anyone—this was quite an attitude coming from someone so ordinarily meek. Rather than take leave, Viviane remained to observe the curious altercation.

"Have I transgressed against you in some way, M'lady?" Mithragog scoffed, his expression and the inflection in his voice insinuating he hoped he had.

Eyes squinting, and the color deepening on her cheeks, Myla barked, "If not for your wickedness, I would dwell in peace at home."

A slight grin played at the corner of Mithragog's mouth. "Pray thee, don't let me keep you from your knitting. But, out of curiosity, how is it my fault we find you here?"

Myla stepped forward until she stood nose-to-nose with him, spittle leaping off her lips as she hissed, "Your incessant quest for the heart of the heir. And in your extreme ignorance, you aren't even pursuing the right woman."

"Your tongue!" Viviane wailed, but it was too late, the words had already left Myla's lips.

Red-faced, Myla pronounced, "I will not allow peril to come to the future queen on my behalf!"

What was this?

"On *your* behalf?"

The assumption startled Viviane at first, but she suddenly understood. All those questions earlier about the true heir...Myla had mistakenly assumed she was the heir. This was Viviane's fault, she should have known Myla would leap to this conclusion and should have been more forthcoming with the facts when Myla made the inquiry—

she had been inseparably close to Gwenevere and seeing herself as Gwenevere's daughter rather than an unwanted, orphaned child had probably soothed her.

"You are not the true heir," Viviane said, hoping her gentle tone might ease the blow.

The expression on Myla's face was the look of a soul shattered.

Viviane grabbed Myla's hand and squeezed.

"But," Myla disputed, "there was only one other child delivered to the orphanage on the day of my arrival...you said there were only two..." Allowing her thoughts to trail off, she struggled to make the connection. At last, her gaze raced toward the bush-infested area where Helga had gone to tend to toiletries. Myla slowly turned back for confirmation. Viviane nodded.

"Helga Dearbourne is Gwenevere's daughter? No!"

"Yes," Viviane sharply affirmed, well aware that Mithragog had suddenly rushed off.

Myla pranced like a caged panther, fists curled to white knuckles. Anger of this magnitude, Viviane supposed, was a rare experience for Myla and it seemed as though she wasn't familiar with the usual methods for expressing a conniption. Breathing short intense breaths, her color bloomed the mortal rose.

Whenever Viviane experienced a similar rage, she would conjure up an earthquake, or produce a violent storm—these events had a way of expressing inner turmoil like nothing else could, but Myla would never imagine doing such a thing. A general introvert, she would take it all in and keep it there, where it might fester for a hundred years, until it caused physical pain. But, to Viviane's surprise, Myla did not intend to suffocate the issue.

"I was bait," she blasted. "Gwenevere treated me like a daughter because she needed those who coveted the heart of the heir to believe I had it. I was meant to *die* for Helga Dearbourne." Ears raised, jaw locked, she glared, her eyes accusing.

"It's true," Viviane calmly replied. "You were brought to Gwenevere for that very reason...to protect Helga Dearbourne should anyone come seeking the heir."

Myla's jaw slackened and her eyes opened wide with the shock of a confession she didn't expect to hear.

Allowing her no time to respond, Viviane took her by the shoulders, demanding her full attention, "I ask you to remember the bond you formed with Gwenevere. Things change over time, unexpected things happen. Love is born, it flourishes, and never dies. To judge Gwenevere based on one instance created out of sheer necessity is to abolish the years of love and devotion she ultimately gave you. No one on this plane of existence, wizard or sorceress, king or queen, escapes the duality of human nature...we all have our secrets to bear. In the end, you must understand, you received the treasures of Gwenevere's heart while her own flesh and blood did without. The pain you feel now is the direct result of your belief that Gwenevere did not love you without fail. She did. Let no one ever claim otherwise."

Myla collapsed into Viviane's arms and wept the tears of an abandoned child. Viviane soothed her with a tight embrace, clinging until Myla's defenses against tortuous truths seemed, in part, restored.

"If we are to safeguard the heir," Viviane suggested, "time may be of the essence."

ξӜξ

The crisp air thinned significantly and the road had grown wide. Farrin's journey over the mountainside had nearly come to an end when she finally asked the question that had begged all along.

"What is this all about, Merlin? I understand the general idea of lust for power and I realize evil requires little motivation to flourish, but I sense there is much more to this encounter and I feel at a disadvantage for lack of understanding."

Merlin made no ploy to dismiss her inquiry as irrelevant, but the apprehensive expression on his face said he wished she hadn't asked. His gaze fell over her shoulder, scanning the nest of forest behind her and she sensed his eagerness to press on. Drawing a deep breath, he nodded, and led her to a small grove on the outskirts of the forest's edge where they settled into the smooth grooves of a large boulder that seemed fashioned specifically to provide rest for the weary.

While he spoke, Merlin observed the frosted landscape, eyes scanning with intense scrutiny, as if expecting a sudden intrusion.

"No life is lived without accruing complexity. Even those whom we are tempted to judge as mundane are burdened with such involution it would boggle the mind to fathom all the nuances that create the knotty tapestries one person is capable of weaving in a single lifetime. This is especially true for Morgana le Fay. She was, you see, half-sister to King Arthur. Her love for Arthur was immeasurable and consuming, but unrequited. This frustrated her and caused great confusion, for Morgana was quite beautiful and highly coveted. In an attempt to force Arthur to accept Morgana as queen, Morgana's sisters, Elaine and Morgause, devised a deceitful plot to bring Arthur and Morgana together using an act of sorcery, through which Morgana conceived a child.

Once Morgana gave birth to Arthur's son, Morgause and Elaine revealed their plot. Morgana carried the news to Arthur, expecting him to legitimize the child by making her queen. To her dismay, Arthur took the hand of the Lady Gwenevere in marriage instead. Not only did this perceived betrayal cost Morgana the glory and admiration of the kingdom, but it bastardized her son, Mordred. To say she was furious would constitute a massive understatement. The curse Morgana cast upon Gwenevere's womb was fashioned from the depths of insane jealousy. Understanding that a queen considers it her utmost duty to provide an heir to the throne, Morgana used the curse as a manner of usurping Gwenevere's very purpose."

The boulder Farrin sat upon now seemed a bit more like a glacier as the cold seeped through her black leather breeches, numbing her backside and forcing her to stand to alleviate the irksome condition. Engrossed in Merlin's expose, she maintained a concentrated focus as he continued.

"Once Morgana realized she would not gain notoriety, power, or control through a political station, she came to me, seeking, she claimed, the skills and talents necessary to help safeguard her son should he become subject to public ridicule later in his life. I was only too happy to provide her with an education for such a noble purpose. Frankly, as time passed between us, I became very fond of Morgana and thought of her as kin. However, it seemed the more she learned, the darker her mood. It was difficult, at best, to witness Arthur parading his bride about, his infatuation so glaring, only a blind man would fail to recognize it. Arthur's devotion to Gwenevere was complete.

Several years passed and when Gwenevere found herself in a family way, she chose to hide her condition by claiming the need for a few months of rejuvenation at the nunnery in Almesbury. There, she gave birth and ushered her child off to an orphanage in Bibury, leaving her husband forever ignorant of his daughter's existence, such was the gravity of the Queen's concern for the child's safety."

"A daughter?" Farrin interjected, shocked at the implications. "But, that would mean I'm not the first female born in the line of Gwenevere, not the true heir."

"Which is correct," Merlin nodded, "you are not."

On one hand, this information came as a dire blow, but on the other, it was a great relief as the weight of the burden of the curse lifted instantly. And yet, how underhanded of Merlin to allow Farrin to test her newfound skills at the peril of Mithragog's ire under the guise of the charade.

"The true heir," she asserted, "must be long dead. Why wasn't the light of this truth brought forward long ago?"

Merlin scratched his chin, meeting Farrin's impatient gaze with a tight grin. "Because the true heir yet lives. She is a woman I would suspect you haven't had the occasion to meet despite the fact she is your great grandmother— Helga, the witch of Dearbourne. She is mother to two sons. You would know the oldest of these as your departed grandfather, Sir Hilary Lockwood, who, as you know, was your father's father. Helga's second son, born less than fifty years ago, is one Phylus Antius, a lad I have not seen or heard of for many a year, though he must still be quite virile if fate did not mark him for an early departure. Now that I consider it, I suppose he may have left the area in search of a new life, considering the poor boy took quite a lashing when some took to calling him Phyllis. Alas, the young do seem to savor cruelty."

"I have a living great grandmother?" Farrin mused, the idea astonishing.

"Indeed," Merlin said, waving his hand in a gesture meant to caution her from allowing hope to run too far ahead of the conversation. "Do not fault your father if he never mentioned Helga Dearbourne. She is not the type of influence a wise man desires for his beloved child."

Farrin drew a long, determined breath. She would never ignore family without severe justification.

"She's Gwenevere's daughter. She can't be all bad."

Merlin chuckled. "Alas," he said, cracking his neck with a sharp twist, "Helga never knew who her mother was. Her kinship to Gwenevere did not provide her with a naturally sweet disposition, trust this. Oh, the witch of Dearbourne had her days of glory, do not mistake that, she was once one of the most desired women in all the land, but that had more to do with a favorable appearance than a warm heart. She never married, quite the scandal, but that's beside the point. Things change and not always for the better. In fact, if my senses serve me, I believe you will soon meet Helga as we join the others on the sacred acre."

"The sacred acre?"

"Ah yes, I meant to tell you about this most magical place. Forgive me. It slipped my mind. No matter, we've come around to it, haven't we?"

ξϾжϾξ

Helga heard someone approaching and assumed it was Myla, who else would be so rude as to interrupt a woman's toiletries? Cutting it short, Helga covered her pile of waste with a handful of dead leaves, urging her joints to bring her out of her squat and see her to her feet. The face emerging from the thicket belonged to Mithragog, smug expression at the ready.

How she despised the sight of him. At least, for once, he had taken her advice and come to join her. Perhaps he had seen the advantage of battling for Merlin's power as opposed to chasing the heart of the heir. If all went well, it was quite possible to obtain both. Who would stop them then? With Merlin's power, Mithragog would gain the glory he sought, and the heart of the heir would restore Helga's youth. What more was there to ask for?

"Good of you to join me," Helga said, careful to curtail any sarcasm that might leak into her tone.

"I am so very happy to see you, Mother," he responded, bending at the waist with a curt bow—a gesture that might have endeared her if she thought for one moment he actually meant it.

Walking with the aid of his staff, he came closer. He wasn't carrying his usual staff, but a ragged stick with a meager gemstone, low-grade quartz of all worthless things, and Helga wondered what happened to the previous staff, but didn't mention it. No sooner had she made the decision to keep her mouth shut than he lifted the staff and pointed it toward her, his tongue fumbling over a line of Latin that would have obliterated her if he had spoken the spell properly.

Stumbling back, she blasted, "What are you doing? Now is no time to settle family disputes. I've told you repeatedly, I named you Phylus after your father, it was a noble name in Rome, no one ever made light of it there. Why bother with all this now? Between the two of us, we can overcome Merlin and take the heart of the heir!"

Mithragog's annoyance and frustration with the failed spell showed in his knotted expression. He really had it in for her. Why now? Why not yesterday, or last week...last year, or ten years ago? Did he come here thinking he could walk away with everything for himself? So it seemed.

We'll just see about that.

Slowly, she circled him, studying his eyes and hands. He joined in the dance, searching for the right moment to attack.

"Haven't you heard, Mother?"

Slipping her hand in her pocket, she grabbed a fistful of silver powder, "Heard what?"

"You already have the heart of the heir," he proclaimed, his gaze filled with certain bloodlust.

And just who had filled his head with this nasty accusation? He couldn't possibly believe it.

"If I had the heart of the heir, would I look like this? Do you think I would linger about this mountain rather than make my way to Paris?" She cackled a hearty laugh, but he didn't flinch and his focus only deepened.

"I have not taken the heart of the heir. In fact, I haven't killed anyone since the battle of Camlann and, believe me, those blighters deserved what they got."

Mithragog was the only person Helga had ever known whose eyes could drool with avarice, they were doing so now. He must truly believe he had something stupendous to gain from killing his own mother. But, what could that possibly be?

"Shut up, Mother. You've missed the point altogether. You *are* the heir."

For the second time in as many days, Helga plunged into the throngs of uncontrollable laughter. As she laughed harder than ever before, she saw, through bleary eyes, her son lift his staff and point it at her. This time he spoke with perfect clarity.

ξӜξ

Lady Viviane stood in the brush, hands pressed to her mouth, staring at the gory spectacle twenty paces ahead. Spattered over the scant dusting of snow, streams of fresh blood flowed, more added every moment as it gushed from severed jugulars.

Viviane and Myla had come searching for Helga and had nearly cleared the thicket when they heard her scream.

'*Capulatio!*' was the cry they'd heard and it had been many years since Viviane witnessed the effects of such a devastating spell.

There was Helga, looking broken and torn, chasing after her son's severed head, much like a child might run after a toy. Reaching it, she bent down to regard his blinking eyes. In shock, he spoke to her, clearly and unencumbered, "Am I dead?"

Shaken, she answered, "I should think so."

Convinced, he murmured, "I should probably commence with it then."

With trembling lips and a stream of tears flowing over her cheeks, the witch of Dearbourne reluctantly nodded.

Viviane recognized the emotion on Helga's face as the onset of a regret that would linger like a heavy fog until it engulfed and permeated her pores, until it was all she could taste, all she could smell, until, once she'd lived with it for a few years, it became such an integrated part of her that no one would recognize her without it.

"Mother?"

"Yes?" Helga grasped Mithragog's head, gently wiping snow, dirt, and debris from his face and drawing it nearer so that she could peer into his eyes while he spoke.

With his last breath, the wizard made his final proclamation, "I hate your guts."

"I hate you, too," she choked, weeping as the light in his eyes went dim.

ξ⅗κξ

Farrin listened to the sound of horse hooves clopping over gravel as Merlin spoke of the sacred acre. She attempted to see beyond the sheltered grove through which she strode, past wide trunks of naked trees, hoping for a glimpse of the riders winding their way to the crest of the mountain, but all she could see was bark, brush, and an occasional eclipse of light as shadows moved past.

In the moments preceding the riders' passing, she had learned much about the sacred acre. Merlin had explained that all forms of life on earth had begun there. He confided the grounds were a high-energy vortex capable of amplifying magic to an extreme degree, adding that this place would offer no advantage to good or evil, as the vortex remains neutral in such matters. When she asked why this was so, he claimed it was a matter of free will directly connected to the duality present on Earth. Without duality, without contrasts, he'd said, there can be no free will. From the pristine light gathered at the sacred acre, the Lady of the Lake had forged the twin swords, Excalibur and Clarent. There, Arthur drew the sword from the stone to become king of all England. And there, one can find the interments of Arthur and Gwenevere, contrary to the prevalent belief that Avalon was Arthur's final burial place.

Hearing this, Farrin pressed to move out of the grove and join ranks with the riders gathering at the crest of the mountain. Merlin, however, insisted on summoning another ally. A fellow, he assured her, she would find most interesting, a warrior of exceptional skill. A Hulderfolk.

The mention of this mythical creature summoned the recollection of another of Farrin's childhood instructors, the lively and wildly imaginative Madam Torramaine who had once mentioned such a being. But, because many held the Madam in wide regard as a prevaricator and because she had purposefully misled Farrin on several occasions, it seemed probable that the Madam's ruminations concerning the Hulderfolk were fanciful and, as such, Farrin had not afforded them much thought. Until now.

From what she could recall of the Madam's claim, the Hulderfolk are Scandinavian fairies who appear human in every aspect but for the presence of a longish tail similar to a monkey tail. They keep these tails bound to long braids of hair, causing the length of their backs to appear seamed. When a Hulderfolk mates with a human, the result is a prophetic offspring, able to see past, present and future with perfect clarity. Consequently, the males are prone to profuse flattery and appear irresistibly attractive to human females.

It would certainly prove interesting to see how much the Madam had exaggerated if the opportunity came to stand face-to-face with such an intriguing person.

Finished with his summoning, Merlin assured Farrin that the Hulderfolk known as Kai Anders would join them on the sacred acre.

Then Merlin did something that caught Farrin completely off guard—he asked her to show leniency toward Morgana, explaining it his wish, if possible, to settle matters with Morgana peaceably. "Hold back," he had requested, "until she has taken possession of the ultimate spell."

As Farrin studied his eyes, she could see he knew as well as she that Morgana was not likely to settle for a peaceful resolution. Nevertheless, she accepted the terms.

At last, she and Merlin left the grove to make their way toward the peak of Bodach Cairn.

ξϪξ

The air seized Sarina's face, gripping her skin with its frozen fingers. She reveled in the invigorating sensation as the cold invaded her nostrils, causing a glacial itch, her lungs burning, clouds of tempestuous mist forming when she exhaled.

The road curling around the mountain seemed to coil in an unending spiral, but the trail had begun to grow wider, indicating the journey had nearly ended. She began to feel Farrin's presence now, so intense it seemed as though they stood side-by-side, so profound, Sarina began to look for Farrin, eyes scanning between the trees, following shadows, ears alarmed by snapping twigs.

Ozzie and Flea had not been engaging company, their silence heavy as they focused on the battle ahead and struggled to ignore the pain kindled by their purulent wounds. Men and their stubborn gallantry seem intent to prove that you can lead a horse to water, but you cannot make it think. It was too late to urge them back to their healing beds. They had bound their determinations—they would die in battle or suffer later beneath the weight of their festering injuries.

ξЖξ

Kai Anders was nothing short of gorgeous perfection. His chest and upper body rippled with sculpted muscle, his bright green eyes glistened as brilliantly as two polished emeralds and his long braid of hair radiated so brightly, it seemed almost white. Farrin forgot everything she thought she knew about fairies, no preconceived assumptions applied. Like anyone else, she assumed fairies were small creatures, perhaps with wings and pointed ears, much like the sprites, Nyx and Fig Knockbottom. Not so. Kai stood over six feet tall. Dressed in earth-tone leathers, he seemed formidable in every way, except one—he carried no weapons. And yet, Merlin had described him as a hearty warrior. What kind of warrior carries no weapons?

The Hulderfolk joined Farrin and Merlin shortly after they arrived on the crest of the mountain. They stood on the edge of the forest overlooking the field that led to Friar John's meager cottage. Kai wasted no time in delivering an unending flurry of compliments aimed at Farrin, which resulted in a blush and a giggle, but no more. Apparently, Madam Torramaine had stretched the truth concerning the irresistible nature of the Hulderfolk male. Granted, Kai was a fine specimen, distinctly superior in appearance compared to other men, but he was still a stranger. As for attraction, Farrin didn't feel the slightest flutter.

Frustrated and clearly perplexed by Farrin's immunity to his advances, Kai rushed her, grappling to deliver a passionate kiss. Sarina's whistle and whoop issued from less than fifty yards away. Breaking Kai's brutish grip, Farrin delivered a solid punch to his midsection and looked up to see Ozzie riding away in disgust. Had he turned away at the sight of the embrace without witnessing the blow?

Face flushed, Farrin turned to Merlin. "Your warrior has no manners. Keep him away from me."

"It's not so much a lack of manners as it is shock," Merlin murmured, "It's a rare experience for a Hulderfolk to be ignored by the human female."

Kai nodded emphatically, his deep voice strained, "Only a woman already in love has the power to ignore the charms of the Hulderfolk."

Sarina dismounted her horse and ran toward Farrin, cloak suspended on the wind behind her as she rushed forward. Smiling, Farrin prepared for the impending embrace, but Sarina pushed past her and rushed to envelop Kai, "Marry me!" she gushed, clinging to his leather like a newborn summer leech.

Merlin laughed a hearty bellow and drew Farrin away for a private word.

"I would be remiss, M'lady," he said, "if I did not ask you to consider the needs of your country where their future queen is concerned and beg you to remain safely out of the fray."

Mouth agape, Farrin thought about the amount of energy and attention Merlin had invested in preparing her for this battle. Truly, this man is an enigma.

"My country," she replied with a tinge of indignation, "will fare no better for having a coward for a queen."

Donning a curt smile, Merlin nodded, "Well said. I suggest we get on with it. I'll gather the others. You may wish to render yourself invisible."

Handing Kai an intricately carved facemask, Merlin instructed him to keep his face covered at all times, until otherwise instructed. The Hulderfolk seemed offended by the idea of hiding his glorious face behind such an ugly mask but complied without complaint.

ξжξ

Morgana dragged Friar John from the confines of his cabin when the sound of horse hooves alerted her to the small group of misfits crossing the field, two on horseback, two on foot. Shuffling the Friar over the threshold, she pressed her dagger to his throat, and called upon Dezva, who immediately joined her.

Despite the Friar's struggle to break free of her grip, Morgana kept a keen focus on the man leading the advancing fray as he marched with foolish confidence. Merlin. The man she had once believed she would never see again, the man who fueled the most passionate loathing she had ever experienced, the man she would mercilessly erase from existence and, if fate had any sense of justice, the man she would watch die a thousand different ways before this day drew to a close.

The closer Merlin came, the more Morgana's rage escalated. She allowed it to flow, to quicken her pulse and intensify her senses until the heat of fury saturated every pore.

This world, this insane reality, never gives anything freely—in fact, it knows only how to take. Without sufficient defenses, this life would eat a woman alive and spit her out for worm meal. But a woman born to greatness, a woman tested and tried in the flames of adversity, a woman clever in her assessments and decisions, a woman in possession of age-old wisdoms and devoid of the weaknesses that burden the mortal heart, that kind of woman stands a chance to give this realm a taste of its own decadence.

But, first, she would free herself from the squirming oaf locked in her grip. An oak tree of sufficient size stood to the right of the cottage, it would suffice. Drawing a handful of powder from her pouch, she flicked it at the tree, intending to create a simple cage. Instead, a pair of hands with long gnarly fingers and dagger-like claws grew from the ends of two large branches and began to flail about as if searching for a victim. Initially shocked at the strength of her spell, Morgana smiled with satisfaction. She had just the prize for those greedy, groping hands. Prodding and dragging the Friar toward the mutated tree, she gave him a stiff shove and sent him sprawling. The enchanted appendages snatched him up by the ankles faster than a starving frog arrests a fly. Head dangling four feet off the ground, the Friar began to vomit and choke, eyes bulging with pressure and fear. His hood dangled behind his balding head as his robe slipped and curled around his chest, the robe held in place by a rope he used as a humble belt. This unfortunate posture had exposed his knickers, along with several unsightly stains in unmentionable places. Morgana made no effort to suppress her laughter. What a delightful sight. And now, her hands were free to deal with Merlin and his addle-headed army.

ξЖξ

Farrin was invisible, but didn't *feel* invisible. Adjusting to the idea that no one could see her, especially those standing less than a foot away, proved oddly difficult. Clearly, no one but Merlin had an inkling of Farrin's presence and he was engaged in a hushed conversation with a woman wearing brilliant white robes. The demon,

Dezva, however, seemed to watch Farrin's every move. Was this a delusion created by Farrin's mistrust, or was it possible the demon had a gift of sight no one else possessed?

As the company drew across the field, they watched in horror as Morgana le Fay cast a spell on a nearby tree, which subsequently snatched a man wearing a monk's robe and dangled him upside down. Of special interest was the fact that the sorceress had used silver powder to cast the spell.

"I thought you said Morgana understood the Principles of Reality," Farrin whispered.

"That I did," Merlin replied, speaking in a hushed tone, careful not to direct his gaze toward Farrin, or to move his lips too much as he spoke. "She is a creature of habit and reluctant to abandon the old ways. Let's hope it works to our advantage."

ξжξ

Merlin observed Morgana as he and the Lady Viviane drew near, not the slightest flinch or twitch of nervousness. Standing resolute and waiting patiently, her long ringlets of dark hair billowed in the wind, her cheeks red from the bite of early winter.

Pointing to the tree where the Friar hung, Merlin spoke with booming authority, "Release him."

Morgana raised her eyebrows in interest but shook her head, her expression one of mild amusement.

Friar John, still moaning and gagging, managed to sputter, "Is it true you were my friend, Barnabus?"

Merlin turned to him. "Yes. Forgive my deception. I meant no harm."

"The witch claims you are my father," Friar John managed to say. The unnatural hands that gripped him began to shake violently, apparently provoked by the sound of his voice and, once again, the Friar vomited.

"That is true," Merlin confessed. "I beg your forgiveness."

Morgana stepped between Merlin and the tree so that he could not see past. "Are you prepared to trade your secrets for your son's life?"

The Lady Viviane's fingers dug deep into Merlin's shoulder.

"Why do you claim this man as your son? The very idea is preposterous."

Morgana cackled with delight, taking extreme pleasure in Merlin's plight. "Tsk, tsk," she sneered, "Have you been keeping secrets from your lady?"

Face burning with indignation, the Lady Viviane shoved Morgana forcefully. "It is a vile lie!"

Snickering, Morgana pointed to Merlin. "Ask him. You need not trust my word."

There was no need to make the inquiry. The moment Viviane looked into Merlin's eyes she knew he had kept this magnanimous secret from her. Her indignant rage displayed itself in the blooming of her cheeks and her hardened glare. Without uttering a single word, she walked away. At which moment, Friar John coughed and sputtered a barely audible, plea for help.

The Lady Viviane abruptly stopped her angry march and returned.

"Whose child hangs from that tree? Do not lie to me."

Taking in a deep breath, Merlin summoned his courage. "He is our child, M'lady. He belongs to you and I."

The Lady's eyes shifted as she processed this information, searching for reason and any semblance of sense. The more pieces of the puzzle she put together, the more her ire ignited.

"The enchantment on the globe," she whispered.

"Was a very good enchantment," Merlin interjected, hoping she might accept the compliment.

She slapped him hard across the cheek.

Facing Morgana, the Lady released her rage, "Let him go. Get him down from that tree at once."

Unfazed by the directive, Morgana laughed. Not dissuaded, Viviane advanced, her resolution set like cold stone, forcing Morgana to step backward.

"I am the first soul born to this plane of existence," Viviane declared, "And, I assure you, I will be the last soul to leave. Any attempt to usurp my will can only meet with defeat. Release the Friar."

Merlin watched Morgana study the Lady Viviane's face and saw a moment of surprise and confusion pass over Morgana's demeanor. Viviane's words had jarred her. In that moment, Merlin remembered why he loved Viviane so—she was simply the bravest woman he had ever known.

ᚼᚵᚼ

Morgana knew the rules of immortality. Unharmed, an immortal can live forever. However, it is not outside the realm of possibility to harm or kill an immortal, she could attest to having killed three or four herself. But stories whispered from long ago speak of the matron of souls, a woman, who cannot suffer harm, cannot die, rumored to be in possession of the original soul from whence all other souls derive. Had the Lady of the Lake spoken truthfully? Was she that one indestructible soul from whom all life originated? Or, was this outrageous claim but a ploy to gain the upper hand through intimidation? There seemed only one way to find out.

ᚼᚵᚼ

Nyx and Fig Knockbottom worked against the grip of the tree's enchanted hands. Their sharp but small daggers had very little effect as the wood seemed constructed of a mysteriously pliant substance able to maintain a perplexingly flexible constitution. Digging into the beguiled appendages, Nyx and Fig prodded and sliced, their efforts thwarted by wood pulp that healed itself almost as quickly as they defiled it. Worse, each time they jabbed into the oak, the hands shivered, shaking Friar John as if he were naught but a soiled rug. Coupled with this impossible challenge, Nyx and Fig remained ever mindful of Morgana's gaze and skillfully moved out of her sight each time she inspected the Friar's miserable disposition. Their efforts failing repeatedly, it seemed certain they had little chance to free the Friar from this terrible curse. But, at times like these, it is advantageous to remember that songs of praise concerning a Knockbottom are always sung as a testament to his resourcefulness and determination.

ξᛜξ

Her favorite time of the year, Sarina delighted in the beginning weeks of winter. She spent a good part of the winter months experimenting with herbs and tinctures, an integral pastime for the seasoned healer. In a few weeks, the blinding snows would come and all of Collingswood would begin its annual hibernation. Trails of smoke would twist and churn, escaping from cabin roofs as each village and its inhabitants focused on managing the necessities required for surviving an oft-times brutal season. Armies remained behind castle walls whilst kings rejuvenated themselves by indulging in extravagant feasts and turning their courts over to the skills of local artisans. Even tax collectors left well enough alone until spring. Winter, though seemingly coldhearted, had always carried in its arms a certain peace.

Here, on Bodach Cairn, the air hung crisp, filling the lungs with a burst of cool revitalization and Sarina could see her breath's fog linger as it misted from her lips. Weather like this kept her alert, her senses sharp and honed, keenly aware of her surroundings. The light snow that had fallen earlier in the day had melted away, leaving only scattered traces. Fallen leaves were stiff with hardened veins, crackling beneath her step as she stood on the edge of the wood watching bizarre scenes play out before her eyes.

A witch had burst out of the cabin that stood across the field, her arms wrapped tightly around a man of the cloth, her dagger drawn across his throat in a menacing manner. Casting a spell, she enchanted a nearby tree, which took hold of the poor fellow and hung him upside down. This witch must be none other than the infamous Morgana le Fay, Sarina's first known encounter with an immortal.

An aged wizard, identified as such by the jeweled staff he gripped, a man who might easily pass himself off as the once great Merlin, had approached Morgana and demanded she release her captive. Standing near the wizard was a woman clad in white, a woman who bore a majestic glow, a curiosity Sarina had never before witnessed. This strangely anointed woman seemed quite unnerved by the ensuing conversation, an argument Sarina could barely hear from such a lengthy distance.

The muscular Hulderfolk also stood on the border of the wood, a despicable mask concealing his glorious allure. Beside him were two women, an aged witch withered by the cruel hands of time and another woman youthful in appearance, each of them content to hold their ground for the time being, looking on with concerned astonishment.

Ozzie and Flea had accompanied Merlin halfway across the field when a wall of stone appeared and barred their passage. Spooked by the sudden appearance of the wall, Flea's horse nearly threw off its rider.

Chivalrous to a fault, Ozzie and Flea once again spurred their horses to cross the field but each time their horses approached the halfway mark in the field, the wall suddenly reappeared, blocking their progression. Three times, they rushed the field and three times the wall appeared. Someone wielding an extraordinary magical skill clearly intended to deny them passage. At a standstill, Ozzie and Flea leaned in toward one another, conspiring, no doubt, a new plan to gain access.

As deeply unnerving as Sarina found all of this, she focused her concern upon Farrin. Where was she? Sarina hadn't seen her since embarrassing herself with the Hulderfolk. What was that all about anyway? Whatever it was, Sarina was grateful the Hulderfolk now wore a gruesome mask. Hopefully, he wouldn't take it off anytime soon.

Oddly, Sarina could see no sign of Farrin anywhere, but she had returned all of Sarina's hailing spells. Curious.

Farrin was somewhere nearby, but nowhere in sight. Perhaps it was part of a befuddling battle strategy. Sarina knew so little about such things. What else could it possibly be?

A sudden blur of wind caught Sarina's attention—a compact area of compressed cloud that circled near the further end of the field, close to the cabin and the group assembled there, and then away. At first, it seemed a trick of the eye, as sometimes happens when a stray hair nestles beneath the eyelid, but Sarina's attempts to blink it away brought no cure and her vision appeared without fault but for that one specific area. Had Morgana cast another vexing enchantment, or was this something else entirely?

Before Sarina had a chance to explore the thought further, something popped out from behind Morgana's cloak, a grotesque creature with a tail planted on the back of its head, its large coal-colored eyes set deep in a gnarled and disfigured face, its long arms reaching past its knobby knees, which seemed to bend in entirely the wrong direction. A horrible sight. This creature, too, seemed focused solely upon the blurring wind, its exposed fangs drooling in much the same way a ravenous cat might stalk a cornered mouse.

The brattle of clanking metal combined with thundering horse hooves drew Sarina's attention as a small regimen of Ozzie's knights rushed through the wood, necks frantically twisting in search of who-knows-what. Dressed in formal regalia, new armor bright and polished, they brandished the flags of Collingswood, holding them high and with firm regard. Although they clearly spied the small gathering at the wood's edge, they did not stop to inquire of Sarina, but galloped past, out into the field where they stopped to exchange words of agitation with Ozzie. Sarina couldn't hear the entirety of their message, but she did catch three words that resounded with the utmost intensity, "Farrin," "Queen," and "Dead."

§※§

A warrior's ears take note of the slightest sounds, things others might dismiss as insignificant. Ozzie heard the regimen approach long before they became visible and knew that Sir Charles led them by virtue of his distinguished tone when he barked, "Ho!" as he approached the apex of the mountain.

A regimen of the king's men would serve this battle well.

Ozzie turned to offer Sir Charles a smile of gratitude, but his short-lived joy was eradicated the moment he saw formal attire and official banners. These men had not come to join battle, but by order of the council.

Sir Charles drew his stallion beside Ozzie's and lifted his visor.

"We come in search of Farrin the Queen," he said, his expression grim.

Ozzie swallowed past a lump in his throat at the sound of this unexpected announcement. Yet, it would not do to hasten to unconfirmed conclusions.

"The Queen?" He asked.

Sir Charles sat higher on his steed and straightened his back, a simple gesture that seemed to require too much effort.

"The king is dead," he confirmed, a flutter of the eyes blinking away the underlying emotion.

Ozzie felt as though an intangible projectile had impacted his chest, leaving his body rigid and unmoving, his gaze fastened but unseeing.

"Have you seen Farrin the Queen? Can you tell us where to find her?"

Ozzie had been asking that same question for the last half hour. He had not set eyes on Farrin since seeing her locked in the embrace of a stranger. This news will crush her.

"She was there, earlier," he answered, motioning back toward the grove. "If you didn't see her on your way here, I can't imagine where she is. Still, she can't be far. Your only recourse may be to use la trompette de la morte."

Sir Charles balked at the suggestion. "The horn is a crude way to deliver such a blow."

"I agree," Ozzie said. "However, you can easily spend hours searching for her. If she's near, she'll show herself at the sound of the trumpet."

Staring, Sir Charles studied Ozzie's face as he considered the prospect.

Understanding his reluctance, Ozzie gifted him the only peace a senior officer could offer, "You may tell her you used the horn solely upon my order."

ξϽжξ

That sound, that most dreadful lament, the low moan and growl of la trompette de la morte. Sarina dropped her chin, allowing a stream of hot liquid to trickle over her cheeks.

The king is dead.

Splicing through the fog of Sarina's newborn grief came the projection of Farrin's guttural scream, resounding from the far side of the field. Sarina lifted her gaze and scanned the field but saw no sign of Farrin, just a cloud of blurring wind, driven to the ground where it hovered, unmoving. Emanating from within that cloud, the sound of a broken heart weeping.

ξϽжξ

A soul-splitting wail resounded from mid-field as the future queen grieved. Selfish, yes indeed, but Merlin willed the young woman to keep her composure and maintain her cloak for the sake of the battle.

Merlin had barely a moment's time to process his own stirring emotions upon hearing la trompette de la morte, as Morgana had used the shock of the moment to her advantage by grabbing hold of Lady Viviane and spinning her around until both women became a blinding whirl. When the spinning stopped, two perfect representations of the Lady Viviane stood before Merlin and he without the slightest clue as to which was which. Overall, an impressive display of shape-shifting skill, but what could Morgana possibly hope to profit from it?

"Kill us both," said the alluring Lady on the left, "and you can be sure."

What a perplexing and clever mesmerism, but which of the women might make such a brave proposal? Would Morgana give this advice hoping Merlin might slay the Lady Viviane by his own hand, or would Viviane make the suggestion, convinced of her inability to suffer harm? Studying the women carefully, he searched for clues that simply did not exist. No matter, the solution to the conundrum seemed obvious enough.

"It will not be necessary to kill either of you," he said, directing his answer to the Lady on the left. "Step forward and embrace me, a man knows his lover's kiss."

The ruse foiled, Morgana shed the likeness of the Lady Viviane and scowled at Merlin. Contempt radiated off her furrowed face and a curse flew past her lips as she thrust her hand forward to summon a boa constrictor, a pale and potent specimen that wrapped itself around Merlin's neck then curled around his body, forcing the air from his lungs. Merlin imagined he had turned blue and then, perhaps, a flattering shade of purple. Keeping those vibrant colors in mind, he tapped the snake behind the neck and transformed it into a lovely knit scarf.

"Thank you, my dear," he said, bowing slightly to accentuate his gratitude, "it is a lovely gift. I shall cherish it always."

There are moments when time stretches beyond all imagination, slow in motion to the point of pain. Thus it was, when the Lady Viviane allowed a trickle of laughter to escape at Morgana's expense and embarrassment.

Morgana cast her spell without words or powder, cast it from the depths of pure hatred, and cast it so quickly Merlin had no chance to defend against it.

Upon the ground lay the Lady of the Lake, the white of her robes no longer brilliant, her voluptuous radiance extinguished.

"She lied!" Morgana exclaimed, her face bright with satisfaction. "She doesn't possess the original soul! It was nothing but a preposterous claim." Squirming with laughter, Morgana inched close to Merlin's face, pointing a rigid finger at the crumpled form lying motionless at her feet. "When you feed her to the maggots, Wizard, carve this into the stone, *Here lies a liar.*"

Ignoring her, Merlin stooped to tend to the Lady, turning her over that he might see her eyes, vacant orbs of gray staring off into the distance but seeing naught, devoid of life. How could he possibly have allowed this to happen? Taking the Lady into his arms, he cradled her wilted form while his soul shattered like shards of fragile crystal.

؏ﮋ؏

The world is disorienting and confusing when it's upside down, not at all a pleasant place. Friar John, however, was not confused about what he had just seen. The beautiful, glowing woman in white, a Lady proposed to be his very own mother, had just collapsed to the ground after taking the brunt of a malicious spell cast by the demented sorceress.

The pressure and throbbing in John's head was enough to justify a man's madness, but seeing the Lady of the Lake lying limp in Merlin's arms spurred him to do the one thing a Friar knows to do in situations such as this.

"Lord of heaven," he sputtered, his syllables interrupted by persistent phlegm, "embrace your child and escort her into your kingdom. Rest her soul in peace."

؏ﮋ؏

Farrin couldn't stand, it was as if the sound of the trumpet had drained away her life's energy, leaving her feeble and limp. How could her father be dead? He had looked so much improved when she last saw him, even sporting a bit of a glow. She assumed Sarina's tonics had set him on a healthy path and that he would at last recover from his fever. But now...

Gone.

A sudden fog infiltrated her mind. Worse, it felt as though the ground had dropped away. This dreadful sinking feeling possessed her, hurling her through space and time... no destination, no end in sight, her stomach churning. The ache deepened. *How long could her heart continue to beat?* Embracing herself, she held tight.

ξжξ

Shocked, Helga watched Morgana le Fay drop the Lady Viviane like a common sack of flour without uttering a single word. The mighty Viviane had fallen to the sorceress, her immortal glow extinguished.

"Do something!" Myla implored, tugging violently on Helga's cloak, by which Helga ascertained that Myla had no magical powers of her own, beyond her immortality.

Helga would do something all right, she would find her way across the field to join forces with Morgana. She had placed her confidence in the wrong witch, an unfortunate mistake that required immediate correction.

Myla dug her nails into Helga's flesh, repeating her supplication, "Please, do something."

Helga jerked her arm from Myla's relentless grip. "The Lady of the Lake was the most powerful woman in the world," Helga seethed, "how much better would an old prune fare?"

ξЖξ

Having witnessed the fall of the Lady of the Lake, Nyx and Fig Knockbottom loaded their quivers and devised an impromptu battle plan. Nyx would take the lead, aiming for the sorceress's eyes, while Fig flanked to the left hoping to send an arrow straight through her ear canals and, with any luck, tear a little brain matter on the way.

Fig seemed to have the more difficult task as Morgana's plush hair covered her ears, leaving him to guess where they might be. Not deterred, he fired his arrows. The sorceress flinched, reacting as if stung by a bee each time an arrowhead pierced her flesh.

One well-placed shot and Morgana le Fay would become a name of the past, a name spoken with a chuckle over large tankards of ale as great warriors told tales that spoke reverently of the valiant resourcefulness of the Knotweed tribe. Because of his size, not despite it, a sprite is adept at discovering advantages.

Where is the wind? One good gust to blow Morgana's locks back and clever bards everywhere would begin drafting the ballads of Nyx and Fig Knockbottom.

The sorceress slapped at her face, agitated by the twenty or so arrows that had missed their intended target but had found flesh nonetheless. At the same time, she searched frantically for the source of her irritation. Her search was fruitless, mainly because when the need arises, a sprite becomes a blur before the mortal eye. Seeing a sprite in battle mode is much like trying to identify which breeze in the wood had turned left and which had gone right.

Morgana yelped and cupped her right eye, slumping forward. Nyx had finally hit his mark and none too soon— the quivers were growing light. If Fig had five arrows left, he would count himself very fortunate.

They would bring this witch down and celebrate her demise, then return to Skitchover glen where their wives and children awaited a triumphant return. On the way home, they would fell a rabbit, which would provide enough meat for the winter season. The Knockbottom boys had won widespread fame when Merlin taught them a method for hunting rabbit whereby Nyx would attach himself to the underbelly and dig into the hide until the creature stopped to scratch, at which point, Fig would move in for the kill. The technique never failed. Fig could already see the image of glowing faces as he and Nyx marched back to the glen toting their winter prize.

Morgana pulled the offending arrow from her eye and stared at it, or at least tried to, using the vision in her good eye. Her expression turned sour, as she seemed to realize she was up against a mighty foe. Laughing, Fig returned to Nyx's side. With so few arrows left, they would work together in an attempt to render the sorceress blind. They each placed an arrow and drew back their bows, ready to fire off a fresh round, when Morgana reached into her pocket and withdrew a handful of silver.

The arrows flew and hit their marks, the center of the pupil of her good eye and, surely, she could see very little after that.

Fig took flight, assuming Nyx would follow suit, but when Fig heard Morgana's curse ring out and turned to watch unfolding events, Nyx was hovering before Morgana's face, caught in the web of her magic, suspended immobile and at her mercy, his high-browed surprise attesting to his shock.

Drawing his blade, Fig rushed to attempt a rescue, but the witch spoke her words too quickly and anger fueled her spell. By the time Fig arrived, Nyx was already dead on the ground.

ξжξ

Farrin felt as though time had come to a halt, even though it clearly had not. The world doesn't stand still for grief, and evil doesn't retire while the broken-hearted heal. This battle would rage on despite shattered souls. Victory would depend upon Farrin's willingness to cast emotion aside, however persistent her heartache might be.

The Lady of the Lake had fallen and Merlin held her in a tender embrace, his face stricken with angst. Morgana seemed in the grip of a maddening fit, slapping herself and flinging silver powder at unseen foes, while Ozzie and Flea continued in their attempts to charge the field.

The thunder of horse hooves drew closer, forcing Farrin to conjure another wall to obstruct their passage. No doubt, Ozzie and Flea would put a world of hurt on Morgana, but without the use of magic, she would have the better of them in the end. Farrin had already lost more than she could bear, she would lose no more.

Did she still have her cloak of invisibility? Waving her arms in Sarina's direction, Farrin noted with fascination that Sarina continued to look past her. Miraculously, the invisibility remained.

The old hag who had been standing on the edge of the wood slowly made her way toward the tree where the Friar remained suspended. Assuming the hag meant well (she had arrived with the Lady of the Lake) Farrin ignored the event. Perhaps the old crone intended to free the Friar.

Keeping Ozzie and Flea at a safe distance seemed enough of a challenge, one that required a keen focus, as all hell would break loose if Flea's frustration spurred him to leave his saddle and make a run for it on all fours.

ξӜξ

Determined never to let go, Merlin clung to the Lady Viviane, her head resting upon his chest. Engulfed in a haze of grief, he was only vaguely aware of the events transpiring outside his misty sentience, but he had witnessed the demise of Nyx Knockbottom, a senseless tragedy that only served to compound the misery ripping at his soul.

Merlin had come to this battle hoping to settle matters without bloodshed. It was his intention to persuade Morgana to see things from a different perspective. Fragments of that hope lingered, but precious lives had already been lost. No matter how things turned out, Merlin would forever regret involving those he loved in a battle that had always been his own. The events transpiring here were his responsibility alone.

Notes of exasperation and frustration mingled in the strained tones of Morgana's voice as she made her demand, "Give me the ultimate spell or more of your friends will die. You're weak from casting the time spell, I am aware. We both know you don't have the resources for further resistance."

As Morgana spoke, Merlin felt the slightest twitch flutter beneath Lady Viviane's ribs and his heart leapt with hope. Only the faintest spasm, it may have been nothing more than a reflex of the dead, but if a man is to make assumptions, he may as well assume that which carries him into the arms of hope. Meanwhile, he must not reveal as much to Morgana.

"The ultimate spell bends the will of the people to follow he who casts it," Merlin said, his tone even. "But, the spell can only be cast by one pure of heart with selfless intention. To cast the spell otherwise will only result in disaster."

It did not seem so long ago when Morgana met the conditions necessary to cast such a spell and Merlin had adored her then, but circumstance and bitterness conspired to alter her former countenance until it was no longer detectable. Had he been a fool to believe it possible to undo such damage?

Spittle flew from Morgana's lips, "Don't toy with me! Your words of warning will not persuade me. I'm in no mood for games."

Flicking a handful of powder toward the hanging tree, Morgana set the Friar ablaze and he screamed in anguish as the flames licked his skin. The fire vanished almost as quickly as it appeared, but Morgana had made her intentions known—she would roast Friar John alive if Merlin did not meet her demands.

"I will give you the spell, Morgana. I ask only that you entertain but one small request. I would like you to meet someone first and if he cannot persuade you to abandon your desire for this spell, it shall be yours, on my oath."

Tightening her lips, she looked perfectly annoyed, but the shifting of her eyes attested to the fact that she was considering the request, which was all Merlin had hoped for.

Not waiting for a reply, Merlin motioned for the Hulderfolk to come forward and watched the warrior cross the field. With long strides and head held high, despite the grotesque mask he wore, the Hulderfolk was a glorious sight.

ξ✗ξ

Morgana knew Merlin as well as anyone and although they had not stood face-to-face for over one hundred years, it seemed clear by the tears that fell for his stricken lover that he was still a compassionate fool who believed in the goodness of humanity, a weakness that would bring about his demise. Men such as Merlin cannot seem to grasp the fact that humanity is comprised of nothing but evil and that the struggle of all the ages has been one bid after another to acquire power and control.

Immortality is the province bestowed upon those who possess the fortitude to seize command—since no other immortal had come forward to claim this right, Morgana would do so. But, because Merlin could not see this and because he had clearly not forsaken his stubborn devotion to the illusion of man's inherent goodness, Morgana was certain he would not rescind his oath to transfer the ultimate spell. She would allow him his benign condition and meet the man crossing the field. She would cast the warrior aside and take the spell. And then, at long last, the once great Merlin would breathe no more.

Sending a sprite to wage battle had been nothing less than an underhanded and cheap blow. Rubbing her eyes, Morgana struggled to clear her vision as Merlin's warrior drew near. Her sight remained clouded, but rapid blinking helped. Oddly, this man carried no weapons. Was he an apprentice hoping to outdo Morgana using Merlin's hand-me-down magic? Morgana stiffened at the thought of another challenge. Had she not already proven herself superior to Merlin's wiles? One more man dying in the grass would only add to her satisfaction.

"I am Kai of the Hulderfolk, M'lady," the warrior said, his voice deep and melodic, his knee settling lightly upon the ground as he bowed in reverence.

How delightfully pathetic. Did Merlin really believe he could win this battle by way of a chivalrous idiot?

Raising his head, the warrior slowly removed his mask.

Blinking profusely, Morgana thrilled at the sight of his sculpted face and the emerald eyes that pierced her gaze as they drank her in. For the briefest moment, she forgot herself and wondered what it would be like to see the world through this man's eyes. That instance frightened her more than any horror she had ever known. She would be better off for never having seen the warrior's eyes, better off if the sprite had blinded her completely.

"Replace the mask!" She demanded.

Bowing once again, the warrior complied.

The mask, grotesque and disfigured, turned the warrior's face into the image of a gnarled tree battered into a lump of scarred bark. Peering at the mask, Morgana expected to experience a revulsion that would set her free from the warrior's allure. Instead, despite the mask, she could still see his eyes, burning away her defenses, calling to her for recognition. She could not un-see what she had already witnessed.

Heart pounding against her chest, head swimming with confusion, she gasped for air knowing it would not satiate her.

"If you remove that mask, you will die," she seethed, wanting nothing more than to see his face again.

Turning sharply toward Merlin, she spoke with contempt, "What sorcery is this?"

"There is no magic in this," Merlin answered. "Connections of the heart are rare. Take this opportunity to live your life with the joy and contentment you have been denied. Every heart deserves fulfillment, yours is no exception."

Think again, pitiful fool. What is more nauseating than an old man who believes love can heal all? Worse, this man had his arms filled to the brim with evidence to the contrary. He sat there, clinging to his one true love, cold to the quick, her flesh stiff, and he, still boldly touting the merits of love.

"It will take more than an improvised love tonic to undo me. I will kill you where you sit once you have delivered your promise. Give me the spell, Merlin."

Reaching into her pocket, she withdrew a pinch of silver powder and cast another bolt of flame at the Friar, who responded splendidly with a terrifying cry of angst.

Acting on an impulse that went against every grain of her being, an instinct, an action completed without thought, she lunged forward and tore the mask from the warrior, exposing his face. Gasping at the sight of him, she quickly turned away.

Whatever the cost, she must find a way to allow this man a place in her life.

What was she thinking? She had no need of this man or any other. Once Merlin gave her the spell, men of all types would surround her with flatteries profuse.

Then again, let no one say Morgana le Fay is a fool. The ultimate spell would give her absolute power over the entire land and every man therein would bend to her will. But they would bend out of fear for losing their own pitiful lives. Here was a man, a beautiful man, appealing in unfathomable ways, offering his heart willingly.

She could have the man *and* the spell, could she not? Yes. But, once she cast the spell, the warrior would no longer have freewill, he would no longer have the ability to offer his willing devotion. Why did that suddenly matter?

Morgana curled her hands into fists and pumped them in frustration. Oh, this was clever. Of all of Merlin's tricks and tactics, appealing to a heart she thought she had successfully chained was the crème de la crème.

Returning her gaze to Kai's face, she willed herself to turn away, but immediately hungered for him. Taking him by the hand, she bid him to stand. His form towered over her, so tall and so mighty. So beautiful. So glorious.

She could not cast the ultimate spell and keep this man. She must choose.

"How long have you known this warrior?" She asked Merlin.

Coaxing strands of hair away from Lady Viviane's lifeless eyes, Merlin answered matter-of-factly, "All of his life. He was born to a man to whom I have entrusted my life on many occasions."

"So, you vouch for him?"

"Certainly, he is a fine lad with a solid heart. He will serve you as he has served me, with kindness and selfless devotion."

Smirking, Morgana gestured toward Kai, "He has a tail."

"Indeed, but he will lose the tail if you provide him with offspring. Any offspring born from your union will be destined to greatness, bestowed with gifts of clairvoyance and the sight to see future events long before they transpire."

"How unique," Morgana noted.

"Replace your mask and undo your tail," she instructed. The Hulderfolk seemed dazed by the request and looked to Merlin for instruction, receiving a nod of consent.

It took the warrior three minutes or more to unbraid his tail and once he had loosed it, he let it drop behind him, thin as a rat's tail and three feet long, a sight such as Morgana had never seen.

Jealous, Dezva snarled and growled at the warrior. Morgana snapped her fingers, commanding the demon to stand down. Despite the order, she could still hear a low grumbling coming from behind where Dezva clung to her cloak, his eyes filled with abhorrence as he glared at the warrior. The demon's devotion to Morgana had always been unconditional, the one constant she could always depend upon, but he was hell to manage.

Upon meeting the Hulderfolk warrior, Morgana had experienced exhilaration, heart palpitations, anxiety, and a certain thrill. She had felt these symptoms before and, although they transpired a very long time ago, it seemed a recent memory.

Morgana's days in Camelot were brief, as she resided there from birth to her twentieth year.

Uther Pendragon, the once great King, had raised Morgana and her half brother, Prince Arthur, within the guidelines of the proper conduct expected of a Pendragon. That is to say, Morgana would not enjoy a normal childhood as she primed for the throne despite the fact that no one expected her to succeed Uther. Arthur, by virtue of his gender, would become king at Uther's passing.

Morgana spent most of her days cocooned in utter boredom. And yet, she had accepted these conditions because, truth be known, Arthur was simply glorious. Everyone in the kingdom, but none so much as Morgana, thirsted to see him crowned king.

Reaching her years of maturation, Morgana began to fixate on Arthur, following him to training sessions, watching with longing each time he rode out for a hunt and waiting at her window until he returned. At first, she worried about the obsession, thinking herself ill or mentally unbalanced. This lasted until Miriam, Morgana's matron servant, a woman not bright in many ways but well practiced in common sense, explained that Morgana was merely in love and that allowing these emotions to run their course was the best she could do for herself. In so doing, Morgana took to learning the art of seduction by surrounding herself with the finest dressmakers, hair stylists, and makeup artisans. Soon, she had managed to bring every man in Camelot to a constant drool. Every man but Arthur.

Many a night the matron Miriam spent drying tears and weathering tantrums as Morgana's frustrations mounted.

"The prince is obsessed with his training, determined to prove himself to Uther, he simply has no opportunity to take notice of you," Miriam would say, and her words comforted Morgana, spurring her to increase her efforts.

Convinced patience posed an ally, Morgana focused on the arts and education, building a strong mind, discovering the mystics and strengthening her allure.

In preparation for high feasts, she would use every advantage at her disposal only to watch with dismay as Arthur spent his time engaged in conversation with Gawain and Percival, giving no notice whatsoever to the women gathered there. It was enough to cause Morgana to question Arthur's manhood. At this, Miriam would laugh, claiming men do not mature in matters of the heart as quickly as their counterparts and insisted Morgana be patient with the ways of nature.

Long were the nights filled with desire and dreaming, harsh were the bleak days.

One bright summer day, Cedric Cador, the Duke of Cornwall, arrived in Camelot, bearing gifts in reverence for the anniversary of Uther's birth.

Travelling with the Duke's entourage, were a number of his students. Among them, the young Lady Gwenevere, daughter to Lord Parronel, governor of Wiltshire, a man highly esteemed for his work in the sciences and most notably regarded for his work in designing a tincture dubbed, 'whiskey.'

Normally, Morgana would take little note of the comings and goings of Camelot's visitors, most of them uninteresting to a great degree, most visiting solely for the sake of propriety, out of duty to the king. The Duke's arrival, however, brought with it grave consequence—a fever that ultimately took the lives of Cedric and Uther, along with many others of lesser importance. This unfortunate event thrust Arthur upon the throne and stranded the Lady Gwenevere in Camelot.

Not blind to Gwenevere's exceptional allure, Morgana volunteered to return the Lady to Wiltshire by escorting the carriage herself, requiring only two knights to accompany the undertaking. Grief, however, had sabotaged all reason as Gwenevere insisted on remaining in

Camelot to oversee the funeral arrangements for her fallen mentor. At the same time, Arthur grieved over the arrangements for Uther.

Bonded by grief, Arthur and Gwenevere found eyes for one another, their hearts forging an instant alliance, a pact Morgana would ultimately find impossible to break.

Recognizing the situation as dire, Morgana's sisters, Elaine and Morgause, devised a plot to undermine Arthur's devotion to Gwenevere by coercing him to lie with Morgana under the influence of an enchantment.

Unaware of these actions, Arthur went about the business of settling into his kingship while continuing to court the Lady Gwenevere. All the while, his child grew inside Morgana's womb.

When the day came to confront Arthur with his son, he turned his back on Morgana, denied his heir and exiled both mother and child from Camelot, decreeing if ever they returned they would face execution. Arthur then sealed his contempt for Morgana by marrying the Lady Gwenevere.

They say the line between love and hate is thin and once it is crossed, there is no going back—no one could attest to this truth better than Morgana. Through the passing of the years, she gave her affection to only one other. To her dismay, she would come to realize that Merlin was so obsessed with the Lady of the Lake that he could not see Morgana's intention any better than Arthur had.

And that is what you get when you give your heart.

Morgana glared at the Hulderfolk's wretched mask.

"Inhero Forem!" Giving the command the full force of her lungs, she thrust a fistful of silver powder at the mask, which was now destined to cling forever to the Hulderfolk's face.

No man would ever again toy with Morgana le Fay.

Shocked, Kai grappled with the mask, attempting to pry his fingers between the mask and his skin, desperate to tear it away from his face, but without success.

As Kai wrestled against his new fate, Morgana slipped behind him and sliced off his tail. Howling, the Hulderfolk writhed in pain. Morgana flung the tail at Dezva, instructing him to bind the warrior with it, the demon all too eager to accommodate.

Sheathing her dagger, Morgana glowered at Merlin, whose hands trembled at the sight of her deed.

ξжξ

Helga Dearbourne stared at Friar John, his purple hue quite the sight, half his beard burned away, eyes bulging, face blistered, robe dangling and seared where Morgana's curses had scorched it. Perfectly still, but for the occasional blink, he seemed exhausted by his fate as his feet drained white under the relentless grip of the tree's enchanted hands.

It seemed a perfectly ordinary tree, but for its gruesome appendages and as Helga swirled around its trunk in her inspection, she snagged a piece of bark out of curiosity, ripping it forcefully away. The tree reacted with a shiver and violently shook the Friar as if he had committed the offense. If the tree could speak, it might have a few choice words to say. Helga chuckled at the prospect.

After mercilessly maiming the young man in the mask, Morgana engaged in a stare down with Merlin.

It takes a special kind of woman to brandish such conviction and fortitude, to know what is required to achieve an end and to pursue that end with unwavering focus and due diligence. Helga admired Morgana's mettle.

The sorceress demanded a spell from Merlin, one she coveted most sincerely, which indicated it must hold a supreme power. Helga cowered behind the tree. Finding a means to offer allegiance to Morgana suddenly seemed urgent.

Inching her way around the tree, she stepped ever closer to the spot where Morgana stood.

It happened so fast, the event was almost lost forever, but sure enough, from the corner of her eye, Helga spied the sight of a sprite, working feverishly to free Friar John from his unlucky entanglement. The blood in Helga's veins rushed to places she had long considered dormant as her fingertips began to tingle and warmth emanated from her chest. This discovery might be exactly what she needed to cement a pact with Morgana. In fact, this situation brought back the words of Helga's mentor, the Witch of Kent, who had once said, 'When opportunity comes knocking at your door, rip its heart out and hang it in a cool, dry place that it might never escape.'

Helga would act as though she hadn't seen the sprite. If he suspected her, she wouldn't see him again. She must devise a way to ensnare the little do-gooder.

Careful to keep her gaze directed downward, she slowly circled the tree, listening to the sound of the sprite's dagger as it fought for advantage. Estimating, she concluded the sprite was located approximately two feet over her head, well within reach. He continued in his efforts, oblivious to her interest.

The Friar quietly begged, "Help me," but Helga ignored his blither. Bending forward at the waist, she pretended to survey fallen leaves. Whilst crouched, she removed her hat, and then slowly stood back up, careful to keep her gaze low. She would make a blind swipe and hope to hit her mark.

ξЖξ

Dezva yanked on Morgana's cloak with such urgency, she was tempted to give him a good swat on the head.

"What? What is it?" She lambasted.

Pointing excitedly at midfield, he cried, "Magic sword," his voice garbled and irritating.

Scanning the area he indicated, Morgana saw nothing at all. Was her eyesight worse than she knew?

"Deadly sword, Mistress, dangerous."

Blinking, Morgana surveyed the field once again but saw nothing. "Be still," she commanded, and the demon whined and whimpered but dutifully obeyed.

ξЖξ

Helga pinched the bulge wrestling in the tip of her hat, amazed that she had bagged the sprite. Morgana, Helga suspected, would want him alive to do with as she pleased, thus, time was a factor. If the sprite still had his dagger and thought to use it against the fabric, all would be lost. To insure against this unfavorable probability, Helga whacked the hat hard against the tree trunk. Sure enough, the bulge in the hat went suddenly still.

"My lady," Helga beamed, arriving at Morgana's side, "A gift, a token." Extending her arm, she invited Morgana to take the hat.

Morgana's gaze seared, her expression a scowl of annoyance, but her regard soon shifted to the hat, which she cautiously accepted. Glancing inside, her scowl faded, replaced by an impish grin as she realized what she held.

"There were two of the little mongrels," she said in awe, and immediately threw the hat to the ground, stomping on it until a crimson stain appeared. Seeing this, Merlin moaned in anguish. Elated, Morgana reached inside the hat and withdrew the bloodied sprite, dangling him before Merlin's tearful eyes. She then handed the sprite to her demon. Surely, an offering so small did not provide much of a snack, but perhaps enough to whet the demon's appetite.

ξ϶Ӝ϶ξ

Sir Charles, captain of the knight regimen, declared the Queen nowhere present and took his men in search of her. They would wind their way slowly down the mountain, covering every inch of terrain. Ozzie would be inclined to agree with the assumption if it wasn't for the fact that each time he and Flea attempted to cross the field they met with impossible obstacles. At first, he had attributed this wretched sorcery to the heartless witch, but had since begun to suspect Farrin's involvement. Why would Morgana be so keen to keep the knights at bay when she believed she had the power to dispatch them with little to no effort? In fact, Farrin had more compelling reasons to create these frustrating conditions. Ozzie sensed she was near. But, where and why couldn't he see her? For now, there was little more he could do but continue searching.

ξ϶Ӝ϶ξ

Dezva yanked on Morgana's cloak with such force it nearly decapitated her.

"Sword! Sword!" He screamed, his gaze intense, his muscles thoroughly rigid as he pointed to the same spot in the field as before, his drool increased to gushing.

Morgana turned sharply toward Merlin, seeking a sign, the slightest movement or gesture that might suggest he knew something about this anomaly. Unfortunately, he gave away no such clue as his focus remained solely upon the stricken Lady.

Turning to her new ally, Morgana asked of Helga, "Do you see anything out there?"

After searching the field with intense scrutiny, Helga indicated she saw nothing at all.

Dezva, however, continued to tug at Morgana's cloak. Even if there was nothing out there, what could it hurt to allow him his folly?

"Go get it," Morgana commanded and the demon rushed off.

ᚷᚳᚷ

Hands clasped to her mouth, Sarina stared at the center of the field scarcely able to believe what she had just witnessed.

It all began when Morgana's demon creature rushed across the field, a hellish sight and startlingly frightening because, at first, Sarina believed the creature was headed in her direction. Very few witches have spells at their disposal capable of dispelling such an ominous evil and so, the sight of the demon barreling across the field at high speed had caused Sarina an instant panic. Reaching midfield, the demon stopped so abruptly it was as if it had run into a solid wall. The impact sent the beast sprawling. Without hesitation, it regained its footing and rushed forward, but the force dispelled the demon once again.

Sarina suspected the old wizard had cast the magic responsible for the erection of the walls that kept Ozzie and Flea from crossing the field and now she wondered if this awesome display of prowess with the demon was his doing as well. If so, she would dearly love to make his acquaintance if anyone survived this fray.

Not dissuaded, the demon grappled for footing, eyes wild with ire, body trembling with vexation.

Watching this grim fiend wrestle against an unseen force was terrifying, and yet, nearly comical. Whatever, or whomever it was that Sarina could not see, the demon clearly had in sight. But, for Sarina, it seemed as though empty air was thrashing the demon.

Stepping back, the alarmed creature paused for a few moments, after which, it held its hands aloft and watched with satisfaction as a set of elongated, knifelike claws grew from its fingertips. Sufficiently armed, it raced forward. This time, the force warring with the demon repelled it with a burst of terrible flame that would have instantly devoured human flesh. Incredulously, the demon was unfazed by the fire and, by Sarina's observation, seemed to enjoy the blaze, licking its lips and grunting a squalid snigger.

Several times, the demon lunged forward and fell back stricken. The magician battling against the demon was giving it a good swat-about.

The demon must have tired of this for, all at once, its resolve seemed strengthened. Determined to gain victory, the demon curled in upon itself and, as it did so, its eyes began to bulge, its reptilian skin turning a beet shade of red, the creature growing at an alarming rate. As it expanded in size, its features became more gruesome and offensive, eyes black as night, fangs long and sharp, horns jutting from the shoulder blades, elbows and knees, and bat-like wings sprouting from the spine, the image branded in the forefront of Sarina's memory where she would never be rid of it.

Surely, she thought, there is no power on the mortal plane capable of defeating such a monstrosity.

Would devouring its foe satiate the demon, or would it take issue with Ozzie and Flea? Would it consider Sarina a delectable dessert? She felt her body quake with fear, heard the thrumming of her heart as it begged for escape, but she stood firm. If fate had chosen this day for her friends' demise, it seemed only fitting to join them.

Ozzie and Flea rode back to the edge of the wood at a gallop, positioning themselves and their horses in front of Sarina and the woman who had since introduced herself as Myla. While the gesture did not provide a sense of security, it did much to steady Sarina's courage.

The blurring wind that she had noticed before seemed to grow alongside the demon until it appeared as a massive cloud. Sarina found this encouraging and hoped that whatever force existed inside that cloud had enough brawn and wit to match rank with the demon.

Brandishing its claws, the demon began to swipe and slash at the cloud in an attempt to rip it to shreds, but the air pocket seemed agile and allusive, moving too quickly for the demon to make contact. Swiping high and then low, eyes frantic to follow the elusive wind, the demon's blows became increasingly desperate and erratic. Frustrated, the fiend became eerily still, standing in mid-field, silent as the peering moon, eyes shifting with thought as it contemplated the predicament.

After several tense moments, the demon began to inhale, slowly at first, but with a tremendous force that sucked in the edges of the cloud. Realizing the tactic was effective, the demon sucked harder, drawing in the cloud, devouring it.

Sarina gasped and Myla screamed.

As the center of the cloud drew nearer to the demon's mouth, a booming clap of thunder issued forth, startling everyone and a beam of light protruded from the cloud, high above the demon's head. When the demon's eyes rose to meet its fate, that glorious beam of light splintered the creature in two, splitting it down the middle from head to toe. Half of the demon's body fell to the left, the other to the right and Morgana's scream pierced the air with a chilling resound as the severed halves of the demon immediately withered like grapes left on the vine.

Realizing that things don't always go the way we plan can be a knotty bitch. Knowing Morgana had gotten a taste of her own tonic provided Sarina with a serious thrill and what an absolute utter relief it was to see that demon fall.

It hadn't escaped Sarina's notice that the Duke of Devonshire had fallen to the same fate, split in two by a mighty sword. Perhaps the old wizard wasn't responsible for the brilliant magic performed at center field after all.

ξഈξ

Patience expired, Morgana blasted an explosive spell at the ground beneath the Friar, igniting a fire.

"That should fry him properly," she warned. "Give me the spell."

Merlin removed the Lady Viviane's body from his lap and gently laid her down. He approached Morgana, his voice saturated with a tone of dread, "I fear you did not hear me when I said only one of pure heart can cast this spell, to speak it otherwise will produce severe consequences."

Fists curled and white-knuckled, Morgana engaged him with a granite stare and spoke with contempt, "I heard you."

Squirming to escape the heat of the fire, the Friar begged, "Please give her the spell, I cannot endure!"

At last, Merlin reached into his pouch and produced a small leather-bound book, an object he clung to as if it were the last gold nugget on earth. Trembling, he extended his hand and allowed Morgana to swipe the book away, a fresh stream of tears rolling over his cheeks.

"I beg you," he beseeched, "put the fire out."

"Put it out yourself." She sneered, mesmerized by the intricate etchings embedded in the book's leather. Opening the cover, she found but one page, scripted with breathtaking calligraphy. Finally, she had obtained the ultimate spell and, at last, she possessed the power to bring the world to its knees.

Merlin cast a spell to extinguish the fire, but in so doing weakened himself, evidenced by a pronounced bend in the knees and a sudden shoulder slouch. He nearly fell over.

Ignoring him, Morgana stepped away to read the words on the page, committing them to memory. Smiling wide, she lifted her arms to the heavens and spoke with conviction. As she enunciated each word perfectly, the syllables tasted like delectable morsels of music rolling effortlessly off her tongue. But, as she spoke the last word, she suddenly lost her smile and thoughtlessly dropped the book, clutching her chest where a searing pain burned like a cattle brand.

"What is this sensation?" She demanded.

Tears still streaming, Merlin lowered his chin and shook his head, responding sorrowfully, "I don't know what else I could have said to you, Morgana."

The pain radiated from her chest and spread quickly, engulfing her entire body with an arthritic infliction.

"What is this!" She cried.

"I suspect you are experiencing the loss of your immortality," Merlin answered, mucus pouring from his nose, as he seemed genuinely remorseful for the turn of events.

How absurd! Merlin's words of warning were a deception meant to keep her from performing the spell. They were an outright lie. But the discomfort, the pain, and the many other sensations she hadn't felt before...is this how it feels to be mortal? The *horror*.

The spell meant to exalt her to the status of a goddess had reduced her to a mere mortal.

Merlin had issued his warnings knowing she would not tolerate them, knowing how the spell would affect her. He had known this would happen all along.

"Damn you to hell!" She spewed, casting a death spell. The impact was spectacular. It seemed as though the light in Merlin's eyes went out before the blow struck. Limp as a weed caught on the blade of a sharpened scythe, his body slumped to the ground.

Revenge really is a bit of honey.

ξэжξ

Well then, isn't this a curious turn of events? The mighty sorceress, Morgana, bound to go down in infamy for slaying the Lady of the Lake and now the great wizard, Merlin, has been sufficiently reduced to nothing more than a mortal, and by her own hand nonetheless.

Helga had retreated to the cover of the oak tree while Merlin and Morgana had their spat but now she brimmed with confidence, being the senior member present and still in possession of her immortality. While Morgana maintained an advantage for her knowledge of magic, Helga's immortality provided a distinct advantage. Who's to say she couldn't give Morgana a proper thrashing? If the bumptious wench had any wits left about her, she would do well to steer clear of Helga Dearbourne. Snickering, Helga dug her nails into her backside and gave it a good scratch.

ξӜξ

Farrin had seen enough. She had more than fulfilled her promise to Merlin to stand down while he reasoned with Morgana. Now, he had paid the ultimate price for offering leniency to a dangerous foe. Farrin would not make the same mistake.

ξӜξ

Morgana may have lost her immortality (of that, she wasn't entirely convinced) but she hadn't lost her senses. Every instinct said danger approached. The force that had dispatched her demon, the cloud at the center of the field, began to bear down upon her at great speed. Someone wielded that magic, someone had robbed Morgana of her dearest Dezva and someone would pay.

Palming a handful of silver powder, she thrust it forward and shouted, "Aperio!"

The translucent mists forming the cloud promptly fell away. A young woman rushed across the field, sword in hand, fire in her eyes. None other than the future queen, Farrin the Fair. How delightful. It would be a pleasure to obliterate the seed of Gwenevere before the tart had a chance to enjoy the throne.

Like a skilled warrior, Farrin ran with her sword held in both hands, raised high over her right shoulder—anyone else but Morgana might have cringed at the sight. No one, however, had ever forged a sword capable of prevailing against Morgana's wiles. And yet, it was a bit unnerving to know this witch had the ability to maintain an invisibility cloak and for such an extended period. Morgana hadn't mastered the feat of invisibility. In fact, she had never come close. Surely, Merlin had schooled this freckled toad-boiler, which added an element of unpredictability. If there was one thing Morgana prized above all else, it was control, she would not lose it.

Two men at wood's edge attempted to cross the field, their determination nearly as resolute as the young queen's determination to keep them at bay. It must be terribly distracting for her. Such a pity.

Morgana waited for Farrin to look away then belted her in the midsection with a pressure curse that drove her to the ground and pinned her there, she should remain immobile for quite some time.

Morgana confidently crossed the field. She would put the young queen out of her misery, leave Bodach Cairn, and go in search of a way to regain her power and strength. Fuming over the day's turn of events, she decided it an asinine condition to require a person of pure heart to cast the ultimate spell. What bleeding heart would have the desire to control others? So, why bother to craft such a spell? She mulled the question over as she stepped closer to her helpless prey. Considering carefully, she arrived at the only viable solution. The spell was a sinister tool meant to disarm anyone seeking extreme power and she had foolishly succumbed to the ruse. She should have known.

But, the day was not an entire loss, she had had her way with Merlin and he would never meddle with her heart or head again. Doing away with the Lady of the Lake also brought a sweet satisfaction. And now, turning the last seed of Gwenevere to maggot meal would provide the pièce de résistance.

ξӜξ

Farrin twisted in angst, struggling to regain her breath. Morgana's spell had knocked the air from her lungs and the weight of two tons pressed in on her. Unable to move, she watched the sorceress approach, not in any great hurry to arrive, but striding with a stoic expression spread over her face. Whatever heart Merlin had given the sorceress credit for had vanished long ago and she didn't seem in possession of a soul. She certainly didn't intend to offer tea and a chat, but meant to kill Farrin and then have a go at Ozzie and Flea, perhaps Sarina as well. Morgana didn't strike Farrin as the type to take satisfaction in anything less than total domination. Given her way, she would leave the field littered with bodies and then go in search of more innocents.

Farrin tried to move, but found it impossible. Morgana's magic must have had an element of immobility in it. At last able to inhale a sliver of air, Farrin closed her eyes and imagined herself a spring monarch with a wide wingspan, light and unencumbered. The picture of the hextress strutting over the field with the wind in her hair and her hands comfortably swinging at her side would not be Farrin's last vision.

The image of the butterfly set Farrin free from the enchantment. Remembering Merlin's words concerning Morgana's tendency to underestimate her opponents, Farrin remained still, waiting for Morgana to arrive.

When Morgana came within a few steps, Farrin blasted her with a wind spell, a terrible tornado that plucked the sorceress off her feet and spun her around, engulfing her in its grievous embrace and racing over the field, captive in tow. When the spell wore off, the wind dumped Morgana a few feet from where the storm had originated. Morgana landed with a thud and a grunt, fear and fury vying for position in her expression. She reacted immediately by projecting another spell, a shredding spell, if Farrin estimated correctly, and if Excalibur hadn't blocked the brunt of the spell's force, it would have been the last of Farrin. As it was, too much of the spell broke through, slicing a gash into her neck and another into her left thigh.

Slumping to her knees, Farrin pressed a palm to her gushing neck. She couldn't see straight, the edges of the world blurred. Fighting to maintain consciousness, she focused on the pain in her leg, hoping it would keep her grounded and awake.

"You should know better than to tangle with your superiors," Morgana chided, already on her feet and hovering, her lips poised in an arrogant grin.

Farrin knew what she needed to do, she had the spell ready moments ago, but now she'd forgotten the incantation. Where were the words? As she struggled to recall them, her head grew light and her eyes began to droop. She had to stand and fight. Squirming over the earth like a worm pulled in two was no way to die.

Using Excalibur for a crutch, Farrin lifted herself to her feet, but as she stood erect, Morgana thrust another spell that pounded Farrin's midsection causing her to drop Excalibur. The sword landed a foot away from Morgana's outstretched hands. Smiling at her luck, Morgana lunged for the sword but couldn't lift it, its weight equal to the weight of her malevolence. Farrin rushed for the sword and swiped it away.

Morgana's shocked gaze met Farrin's glare.

An opportunity had arisen, a fleeting moment to capitalize upon Morgana's confusion, but what were the words for the spell?

Morgana's expression changed, she was finished toying about—her next spell would kill.

True to her nature, Morgana reached for a pinch of silver powder. Merlin was right about the sorceress, she hadn't allowed old habits the space they needed to die.

Words that had eluded Farrin moments ago, rushed back. "Incohare calx!"

As the command spilled from Farrin's lips, a stone encasement grew around Morgana, forming a massive boulder, locking the sorceress within. Unwilling to give Morgana time to devise a way out of the predicament, Farrin sheathed Excalibur and began to scale the boulder. Because the rock had formed smoothly, with only a few fissures to grab onto, and because her bleeding leg proved reluctant to perform its proper function, Farrin lost her footing several times.

The sound of horse hooves thundered, coming from behind. No need to inhibit the boys now, let them come.

Once she reached the crest of the boulder, Farrin quickly surveyed the field. Sarina had climbed aboard Flea's horse and raced toward the Hulderfolk. There, Sarina freed Kai from his binding. Ozzie headed for Farrin.

Concerned Morgana might rediscover the principles of reality in time to escape her encasement, Farrin unsheathed Excalibur and gripped the sword with both hands. A sudden wave of nausea rippled through her stomach. For a moment, she thought she might lose consciousness and topple off the rock.

Doing the right thing is rarely the easiest thing to do and Farrin knew the possibility existed that more than one ghost might haunt her memory after this day drew to a close. Yet, she had learned long ago that fear is the firmest foundation upon which to build courage. No choice remained. Where evil lives, it breeds.

Thrusting with every ounce of might she could muster, she plunged the sword into the center of the stone where it ignited a fiery explosion, entering the stone as if cutting through butter. When the boulder swallowed the blade to the hilt, she slowly pulled it out.

No one, mortal or immortal, could have survived that.

Positioning his horse alongside the boulder, Ozzie held his hand up, inviting Farrin to join him on horseback.

Without exchanging words, they somberly watched a pool of blood amass at the base of the boulder.

ξЖξ

The Friar profusely thanked the witch of Dearbourne for casting the spell that set him free, her reaction a grunt of perturbed annoyance. Sarina left Kai's side long enough to bandage Farrin's wounds and to position the Lady of the Lake in Merlin's arms, as only seemed fitting. The Friar began to recite a lengthy prayer, his voice breaking beneath the weight of a heavy heart.

Ozzie removed Merlin's sword from its sheath and had asked Farrin for Excalibur, which she gave without question. Placing the swords beside the heads of the stricken lovers, he positioned them to form an arch.

"I don't know what this is about," he explained, unbidden, "but I feel compelled."

Farrin nodded, knowing what it meant to follow instinct. Some things must be done, even if we never understand why. Ozzie's desire to perform this ritual seemed shaped out of reverence for the fallen, a small token of honor—fitting, admirable and just.

Finishing the last touch, Ozzie moved the sword hilts together, locking them in a symbolic embrace. As the hilts connected with one another, the sky spit a fearsome flash of lightning and the earth began a series of ground-splintering shivers, quaking until all who stood had fallen. The last thing Farrin remembered was watching the previously enchanted oak tree uproot and fall toward her as Ozzie's horse stumbled into a burgeoning crack in the earth.

ξЖξ

"It's been nearly a week," Farrin heard the owner of a small feminine voice say. The smell of medicinal herbs permeated the air.

"Give her time, she'll come around," a gentle tone replied, and Farrin felt someone tuck a linen about her, followed by a light patting on the back of her hand.

The next sensation to arise wasn't so endearing—her head felt as though it might split wide open and promptly eject its contents onto the floor. She moaned against the pain.

"She's waking!" The timid voice said, and Farrin listened to the sound of scurrying feet as attendants rushed to her side.

A full week of recovery passed before the headaches subsided and Farrin finally felt well enough to lift herself into a sitting position.

Throughout the recovery, Sarina insisted on remaining at Farrin's side, barely leaving long enough for a sufficient tinkle. Several times, Farrin woke in a panic, convinced the earth had swallowed Ozzie along with his horse, but Sarina assured her he was fine. Farrin would soon see for herself as Sarina had finally agreed to allow visitors.

The first callers to arrive bedside provided quite a shock, requiring several minutes of brow patting with a cool cloth and a great deal of convincing before Farrin realized what she saw wasn't just another hallucination— Merlin and the

Lady Viviane, perfectly radiant, wonderfully healthy, and oddly alive.

"I cannot imagine how Sir Oswald knew to place the swords just so," Merlin mused. "Perhaps he is not so far removed from my family line as he might hope. By placing those swords in the right position, he performed the one ritual capable of restoring my spirit to flesh. I owe him my life."

Hearing this, Farrin quickly turned her gaze to the Lady of the Lake.

Chuckling, the Lady answered Farrin's unasked question, "I would have survived regardless of the ritual. I really do possess the original soul, although I am sadly not immune to losing consciousness. I, too, am forever indebted to Sir Oswald for restoring Merlin."

After several minutes of lighthearted conversation, Merlin and his Lady took their leave.

Kai of the Hulderfolk entered the chamber next, no longer burdened by the gruesome mask, as Merlin had devised a spell to remove it.

"I've been dying to tell you," Sarina gushed, "but until now, I didn't think you well enough to hear the news." Sarina grasped Kai's hand and flashed a wide smile, "We're nesting and talking about marriage. Isn't it wonderful?"

Farrin feigned surprise. Even those dimmer than a newborn wart could have seen this coming. Extending her arms, she took Sarina in for a tight hug.

"Blessings for you both," she said sincerely, kissing Sarina on the forehead.

Expressing gratitude and admiration for Farrin's feats on Bodach Cairn, Kai bid her farewell and left Sarina hungering after him as he exited the room.

"He really is a lot to look at it," Sarina gushed.

Finally, Ozzie stepped through the door and sat on a stool next to Farrin. Keen to provide them with some privacy, Sarina left to tend to a young boy who had broken his leg when he interfered with a jousting match.

"Feeling better?" Ozzie asked, his smile momentarily bright before a sudden seriousness took over his expression. "I had no idea putting the swords together like that would cause an earthquake and if I'd known the oak tree would mistake your head for a batting ball, I never would have..."

"I know." She gave his hand a reassuring squeeze.

Guilt somewhat assuaged, Ozzie recalled his adventures in Glastonbury where he and Flea had taken the boulder and the demon's remains. The artifacts would rest inside a guarded crypt, just in case some insane blighter had a mind to try a bit of necromancy.

"Your dear granny is being held in the dungeon awaiting your orders," he informed her.

"In the dungeon? Whatever for!"

"Seems the Lady Myla let slip Helga is Gwenevere's daughter, the true heir. Granny became quite irritated and vowed revenge against Myla for spending all those years with Gwenevere while Helga remained banished from the king's court. It really was an unpleasant scene and we had no recourse but to take her powder and restrain her. Meanwhile, her toad sits outside the castle looking forlorn and depressed."

Farrin chuckled at Ozzie's description of the toad, but somewhere along the way, she would have to decide what to do with Helga Dearbourne, not at all a pleasant thought. Farrin had seen what Helga had done to that poor sprite on Bodach Cairn and the memory had not endeared her to her great grandmother.

Ozzie stayed for several hours, reminiscing about the day's events, ultimately winding his way to the subject of Farrin's coronation.

"I suspect," she suggested, "You might find a proper tailor in Drivensdale."

Furrowing his brow, he leaned back and crossed his arms over his chest, "Whatever could I possibly require from a tailor?"

Grabbing hold of the lapel on his raddled leather coat, Farrin tugged, coming away with a fragment of deceased fabric.

"You can't get married in rags," she said.

Jaw slack, he replied aghast, "Married? Who would marry a no-good rogue like me?"

"A queen needs a king," Farrin declared, leaning to give her valiant knight a kiss. A kiss hungrily received.

"M'lady," Merlin's voice boomed from the doorway, "Get your rest, you have a month of instruction ahead of you."

THE END

BK CRAWFORD

About The Author

B.K. Crawford currently resides on the coast in New England with the love of her life, two menopausal tomato plants, and several purse-snatching poltergeists.

You can connect with B.K. on Facebook at the following address:

https://www.facebook.com/authorBKCrawford

A band of infamous pirates have deeply angered a voo-doo priestess. Fujo Sinclair will not leave Port Royal before she has placed a dreadful curse on the souls of the rogues responsible for the loss of her sister, Catti. Two hundred years later, a young ballet dancer is faced with the burden of breaking the curse while attempting to solve a more recent murder. But, if you ask Jillian Miller, surviving the small town mentality prevalent in Devil's Edge may be the most difficult task of all.